Eric Malpass was bc in a bank after leaving s ; to become a novelist an many years. His first book, *Morning's at Seven,* was published to wide acclaim. With an intuitive eye for the quirkiness of family life, his novels are full of wry comments and perceptive observations. This exquisite sense of detail has led to the filming of three of his books. His most engaging character is Gaylord Pentecost – a charming seven-year-old who observes the strange adult world with utter incredulity.

Eric Malpass also wrote biographical novels, carefully researched and highly evocative of the period. Among these is *Of Human Frailty*, the moving story of Thomas Cranmer.

With his amusing and lovingly drawn details of life in rural England, Malpass' books typify a certain whimsical Englishness – a fact which undoubtedly contributes to his popularity in Europe. Married with a family, Eric Malpass lived in Long Eaton, near Nottingham, until his death in 1996.

BY THE SAME AUTHOR
ALL PUBLISHED BY HOUSE OF STRATUS

AT THE HEIGHT OF THE MOON
BEEFY JONES
THE CLEOPATRA BOY
FORTINBRAS HAS ESCAPED
A HOUSE OF WOMEN
THE LAMPLIGHT AND THE STARS
THE LONG LONG DANCES
MORNING'S AT SEVEN
OH, MY DARLING DAUGHTER
PIG-IN-THE-MIDDLE
THE RAISING OF LAZARUS PIKE
SUMMER AWAKENING
SWEET WILL
THE WIND BRINGS UP THE RAIN

ERIC MALPASS

Of Human Frailty

This edition published in 2001 by House of Stratus, an imprint of Stratus Holdings plc, 24c Old Burlington Street, London, W1X 1RL, UK.

www.houseofstratus.com

Typeset, printed and bound by House of Stratus.

A catalogue record for this book is available from the British Library.

ISBN 0-7551-0200-2

PROLOGUE

All his life he had known what it was to wake from nightmare to the safety of morning: nightmares of Blount, his brutal schoolmaster; nightmares of the terrible Old King whom he yet loved, of his implacable enemy the bitter-lipped Queen. But now something more frightful. His dreams were gentle and peaceful, so that as he slept tears of happiness and thankfulness squeezed from his tired lids. He galloped through forest rides, his head his thighs scattering the dew from the crowding laurels. He ate a peaceful meal with his sweet Margarete, and they were courteous and loving one to another, as they had been in life. He walked, in a monk's habit, his face hidden by his cowl, the echoing aisles of Canterbury. But the people knew. He saw them nudging each other. ''Tis his Grace. 'Tis Doctor Cranmer.' And down on their knees for a blessing from his Grace.

Yes. Sweet, lovely dreams. Only, unnaturally now, it was the waking that was nightmare. 'One o'clock of a fine morning, and all's well.' And the bells of Oxford telling away his last hours before – O gentle Christ, if it be Thy will – ? One o'clock, and all's well. All well. The faggots laid, covered with a cloth to keep the dew from them. The Realm soon to be rid of one more heretic. All's well.

He slept again fitfully, worn out in body, mind and spirit. And, waking again to nightmare, upbraided himself for sleeping away a tenth of his remaining life. 'Two o'clock of a fine morning, and all's well.' Our Sovereign Lady Mary, safe on the throne, with Reginald Pole, the new Archbishop of Canterbury, to protect her in the Faith. And one heretic the less. One old enemy, the most hated of them all, held safe and ready for the fire: the fire that would not only destroy him but would also cauterize the bitterness and the hatred (and perhaps the guilt) in her very bowels.

Weak, exhausted by suffering, he drifted towards sleep once more. And this half-sleep was the most wonderful thing he had ever known. He seemed to float in a soft and balmy air, in a silence deeper than the grave. He was a child once more, cradled against his mother's breast. Before it all began. Before Blount; before Joan and Margarete, those two sweet tempters of the urgent flesh; before that chance meeting with Gardiner and Foxe that pitchforked him into an unwanted greatness: the chance meeting that had set him on a long and fearful road, through fame and honour to degradation and torment. But for that chance meeting, where would he be now? Sleeping in his study in Cambridge, preparing for another day with his books. Not lying on a bed of straw, in a worn habit, in a stone cell with jailers guarding the locked door. 'Three o'clock of a fine morning. And all's well.'

He woke and dragged himself on to his knees. He gazed up towards heaven, tugging his fingers through his dirty beard. He was not praying. He was experiencing a miracle. He felt strength flowing into his limbs; and knew, wonderfully, that he was no longer afraid. After the years of weakness and vacillation he was strong again. The fire would pass. And beyond the fire, dimming it to a sulky glare, would be the effulgence of the Throne, and the voice of the Most High: 'Well done, Thomas, thou good and faithful servant.' If only, that is, he could *remain* strong, renounce all his written recantations. He held out his right hand and stared at it in the darkness for a long time. 'Judas!' he whispered, with fond reproach. Then he wrapped it in his habit, holding it tenderly against his breast. And lay down, and slept again.

And then, it was the morning...

Chapter 1

And then, it was the morning. But of an earlier and, for young Thomas Cranmer at least, a joyous and long-awaited day.

The sun, in its rising, peered over the edge of the world. It flashed fire from the vanes of Oxford, it gave its benison to the spires of Cambridge, it lent its own effulgence to the honey-coloured stone of Canterbury.

And, at the Dolphin Inn at Cambridge, it awoke Joan, the proprietor's niece, to a gentle knocking at the front door.

Seventeen-year-old Joan rolled out of bed, tugged her clothes about her, and floundered downstairs. It was only six hours since the last customer at the Dolphin had staggered out through the door; and after that Joan had been busy cleaning up vomit and urine and spilt beer and putting down clean rushes and sawdust. And now, already, here was another day of making beds and emptying slops and fending off the groping hands of drunkards. She opened the door.

And found, not a loud-mouthed oaf demanding horses, or sack and sugar; but a fresh-faced, eager, shy-looking boy somewhat younger than herself.

Drowsing happily on the carrier's cart, young Thomas had suddenly awakened to a suffusion of joy. The stars were fading, and the carrier's lantern, from being the earth's only radiance, had dimmed to a smoky yellowness. He became aware of the smells of people and animals and excrement and decay. Houses, churches and the harsh new brick of colleges loomed out of the mist. Cambridge! It must be! A cramped but noble city, even further from Nottinghamshire in spirit than in weary miles: a city far from the tyranny of his schoolmaster Blount, and the shattering tragedy of his father's death. A new world, a new life!

Sudden as an arrow from the bow, the rising sun lit the golden vanes on church and steeple. 'The Dolphin,' said the carrier, jerking his head to the left. 'Black Joan will look after you.' He leered. 'Thank you, sir,' said Thomas, climbing down with his bundle (ten books, a spare shirt, and a pair of good riding boots. It was the best impoverished gentry could do for a son recently made fatherless).

He bowed courteously to the carrier, and hurried eagerly towards the inn.

From the stables came the whinny of horses, the smells of leather and manure and hay. His cup of happiness had been full. Now it was running over. Horses! To lodge at an inn where there were horses!

But now he found that the inn had something else. A girl, soft and drowsy from sleep, had opened the door to him.

Apart from his sisters, he had scarcely met a girl. It was a revelation. He thought the wanton cascade of her black hair the most beautiful thing he had ever seen, and then crossed himself fearfully, knowing such thoughts to be sinful.

So the fourteen-year-old boy met the seventeen-year-old Joan. In the bright morning of a new world: a morning on which he had left behind *for ever*, Blount; the cheeseparing gentility of Aslockton Manor; his loved yet foolish mother; a morning that glowed with promise: books, knowledge, the company of learned men; the stirrings in Europe, strange and exciting, against the stranglehold of Rome; the exhilarating air of new thought, a new knowledge and, in the background, never intruding on *his* world, of course, yet seen, comprehended, the disturbing loveliness of women.

And there, on that sunlit doorstep, the girl and the boy each found something they had not known existed. She: gentleness, and a kindly cheerfulness. He: a dark beauty, however tousled; and the solace and comfort of femininity.

'Master Cranmer?' she said.

He nodded, savouring the first time he had ever been given the title 'Master'. Though he was too quiet a person to exult openly, inside he was bubbling over. 'Would you like breakfast, Master Cranmer?'

He nodded, again with that grave smile. She set him down at the oak table, brought a mug of small beer, a platter of beef, and a crust of bread. She sat and watched him eat for a few moments. Then, to his disappointment, she jumped up. 'I must not sit here. My aunt would scold.' She looked down at her jumbled clothes. 'Besides, it is not seemly.' They both blushed. Had she noticed, he wondered, how his eyes would not leave her breasts. She ran upstairs. He sat on. A new day. A new life. And here, awaiting him in this teeming city, the world's learning.

And a soft and tender creature as rare and unexpected as a unicorn.

So. A boy and a girl, meeting: a gentle thing, an innocent thing; a thing filled with hope and promise, surely?

But their world was not a gentle world. It was a cruel and brutal world. And already the actors were assembling for the working out of a tragedy that would end only in betrayal and torture and violence and death. They, by their own decisions and lusts (for the flesh, for power, for revenge) by their own weaknesses and folly, they would write the plot. But, unlike actors, they would not be left unscathed when the play was done.

For instance, a Princess of Aragon had been brought from a sun-baked land to the cheerlessness of Ludlow Castle in November. There, a child of fifteen, she spent the winter watching her young husband die. Then, when at last the June suns brought a touch of warmth to the stones of Ludlow, they betrothed her to her late husband's brother Henry, now heir to the Throne of England. (With a dispensation from the Pope, of course.)

And perhaps, as he and her betrothed danced a cheerful measure, she thought it would be always thus, not seeing the dark ways ahead, not hearing the triumphant laughter of a rival as yet unborn.

And the Prince Henry, her betrothed? A young man of the utmost promise, everyone agreed: a golden youth, merry yet devout, already learned; athletic, noble, a future King who would rule with wisdom and compassion. And no one then saw the canker at the heart.

And the other actors: countless men who would sell their souls, or suffer heroically; or finally, after many twistings and turnings, be trapped like rats and cast into the ditch.

And one of these, even now, sat shyly at the table in the Dolphin Inn, Cambridge, in the sweet summer of 1503.

So he met Joan, in the bright morning. And the day passed, and other days; and months and years. Passed, for Joan, in long hard days at the Dolphin; for him in poring over books; in becoming a Bachelor, then a Master, of Arts. Passed, in the great world outside Cambridge, in the birth pangs of a new and fearful struggle: a few stubborn, black-robed scholars against the power and magnificence and cruelty of Rome. Passed, joyously, at Court with the wedding of that most devout Prince Henry to his loved and loving Katherine, Princess of Aragon. (A fairly simple wedding, with the bride's chief ornament her thick red hair, hanging down to her waist; and the bridegroom's rich velvets and gold and ermine, quite eclipsed by his graciousness, courtesy, and his own physical beauty.) Passed with the accession to the Throne of England of a Sovereign unparalleled in princely virtues; with the crowning of King Henry VIII and Queen Katherine in splendour and majesty and the rejoicing of an entire people.

So the days and years passed; until the day when Thomas Cranmer, now in his twenties and a grave, learned and respected Fellow of Jesus College, came face to face with the first crisis of his storm-riven life. And it had to do with Joan.

It began with screams, the frantic clatter of hooves, a wild and desperate neighing. Out of the carriage archway of the Dolphin bolted a horse, wide-eyed with terror.

A woman appeared at the door of the inn, well-built, handsome, with a crown of raven hair. A capable-looking woman. But all she was capable of at the moment was wringing her hands.

The horse, finding himself faced by a row of houses, checked, and in that moment a young man, in black habit, caught its bridle and, with soft words of tenderness, miraculously quietened the poor beast. Five minutes later, with more murmurings and strokings, he was able to lead the horse back into the stable yard.

The raven-haired woman was waiting for him. 'Sir, that was well done. And brave also.'

Brave! Thomas was used to praise for his learning, even for his horsemanship. But it was a rare and heady thing to be praised for his courage. He was exalted. But: ''Tis nothing,' he said, still in communion with the frightened animal.

But the woman persisted. 'You must tell me your name, that I may thank you properly.'

'Thomas Cranmer.'

She looked at him with sudden eagerness. 'You lodged at this house years ago. Oh, you were such a boy, so far from home. I vow I longed to mother you.'

'I longed to *be* mothered,' he said wryly. He looked at her for the first time. 'And you were – Mistress Joan?'

She nodded. 'The drudge. But now – my aunt puts much trust in me. I am no longer the drudge. Come, sir. You must refresh yourself.'

'First the horse,' he said.

'John will see to him. John,' she called. The horse was handed over somewhat reluctantly. She led Thomas inside, sat him down, poured wine. 'And you are a famous scholar?' she asked.

'No, no. But I am a fellow of Jesus College.' He gave her his shy smile. 'I confess to a little sinful pride about that.'

'A little?' She threw back her shoulders, tossed her head. '*I* should strut and crow like a cock. I should want *Fellow of Jesus* written on my cap.'

They both laughed. Then: ''Tis nothing,' he said again quietly. 'I am not an ambitious man. All I really want is my books.' He looked up at her rather pathetically. 'People frighten me somewhat.'

'*You*? Afraid of people? A clever, good-looking, charming fellow like you?'

He smiled, shook his head. 'Books – and horses – and longbows, I can understand. But men – ? Built in God's image, they yet have dark caverns in their souls.'

'Indeed.' She nodded. She probably knew more about those dark caverns than he did – yet. But her bent was for practicalities rather than philosophy. 'John is not good with horses. If you were not a Fellow – ?'

He looked up again, this time with interest. 'What are you saying?'

'You could teach him gentleness,' she said quietly.

He jumped to his feet. Two minutes later they were in the stables. And the years melted away and he was back in the yard at Aslockton, the acrid smells, the stamping and whinnying, the gentle, patient devotion of the noble creatures. Oh, if only she were to say, 'Let me see you ride, Master Cranmer.'

'Let me see you ride, Master Cranmer,' she said.

And he was away, over the cobblestones, out of the little town, nothing but the thudding of hooves and his own murmured endearments and commands. Then back, flushed, eyes shining. And Joan looking up at him, with a certain wonder. 'You ride well, Master Cranmer.'

He dismounted. He said solemnly, 'I would rather be a horseman than Master of King's.' He bowed. 'Thank you, Mistress.'

She curtseyed. 'You call a tavern-keeper Mistress?'

Suddenly embarrassed, completely at a loss, he gave her a brief nod and left her. He did not sleep that night. The powerful horse; and the reincarnation, in a nobler form, of the young Joan's femininity, was too much for him. What a happy life it would be, he thought, to be a tavern-keeper, with Joan to wife and a dozen horses in the yard. And his books? No. He had to admit. He could not live without his books.

But he had rediscovered an old delight. The next day he was back at the Dolphin. 'Mistress. I would hire a horse.'

They smiled at each other like old friends. She gave him a handsome chestnut, powerful, worthy of his horsemanship. And then he was away, his whole body exulting in swift and urgent movement, but his mind returning more and more to the beauty and the tenderness of Joan. Surely, he began to think, an unmarried man is only half a creature. Only a woman's body, a woman's mind and spirit can make him whole, can bring moisture and flowering to the arid soul of the scholar.

That day, the first time for many days, his books lay unopened on his desk.

And, on other days, the same thing happened. For now Joan sometimes rode with him, straight and slim in a scarlet habit, dappled with sunlight in the deep forest rides. Wonderful days, when they both learned laughter, and companionship, and heart's ease. Yet also he was troubled, deeply troubled. Unschooled as he was in womankind, there was yet a look in Joan's eyes that even he must recognize: a hungry look that spoke of a lifetime of shared meals, a shared bed. And she was a tavern-keeper, no matter how beautiful. And he was the son of a Squire, no matter how poverty-stricken, and a Fellow of Jesus College, destined for the Church: a man to whom celibacy was a part of his stock-in-trade.

The choice was stark: marry Joan, and be forced to abandon his career, since neither a Fellow nor a priest could have a wife; or tear Joan from his side for ever: an amputation which would drain him surely of his very life blood.

Such a situation called for a fighter, a man of decision. And he was not such a man. Blount's floggings had taught him deviousness, the avoidance of commitment and direct action. Yet he and Joan *must* come together, without her his life would be an emptiness, a desert.

The chances of a letter from Cambridge ever reaching the tiny Nottinghamshire village of Aslockton were not high. He dutifully wrote to his mother, and gave the letter to the

Peterborough carrier, and felt he had shot an arrow at random into the treetops. Then he went to resign his Fellowship. But somehow he never reached the Master of Jesus. In his craven folly he married his Joan instead, quietly, almost furtively.

Despite their fears and anxieties for the future, it was a time of intense happiness for them both. They managed to keep their marriage secret. The letter to Aslockton might lie at Peterborough for weeks; and even if someone did send it on the next stage of its journey, it still had weary miles to go.

Yet somehow, it did eventually reach its destination.

John Cranmer, Thomas' eldest brother, had been squiring it since the father's death in 1501. A red-haired splenetic, thick-set fellow, he was the last man who ought to receive such a letter. He read it with incredulity and shock. His mother took immediately to her bed. But John called for his carriage and a change of clothing; and, in a brilliant stroke, pulled Schoolmaster Blount into the carriage with him. 'My brother! And a tavern wench!' The moon should have run blood, to herald such a calamity.

It was a terrible meeting.

Thomas, arriving at the Dolphin, was greeted by a white-faced Joan. 'Thomas, there are two gentlemen in the private room awaiting you. One I think may be your brother. The other – I know not. But… ' She looked up at him fearfully.

So. Despite all his hopes, the letter *had* reached Aslockton. But why *two* gentlemen? A sudden, even greater fear tugged at his nerve-strings. He squeezed his wife's hand, and went into the private room.

Dear God! His fear was confirmed. The two gentlemen rose, grim-faced. One was his brother. The other was a bear of a man, stooped, scowling from under heavy brows. A man who still leaned on a heavy ash stick. Blount!

John Cranmer shouted, 'Are you out of your mind? A tavern wench? I forbid the marriage, forbid it utterly, do you hear?'

Thomas licked his dry lips. 'I – thought my letter to have gone astray. I – am already married, brother.'

Blount gave a bear-like growl. But John flopped back on the settle, a look of comic disbelief on his face. 'Then you *have* lost your senses, sir. The brother of the Squire of Aslockton married to a – slut? And your vocation? Do you imagine that because of all this New Learning tomfoolery, you will still be allowed to take Orders?'

A knock at the door. Joan, her paleness intensified by the darkness of her hair, came into the room with a tray. 'Wine, gentlemen?' she asked, her voice trembling and unsteady.

'Get out,' said Blount with a savage sweeping lunge of his stick.

Thomas felt his body change in a moment from a quaking jelly to a ramrod stiffness. 'Master Blount, you will ask my wife's pardon for those words.'

Squire Cranmer might be a foolish and hot-tempered young man, with all the prejudices of his time. But he had more wit than the uncouth bear beside him. If this was Thomas' wife, she was no slut. She had a beauty, a presence. And though that did not mean that someone of his class was not free to insult her as much as he wished, it did remind him that she was his sister-in-law. He said. 'Master Blount, I think it would be as well… '

Blount squinted up at Joan, and said nothing. Joan said, 'No pardon is needed, sirs. I have heard far worse in my time.'

'And used far worse, no doubt,' muttered Thomas' brother scornfully.

'Indeed, sir,' said Joan, bobbing. 'I will leave the wine, gentlemen. Thomas will call me if there is aught you need.' She went.

'Well, sir?' demanded John.

Thomas said, 'I'm sorry, Brother, to have caused you distress. But Joan and I – '

John cut in with a piping, whining voice. 'Love one another. Can't live without one another. Oh, I know. Spare me that cant at least.' He rose. 'Well, Thomas, how you intend to keep alive is your affair. I don't imagine Father's annuity of twenty shillings will keep you from the gutter. And obviously you will have been stripped of your Fellowship.'

'No.'

'No? Why not? Surely the College know of your lecherous folly?'

Thomas was silent.

'Then I shall certainly inform the Master immediately. And if you have come down to earning your bread as an ostler, don't come crying to me.'

'I shall not come crying to you, Brother.'

Blount waved his stick. 'I wish I could still use this on you. *This* would knock some sense into you. It always did in the past.'

Thomas said, 'If you had used it less, sir, I might – ' and suddenly his voice was full of tears, 'I might have been a better specimen of manhood now.'

His brother stared at him in silence and, Thomas suddenly realized, helplessness. John *was* helpless. Oh, he could still hurt, could still cause mischief for his brother. But he couldn't unmarry him. And immediately, in this moment of victory, the gentle-hearted man began to feel compassion for the vanquished. He said, 'John, I am sorry to have given you pain. But Joan is a good woman, and I need her: her comfort, her companionship. I need – God help me – her strength.' He tried to take his brother's hand. But the Squire shoved him violently to one side and groped for the door handle. Thomas watched him leave, the ungainly Blount shambling after him.

That night, as they lay in their truckle bed, he said, miserably, 'By now, my brother will have told the College. They will take away my Fellowship. They will say, what is true, that I have been deceitful, underhand, and wilfully disobedient. I – do not know what we shall live on, Joan.'

She said, 'My aunt pays me a little for my work.'

He said, bitterly, 'I should never have married you, knowing I could not support you.'

'And robbed me of so much happiness?' said Joan, touching his lips with her finger.

Dear Joan! *A virtuous woman is a crown to her husband,* he remembered. A crown that will last a lifetime. For though the coming days and years might be harsh and heavy, yet he would require her for the harsh times. He would make himself ambitious for her happiness. And despite his brother, despite coming penury and hardship, he knew for that night a courage and a faith that was seldom to be his.

But not for long. That next morning he was summoned to Jesus College. There, having been charged with deceit, disobedience, lechery and carnal lust, and threatened with dishonour, starvation, and the flames of everlasting Hell, he was stripped of his Fellowship and his livelihood, and then contemptuously dismissed.

Yet they survived. Joan's aunt let her go on living (and working!) at the Dolphin. And he was often there, tending a sick horse, grooming a well one, and occasionally being allowed to stay overnight by the grudging aunt. He earned a small stipend, and a bed, as a Common Reader to the monks of Buckingham College. Books – and horses! The two things which, apart from Joan, he needed for his happiness.

And for most of the time he *was* happy. Joan was strong, and loving, making light of his fears and anxieties, praising him and encouraging, until he began to feel a confidence he had never known. He filled out, his tread was firmer, his smile ready and open, he exuded warmth. He was Thomas Cranmer, Magister Atrium Cantabrigiensis, married to a beautiful and popular woman.

And now he had another cause for pride and hope. Joan was with child!

Yet he was no fool. He had his black moods, moods almost of despair. He, a Master of Arts, could not even provide a home for his beloved wife, now heavy with child. They could not even live together. When they came together it was like a pair of illicit lovers, in dark alleyways, in the windy fields, in Joan's maiden bedroom. In the eyes of Cambridge, his own lasciviousness had destroyed him. He was a monster of depravity who had brought disgrace (to say nothing of eternal damnation) on to his own head.

Unworldly though Thomas was, he did realize that it would not be seemly for a child of an armigerous family like the Cranmers to be born at an inn. But fortunately Joan had another aunt, more amenable and more respectable than the Dolphin one. She lived at St Ives, loved Joan, loved even more the women's drama of a confinement. Thomas set off on horseback; his one valued possession, his wife seated precariously on the horse's withers.

He left her with her aunt. Then he returned, the lonely miles to Cambridge. He left physically empty.

Still, he told himself, in a month at the most I shall ride this way again, my wife before me, our child in her arms.

Then: our child, he thought. The living proof that I, a university Fellow, destined for the service of God, chose the voluptuous way of marriage instead of the godly path of celibacy. And he shivered in a sudden breeze of evening, that was as cold as the disapproval of God. He crossed himself as he rode, and he prayed that if God wished to punish him on earth he would not touch Joan with His anger. And from that moment on he was full of anxiety and trouble. His new-found confidence deserted him on that lonely journey, and there was no Joan to tease him into cheerfulness.

But the days passed and the news remained good. It was only thirteen miles from Cambridge to St Ives, so he was able to walk there comfortably and see for himself how Joan did.

And she did well. He would approach her aunt's house with a pounding heart, his eyes fixed desperately on the front door. And then the door would open, and Joan would stand there, holding out her arms in loving welcome like a statue of Our Lady herself, her face smiling, serene. And Thomas, gazing on this radiance, knew that even a jealous God would not bring Himself to touch so lovely a flower.

In the Refectory of Buckingham College, the good monks were having their lentil stew enlivened by a reading from St Jerome.

The reader was a man of perhaps twenty-seven, clear-complexioned, with a face that showed gentleness and indecision. But he read sweetly savouring the ponderous syllables.

But neither lentil stew nor St Jerome fully captured the monks' attention. So that when a doorkeeper padded into the room and whispered urgently to the Father Abbot, the Brothers' interest focused completely on the newcomeer.

Thomas Cranmer went on reading. *He* was interested in St Jerome, even if no one else was. But now he realized that Father Abbot was beckoning to him. Apologetically he closed the book on the lectern, and crossed the room. 'You wanted me, Father?'

'There is a woman who would speak with you, my son.' He indicated the doorkeeper. 'Brother Matthew will take you to her.'

Thomas bowed, and followed Brother Matthew. His mouth was suddenly dry. 'What is it?' he whispered.

'The child is born dead,' said the monk.

'And the mother? My wife?'

'She too is dead, Master.'

They were still only half-way to the massive door. There must be some mistake, he told himself. Why, I saw her only yesterday. This oaf must have bungled the message. He felt a most unusual and savage anger. 'What business is it of yours?' he shouted. 'Take me to the messenger.'

'I am taking you, Master,' the fellow said with patient reproof, just this side of insolence. He pulled open the big door. There, in the vestibule, stood Joan's cousin from St Ives. He stared at her face. It was tear-stained and drawn. 'Is it true?' he asked. His voice was a whisper now, almost a croak. 'Is it true?'

She nodded. 'Mother and child,' she said. 'Both.'

'Both,' he repeated dully. 'And – there is no mistake?'

'There is no mistake, Cousin Cranmer.' She gave a sudden wail. 'Oh, I wish there were.'

Afterwards, he could remember nothing about the journey to St Ives: whether he walked or rode. But actually he walked, and sometimes ran madly, holding out his hands before him like a blind man. And he muttered as he ran: prayers, self-reproaches, blaming himself that his lust had brought her to this, calling himself murderer; moaning her name, over and over, to the grey heavens. Yet afterwards all he could remember was the dead face of Joan: Joan who had given him strength and courage, the face of merry Black Joan now incredibly, unbelievably, stern in death.

He got little sympathy from Cambridge. Sly laughter, sniggers behind his back: Cranmer, the scholar who threw away his career to marry a wife; and then lost the wife! Why couldn't he have taken her as a concubine, like the rest of them, thus getting the best of both worlds? But no. That wasn't good enough for Master Cranmer.

Then, one day, he met the Master of Jesus. In a narrow street where the tops of the houses almost leaned against each other, and where, when two men met, one needed to stand in the foul ooze of the open drain. It was a day when Thomas felt most alone. Nor did the Master seem in a mood to do anything but gloat. 'Ah, Cranmer, your wife is dead, I hear.'

'Yes.' He felt the filth of the kennel soaking into his shoes.

'Your child also.'

'Yes.'

The Master's pale, ascetic face looked at him long and thoughtfully. Then: 'God is not mocked, Cranmer,' he said with considerable satisfaction. 'Doubtless, you have now learnt that lesson.'

Thomas inclined his head.

The Master pursed his long lips, nodded, and moved on.

So it was a surprising thing that a month later the College offered a Fellowship to Thomas Cranmer, MA, widower. An offer he listlessly accepted.

Chapter 2

The earthquake of the Reformation might not have come so soon had it not been for a thunderstorm…

Martin Luther, a law student, very laudably went to visit his parents in the small village of Mansfeld.

On the return journey he was caught in a terrible thunderstorm, a storm that frightened the life out of the poor man.

Now his pious and devout upbringing came to his rescue. 'Walled around with the terror and agony of sudden death,' as he so dramatically expressed himself, he cried out, 'Help, Saint Anne, and I'll become a monk.'

The storm began to creep away, grumbling and growling like a whipped cur. Martin Luther went safely on his way.

Now most twenty-two-year-old students would have forgotten that light promise even before the storm had become a soundless flickering among the distant hills. But Martin Luther did not forget. Two years later he took orders in the Roman Catholic Church whose power he was about to challenge.

From now on he was the catalyst for all that happened. Even the bloody upheavals at the English Court were helped by him who, but for that storm, might have lived and died a lawyer in Thuringia. And, suddenly, in 1517, he started a fire in Wittenberg that burned for centuries and is still smouldering: and this in the very year that the bottom fell out of Thomas Cranmer's life in Cambridge, leaving him broken, unpurposed, uncomforted.

But he was not a weakling. Final defeat never occurred to him. So. He would go back to his life as it was before Joan so sweetly, so terribly, disrupted it. Books. And the church. And grave discussions about the New Learning.

And the more he read and discussed, the more wonderful, the more bewildering, everything became. He discovered that the world might not be a flat piece of earth but was instead a spinning ball which incredibly went round the sun; he discovered that if you travelled east or west across the oceans you did not eventually fall over the edge of the world. Doubts even began to arise in his mind about the three-tier universe: the earth on the ground floor, Heaven on the floor above, and a Hell of unimaginable torments in the basement.

And, if the material universe was being questioned in this way, so he found was man's spirituality. Scholars like Colet and More and Erasmus and Wareham were clasping men to their hearts: rediscovering Christ in His glory, and through Him the pathetic, struggling creature man.

Two years later Thomas Cranmer was ordained priest. And his response to Luther's defiance was typical. Whereas Cambridge was in a ferment, the authorities alarmed by campaigns for Luther and against Masses for the Dead and praying to Saints, Thomas settled down quietly with his books and his Gospels to decide the validity or otherwise of Lutheranism. And, despite his weakening sight, he continued with this task for years.

And yet? Thomas, sitting there with his aching eyes (and his aching heart) while outside in the streets the battle of Luther and Papal Indulgences ebbed and flowed nightly, Thomas knew he was already proving himself a heretic. Now an ordained Priest, it was his duty to condemn Luther, not to weigh him.

Yet it was only an intellectual bookish heresy. Thomas sprang neither to help Luther nor to rescue the Pope. Europe, and the known world, were splitting apart. Already men were arming, burning, fighting at the beginning of a terrible struggle. Thomas was interested in the struggle. He deplored it. But he would not fight. He would live, and die, unknown, in little Cambridge.

Only once did the Tempter appear to him, and show him the earth, and the cities thereof. The Tempter took the form of William Capon, Master of Jesus, and he held out a glittering prize: a tutorship at the new Cardinal College in Oxford.

It was a distinction and an honour; for the great Wolsey himself was founding the College.

With typical lack of decision, Thomas accepted, despite his simple aim to live and die in Cambridge. He set out for Oxford. But on the way he met a friend who persuaded him that his own simple ambition had been best. Thomas, half disappointed, half relieved, returned to his loved study and his books.

Unfortunately, the next time Thomas Cranmer was visited by the Tempter, he met no good friend by the wayside.

While Thomas was studying quietly at Cambridge, making up his careful mind about things for which other men were already killing and dying, the English Court was looking back incredulously and wistfully at the rejoicing with which they had welcomed King Henry to the Throne. For, over the years, the golden youth was growing into a massive middle-aged tyrant: still devout, still learned and brilliant, still merry when he felt like being merry, he was nevertheless beginning to show signs of a dangerous temper. The phrase 'Le Roi le veult' was being heard more and more. Anyone delaying for a moment to do whatever it was that the King wished soon learned the force of another phrase: 'The wrath of the King is death.'

So. When the King was merry, the Court was merry. It daren't be anything else. But when the King raged everyone, from the High Officers of State to the scullions, grew white with fear for their very lives.

And that Princess of Aragon, who had come to these cheerless shores so many years ago, and since then had soldiered bravely on as Henry's Queen?

She too feared for her life. Her beauty was growing heavy and masculine. Worse, far worse, she seemed unable to bear a male child. Miscarriage after miscarriage was her dreary achievement; that, and one whey-faced daughter. (And what the Country needed above all else was a male heir, to make safe the succession. The long and bloody agony of the Wars of the Roses was too recent to be forgotten.) Yet once Henry had finished raging over the disappointment of each latest miscarriage, he treated her kindly...

Until, one day, strolling in the gardens of Durham House, Thomas Boleyn's house in the Strand, he passed through a wrought-iron gate and startled two young girls gathering roses.

They dropped their flowers and curtseyed. But whereas the elder lowered her eyes and was most sweet and respectful, the younger allowed her eyes to glance up at his great stature admiringly, and he felt she only just managed to suppress the disaster of a giggle.

Henry was not over-pleased. Nevertheless, two pretty girls alone in a garden of roses was the sort of picture he wrote madrigals about, so he decided to be pleasant. 'What are your names, ladies?'

The elder curtseyed deeply. 'Mary Boleyn, if it please your Grace.'

'Anne Boleyn, your Grace,' said the younger, with a perfunctory bob.

Henry surveyed them both. 'You are pert, Mistress Anne,' he said without warmth.

In contrast to his powerful bulk, Henry's voice was surprisingly high-pitched and thin: a fact that seemed irresistibly comic to Anne.

Henry Tudor was not used to being thought comic. He stumped on his way, curiously ill-at-ease. Thomas Boleyn's girls had unsettled him. He thought of his ageing, swarthy Queen. He saw again the sweet, dark, liquid eyes of Mary Boleyn. (*There* was a gentle, submissive wench for you!) He simmered at the memory of young Anne's near insolence.

Yes. The King was put out. His Fool, who studied his moods as watchfully as a lone mariner studies the moods of the unpredictable sea, was at a loss. He didn't try any jokes. There was, he sensed, a surging, unsatisfied anger troubling that enormous frame. But he, the Fool, who knew the King perhaps better than any other man was reminded of occasions when his Grace had found himself in love with one or other of the Ladies of the Court.

And Will Somers was not the only one watching the King. The courtiers spent their lives watching the King: for the first signs of tedium, irritation, or demonic rage. But they had not the perception of a Fool. They had their ears cocked for approaching thunder; not for the music and the poetry of love.

Henry, lowering in his great chair, suddenly beckoned to Will Somers. 'Fetch your lute, Fool.' He sighed deeply. 'I would hear a song of unhappy love.'

Will, relieved, somersaulted out of the room. It was good to know that one's perceptions were still in good order.

Perceptions could save one from a whipping, even a hanging. He returned with his Lute, settled cross-legged at the King's feet, struck a chord, began to sing in his thin tenor a tale of unrequited love.

Resting, as he so often was, against the King's knees (the better for a bit of quiet bawdy, even a crumb of wise advice from Fool to Majesty), resting so, he was aware that the royal legs remained tense and unrelaxed. In fact he had a well-remembered feeling that after another bar or two a powerful kick might send him (and his lute) sprawling down the steps on which the great chair stood.

Instead, a voice spoke quietly in his ear: 'Will?'

'Uncle?'

The King signed, and was silent. The Fool sensed a man overcoming shame. Then: 'Have Mistress Mary Boleyn brought to the Privy Chamber, Fool. Secretly.'

At Durham House lanterns moved urgently in the Courtyard, messages were given to footmen who sought out the Chamberlain who, so important was the message, disturbed Sir Thomas Boleyn at cards. 'Sir, Mistress Mary is commanded to Court.'

These words were meat and drink to Sir Thomas, as they must be to any man who has two fair daughters and a not over-scrupulous ambition. Then: 'Commanded? Who commands a Boleyn, Chamberlain?'

The Chamberlain gave him a long look and was silent. Sir Thomas said, 'When?'

'Now, Sir Thomas. She is bidden to – the Privy Chamber.'

'God's Blood! Then find her, man, find her.' Hell fire! Men had been made Dukes for less than this. And now everything waited on a silly girl and getting her to Court in clean underclothes.

But here came a gaggle of girls, chattering along the corridor like a flock of birds. He managed to grab the arm of a fleeting girl. 'Mary! Be silent girl, and listen to me.' He began to speak, quickly and earnestly, while she for her part grew pale, and those huge dark eyes stared at him in horror. 'Father! I had rather die.'

'And that's just what you will do if you behave like some green ninny. And so, which is more important, will I.'

Henry, alone in the Privy Chamber, waited, and fumed, and muttered, his jewelled fingers clasping and unclasping the carved eagle's heads on the arms of his chair.

Sudden desire, guilt, and self-hatred were the emotions that were tearing that huge frame. Henry was a devout man; and though he was learning quickly, he was not yet used to giving power its head and damning the consequences. Besides, Hell Fire was a very near and real thing. And everyone new that there was a very special fire reserved for the seducers of virgins.

He swung round suddenly. A small door in the panelling had opened. A beautiful, scared girl stood in the doorway, her liquid eyes gazing at him fearfully.

The door was closed silently behind her.

Henry forgot about devoutness. He even forgot about Hell Fire. He held out his vast arms. His smile was all of welcome and joy and love. 'Mistress Mary! How you honour your poor servant with your speed.'

She stayed in the doorway, curtseying deeply. He walked slowly towards her, took her hands, pressing them warmly. Then he released them. She stared down at her palms. In each lay a vast pearl.

He laughed hugely at her surprise. But, as time went on, his laughter fell silent, his smile faded. 'Well, Mistress, have you no word of thanks for your Prince?'

Staring down at the carpet she said, 'Your Grace, I cannot accept.'

He flung himself back into his chair. 'God's Body, but you will accept. Aye, *and* pay for them before this night is out.'

'Your Grace.' She began to weep piteously. 'My honour...'

God, how they always prated about their honour! But power had still not yet quite eroded humanity. And by now, he thought with shame, the whole Court will know what's happening.

Still, there could be no going back. Neither his pride nor his desires would consider such a thing. He said, gently now, 'Your honour? Can't you see, child, that I am offering you the greatest honour an Englishwoman could possibly have?'

She stood before him, shaking her head vigorously, so that the tears scattered from her cheeks.

He said quietly, 'Le Roi le veult, Mary.'

She stood silent, weeping.

But, he began to wonder, did le Roi wish it? *Did* he want this snivelling virgin? He suddenly pictured himself in connubial bliss with comfortable, friendly Katherine always willing when she wasn't having a miscarriage. It was so much easier. He said, 'Very well, little sniveller. Knock on that door and they'll let you out. But listen. You will keep those pearls, and eventually you'll pay for them. However, first we'll see whether a few years at the French Court will put a bit of heart into you. And you can take that pert sister of yours with you and lose her for all I care.' And he went back into the Presence Chamber, to the great discomfiture of the Courtiers, who thought they'd got rid of him for the evening.

And the decadent Court of Francis I did indeed put some heart into her. On her eventual return Henry found her not only still desirable but now also complaisant. He promptly married her to his Esquire of the Body, William Carey, a gentleman of some breadth of mind who was by no means averse to sharing his wife with his Sovereign. The King also began to notice the improvement in Mary's sister Anne since her sojourn in France.

Yes. That mighty Prince, King Henry VIII of England, still had a conscience: a conscience that was suddenly becoming somewhat overloaded.

Not, this time, about a few ravished virgins. But about a far greater matter: something, in fact, that had grown into the King's *Great* Matter, something that wholly engrossed the high Ministers of State, the Princes of the Church, the University Divines, even presumably God Himself; and not only in little England, but in mighty Rome itself.

The problem was this: twenty years ago Henry had married his deceased brother's wife, something expressly forbidden in Leviticus but approved by the accommodating Pope of those days by the granting of a dispensation.

Now, after twenty years of comparative happiness, Henry was suddenly worried and afraid. There was still no male heir, and Katherine's miscarriages came round as regular as Christmas. Could this be God's anger? Had he and Katherine ever been really married? If, as Katherine always swore, her marriage to Arthur had never been consummated, how did that affect things? It seemed to Henry that the only way to ease his conscience (and to assuage God's apparent wrath) was to divorce Katherine. But that needed the Pope's blessing. And the Pope had a lot of other things on his mind, perhaps the most important being that the Emperor Charles V was holding him virtually a prisoner. And Charles was nephew to Katherine of Aragon: all in all, a difficult situation for even a Pope to find himself in.

Even Thomas Cranmer, living his undistinguished life in Cambridge, gave his mind to the King's Great Matter.

But his was an academic interest. Unlike the great Officers of State, he was not being driven to find a solution, and his life did not hang on his obtaining a divorce for the King.

And then, with the inevitability of Greek tragedy, Thomas Cranmer was suddenly caught up in this Great Matter. He, the pawn, was moved to Waltham, the King to Waltham Abbey. And suddenly the pawn seemed the only possible protector of the King. Once again for Thomas a path lay open to fortune and honour.

CHAPTER 3

In Spring, 1529, the sweating sickness broke out in Cambridge.

That same summer, Henry Tudor decided to go hunting at Waltham Abbey. The harbingers were sent out to arrange lodgings for the Court. They billeted the King's almoner, Edward Foxe, and the King's secretary, Stephen Gardiner, at the house of Master Cressey: two men both deeply involved in finding a solution to the King's Matter, both of whom had known Cranmer in their Cambridge days. And Master Cressey's two sons were being tutored at Cambridge by Thomas Cranmer. And men were dying in the streets of Cambridge, dying horribly of a foul and stinking sweat.

With terror and death walking the streets of Cambridge, Cranmer very wisely took the two young Cresseys to their home to continue their studies. And, apart from a brief return to his College during July, he spent the summer in the Cressey household. So he was an established guest when the family first sat down to supper on August 2nd with their distinguished visitors from the Court.

But he was an uncomfortable one. He was a man of forty now, a man who had lived these last twelve years nursing an old sorrow, a naturally shy man who, once Joan's cheerful influence was lost, had reverted to a solitary, myopic poring over books and manuscript.

But now here he was in a very different world: in a room brilliant with candles, and silver, and glass, noisy with the chatter of women, the laughter of men; a room charged with the gaiety and the excitement of that first meeting before guests have begun to pall and hosts to become tedious.

He was lifted up by this charged atmosphere. He longed to be part of it, to be as merry as the others. Yet this shy and charming man stood apart, black-robed, alone, Master Tutor, even though Mistress Cressey was a distant cousin and he now had the honour of being *Doctor* Cranmer. It was not for him, he thought sadly. He felt safe only when immured in the stone walls of his Cambridge study.

A voice said, 'Isn't it Cranmer?'

He stared. 'Gardiner,' he said, holding out his hand gratefully. It was good to be noticed, even by a mere acquaintance, someone who had risen meteorically at Cambridge; someone who, in spite of his royal service, was still Master of Trinity Hall; someone to whom Thomas must have seemed a dusty nonentity.

Stephen Gardiner was also, unfortunately, a man with whom Thomas could never feel at ease: a rough bully of a man whose smile was a glint in the eyes and a tightening of the long lips, whose voice to inferiors was the voice of a man calling to heel his dog. Now he said, 'The last I heard, you were still at Cambridge.'

Thomas smiled modestly. 'I still am. And likely to be.'

'Tush, man. How old are you? Forty, I would guess. You should have been out in the world these twenty years. There are great things happening, Cranmer. Whereas in Cambridge – men's beards and the spiders' webs grow longer. Nothing more.' He gave a harsh, discordant laugh, gulped his wine, and stared hard and unsmiling at his companion.

Thomas said, 'Cambridge is my life, Gardiner. I ask nothing more.'

Gardiner snorted with disdain. With one hand he deftly snatched another glass from a passing tray. With the other he seized a man by the arm and dragged him round to face Thomas. 'Edward, you remember Cranmer? Fellow of Jesus.' Then he smiled, muttered something Thomas could not hear, though he imagined he caught the name 'Black Joan'.

But, if the name Black Joan had indeed been mentioned, it did not amuse Edward Foxe. He took Thomas' hand with great courtesy and said 'I believe it is *Doctor* Cranmer, now?'

Thomas inclined his head. 'I remember you well, Master Foxe. And now, I hear, you are King's Almoner?'

'So. So. And you are still at Cambridge? How I envy you. The world is a dangerous place, these days.'

'Especially for those of us on the King's business.' Stephen Gardiner dug an elbow roughly into his companion's side. 'Eh, Master Foxe?'

'Indeed.' Edward Foxe gave Cranmer his sweet smile. 'Gardiner and I have travelled Europe on the King's Matter. And met Popes and Prelates and Princes. And all to no avail.' He placed a hand on each side of his neck, smiled ruefully. 'I vow I feel my head loose on my shoulders.' Now it was his turn to seize a glass from a tray. But *he* gave it to Cranmer. 'Drink this, my friend. It distances us from death – and Hell.'

Thomas drank. And whether it was the wine, or the friendliness and warmth of Foxe, he was suddenly confident and happy as he had not been since the death of Joan. And after supper, when the ladies had retired, and the candles stank and guttered in the sockets, he and Gardiner and Foxe spread their elbows wide on the table, and laid their chins on the backs of their hands, and talked. And Thomas, for perhaps the first time in his life, felt himself uplifted to be a man among men.

And the things he heard! They were beyond belief. They were to the rumours of Cambridge what fire is to smoke. And he, Thomas Cranmer, was hearing it from two brilliant young men who seemed well on the way to tremendous personal power. Sitting here with them, cheek by jowl!

Yes. The things he heard! How, if the King did not get between the sheets with Mistress Anne Boleyn soon, half the noble heads of the Council could be hacked from their shoulders. How the King himself had devised a scheme whereby he might at last be relieved of the sinfulness of living with his deceased brother's wife: that Cardinal Wolsey, as Papal Legate, should summon the King to answer the charge that he and his loving, pious Katherine were living in open sin; and that Wolsey, the charge accepted, should then annul the twenty-year-old marriage. How this scheme was ruined by the unforeseen and unlikely event that the Pope was made a prisoner by Charles V's army, so that Wolsey's standing as Papal Legate was cut from under his feet. How Gardiner and Foxe were then sent to Rome to see what *they* could do. They were to stress that the King's sole reasons for wanting a divorce were his troubled conscience and his desire for a male heir: and that Anne Boleyn was a woman of 'purity, constant virginity, maidenly and womanly pudicity, humility, and an apparent aptness to procreation of children'. Were she otherwise, in any particular, they were to stress, the good Cardinal would naturally have refused to have anything to do with this matter. They were to offer bribes and, if necessary, threats.

But, though they 'spake roundly unto him', His Holiness would not budge. Even the threat that England's King would cease his allegiance and embrace Lutheranism troubled but did not move him. He fell back on delay, while the whole of Christendom could think of little else but the King's Matter.

And Stephen Gardiner and Edward Foxe were at their wits' ends.

A strange thing happened. It was almost like a moment of revelation. All Thomas' reading, all his academic weighing up of pros and cons suddenly crystallized into convictions. He didn't like Rome. He thought the Pope far too powerful. He came back to an old theme of his: that all truth lay in study of the Scriptures. And he, Thomas Cranmer, knew that truth. Most shattering of all, he realized he had travelled a long way down the road to Lutheranism.

He began to speak.

Was he inspired? Or had the wine, by its own superb alchemy, sharpened and concentrated his mind? Anyway, he spoke: at length, and to some purpose. He began by telling them roundly that, though he had not studied the subject, it seemed to him 'that you go not the next way to work, as to bring the matter to a perfect conclusion and end.' That it was no good expecting anything from the Ecclesiastical Courts; that there was 'but one truth in it, which no man ought or better can discuss than the divines.' Once they had pronounced, the King could act on their advice, and the Holy Father and the Ecclesiastical Courts could both be ignored.

That Foxe and Gardiner (and especially the canonist Gardiner) allowed themselves to be thus lectured by a dusty scholar; that they even listened to the breathtaking suggestion that a twenty-year-old royal marriage, publicly celebrated and unquestionably consummated, could be set aside by the decision of the theologians, without any confirmation from Ecclesiastical Court or even Pope – this shows perhaps the desperation of men drowning in the quagmire of Papal 'frustratory delays'.

Gardiner was the first to speak. He looked at Thomas with a sort of bewildered anger. 'But the canonists, Cranmer? They cannot be ignored.'

'Why not? If the theologians' opinion is that the marriage is invalid (as it should be), and his Grace acts upon their advice, and declares his marriage null and void, who shall stop him?'

Gardiner was silent. Foxe said, 'Dr Cranmer. Would you forgive Gardiner and me if we walked apart a while?'

Thomas inclined his head, and rose. Gardiner and Foxe also rose and began to pace the room, deep in conversation. Thomas sat down at table again, and watched them anxiously. He was suddenly afraid. What had he said? Worse, what had the wine said? He went quickly over the conversation. Treason? Heresy? The penalty for one was a slow, bloody and agonizing death; for the other, death by fire. And he, wishing to show off his cleverness after the long years of neglect, had risked both by talking freely to two near-strangers who had the ear of Wolsey, nay, of the King himself!

When they returned they were smiling (not that there was ever much comfort in Gardiner's smile). Thomas rose. Foxe put a hand on his arm. 'Nay, Doctor Cranmer, be seated. More wine?'

The three men sat down. Gardiner said, 'How read *you* this question, Doctor Cranmer?'

Thomas was cautious now. 'I have not studied the matter, sir.'

Gardiner said, with some acerbity, 'If you were to study it, sir, how think you that you might decide? That the King's marriage is valid. Or invalid?'

Thomas' mouth was dry. He was silent. Then he said, almost in a whisper, 'Invalid. Most certainly invalid.'

The tension suddenly snapped. Foxe slapped a hand on his shoulder. 'Good. Good. If *one* theologian thinks so – '

Suddenly he gave Thomas a long, hard look. 'Could you persuade your fellow theologians? Starting with Cambridge, say?'

What *was* happening? What were they asking of him? He was afraid, bewildered. He was also flattered, exalted, filled with a tremendous, nervous excitement that he, and he alone, from his long reading of the Scriptures, knew the truth of this matter. He said, 'I am a simple scholar, gentlemen. How can I – ?'

Foxe said, 'Do not fear, Thomas. Simple scholar you may be. But you have a golden key in your hand: a key of your own shaping.'

Gardiner cut in roughly. 'Never mind golden keys. Now listen, Cranmer. The King has arranged a disputation about the Divorce at Cambridge. Six Cambridge divines. Six Oxford divines. *I* will see that you are one of the disputants. And if you can persuade them to agree with you that the marriage of King Henry and Queen Katherine is invalid – ' He paused, took a deep breath. 'Then, my friend, you will have earned the King's gratitude.'

'And the King,' said Foxe, laying a hand on Thomas' arm, 'the King is a man most full of heart, only too eager to reward those who serve him well.'

Gardiner rose. 'Study the matter,' he said harshly. 'And do not fail.'

Thomas went to bed in a daze. Who was he, to influence the decisions of twelve learned divines? Did he even want to? No. *This* world was not for him. And why had he let Stephen Gardiner order him about like a servant? He began to fume at the man's arrogance. And Foxe, friendly though he was, bribing him with talk of the King's generosity! No. He would have none of it.

Yet, even as he thought thus, another part of his brain was already producing arguments for the annulment of the marriage: the uncompromising words of Leviticus; the fact that God had undoubtedly cursed the marriage; the inability of the Pope to dispense over divine law; yes, he, who understood the truth so clearly, had a moral duty to persuade these mistaken divines.

But the next morning, fear had taken over: fear of men in high places, fear of change, fear of failure. Meeting Gardiner he said, firmly, 'I cannot do what you ask, Gardiner,' and braced himself for the storm.

The storm did not come. Only a gust of ice-cold wind. 'Do as you please,' Gardiner said contemptuously. And went on his way without a backward glance.

There was a peremptory knocking at Cranmer's door.

Thomas froze. He had not forgotten his unguarded talk last month at Waltham. And, if he *had* spoken treason or heresy, such a knocking might be the first step on the long journey to Tyburn or the Tower.

Nervously he opened the door and peered into the dark corridor. Torn from his books, his eyes had difficulty in focusing.

But he was not kept in suspense long. Stephen Gardiner was already filling the tiny cell. 'Cranmer, I want you to go and talk to those twelve fools. Now. Today. You know what they've done? They've decided the marriage is *valid*. If you can't change their addled brains the King will have all our heads.'

'But they're wrong,' Thomas said in disbelief.

'Of *course* they're wrong. Well, you go and tell 'em they're wrong.' He looked at Thomas and smiled. Unaccountably, he seemed in the best of humours.

Thomas had been afraid. He was still afraid. But error was abroad. Error had to be corrected. He hurried off at Gardiner's side. Gardiner introduced him to the twelve divines, in a short speech in which he hinted that their heads might have been safer on their shoulders if their verdict had been '*in*valid'.

Then Thomas addressed them: vigorously, gently, thoughtfully, prayerfully. Then, after a short discussion, they gave a new verdict on their disputation. All but one now thought the King's marriage invalid. It was a remarkable piece of persuasion on the part of an unknown scholar.

The King's head was down like that of a wounded bull. His eyes, which through the years were growing smaller and closer, ranged round the Presence Chamber seeking whom they might devour. For the sake of his conscience and the Succession, he wanted his marriage annulled. God wanted it annulled.

Besides, there was no doubt about it, Mistress Anne Boleyn was making his life hell too.

And now, twelve stupid old men in Cambridge had publicly decided that he was truly and honourably married to Katherine. God's Blood, he'd have the heads off their shoulders and the skin off their backs!

Oh, here came Master Secretary Gardiner, bowing and scraping. God, he'd have the skin off his back, too.

'Good news, Your Majesty.'

'*Good* news, Master Secretary? Is the Pope dead? Has my Lady Katherine been taken in adultery?'

'Your Grace, the Cambridge Disputation. They have now decided your Grace and Queen Katherine are living in open sin, to the danger and detriment of your immortal souls.'

'But – yesterday the fools had bound us together for life.'

'That was yesterday, your Grace. Today a Doctor Cranmer has persuaded them of their error.'

'A Doctor Cranmer, you say?'

'A man powerful in argument, though his manner is gentle, almost hesitant. A theologian, he thinks there is but one truth in your matter, and only the theologians are fitted to finding it.'

'And that truth is – ?'

'That your Highness fornicates every time he lies with the Queen.'

'God's Body!' There were times when Henry found Master Secretary Gardiner's direct way of speech unacceptable. But he was too eager to hear more to waste time on niceties. 'What kind of man?'

'Pliant.'

'Ah,' said the King with a long expiration of breath.

'A Doctor of Divinity. Yet – so far – undistinguished. Clever.'

Now the King's look had become concentrated, keen, intense. It was a look his advisers knew well: a look that could augur high rewards or callous dismissal. 'This golden-tongued cleric who can persuade the old fools in Cambridge to see sense. Could he equally persuade the Universities of Europe? Orleans, Paris, Wittenberg?'

'I think it likely, Your Grace.'

'I like not your "likelys". Could he, or couldn't he?' It was an angry growl.

'He could, sire.' But Gardiner's mouth was dry. When advising Majesty you were not allowed to hedge. You were forced to commit yourself, so that, if the man you recommended failed you, your head was on the block with his.

'So far,' Henry said, slowly and venemously: 'so far this Great Matter has been handled by fools. But it could be this man hath the sow by the right ear. Send him to me, Master Secretary.'

Chapter 4

It was not a happy dinner party at Aslockton Manor. The black sheep of the family was present: he who had blackened the Cranmer name by marrying a strumpet.

Well, God had done His best to put matters right. The strumpet and her brat had been removed and Thomas was leading the sort of life he deserved: dull and undistinguished.

Outside, the October afternoon was grey and still: so still that the sound of a distant horseman could be heard, an ancient, evocative sound from which Thomas drew pleasure and comfort, knowing that this time tomorrow he would be creating the same, peaceful sound as he clip-clopped towards Cambridge.

John said, 'Harvests have been bad again.'

Every year the same conversation. Yet suddenly Thomas wanted it to go on, he wanted to belong to it, to the waking in his old room beside the chimney (the room where so often a beaten child had cried himself to sleep), to the quiet, leisurely meals with scarce a word spoken (and that a wholly predictable one).

Yes. Since the disputation at Cambridge, he had been fearful. He had been made aware of another world: a world that had almost touched him, a harsh, hard, brutal world, aclash with the strivings of powerful men; a world that made little Aslockton, however dull, seem like a paradise.

The horseman was very near now. In fact, they heard him clatter into the yard. Then, moments of silence. Then a servant entering the dining room with a letter.

Looking rather pale, Squire John put out his hand to take it. But to his surprise, and undisguised annoyance, the servant moved on and presented it to Thomas.

Thomas turned even paler than his brother. He took the letter. Dusk was beginning to fill the room, and he moved over to the window. That was better. But now incredulity caused him as much difficulty as had the darkness.

'I am commanded to Court,' he stammered.

'To Court? You?' his brother said scornfully. 'Whatever for?'

Thomas was silent. Then: 'To meet the King.' He said with a quick, nervous, slightly hysterical laugh.

'To meet the King,' said Thomas, in wonder. He was in a daze. He went through into the kitchen, where the messenger, despite his royal livery, was gnawing on a hambone, swilling beer and ogling the wenches.

At Thomas' entry he sprang to his feet and, hambone in hand, asked a blessing.

Thomas blessed him. Then: 'When do we start?'

'Now,' said the man. 'We have a horse for you, saddled, and there are relays. We shall travel by Cambridge, where you will be given time to augment your wardrobe. Then we travel, night and day, to Greenwich.'

Clearly, the man had learnt his instructions by rote. It seemed to the anxious Thomas more like an arrest. The only comfort was that his destination was Greenwich and not the Tower. He took a hurried farewell of his intrigued family, and clattered off.

Now, at last, he had time to think.

To meet the King? How *did* one meet the King? Bow, kneel, throw oneself full-length on the floor? No. The rhythmic exercise, the cantering horse, the quiet evening helped him to gather his wits. He, Doctor Thomas Cranmer, son and brother of the Squires of Aslockton, knew how to behave to his fellow humans. And even King Henry, all powerful, all terrible, was a child of God like himself.

But his first sight of London revived all his fears. Riding through the grim city gate, being scrutinized warily by the guards, was like entering a prison, and, once inside, the uproar of buying and selling, the clatter and neighing of horses, the squeals and shrieks and laughter of children at play almost among the horses' hooves – all this noise and bustle, held in and pressed down as it were by the crowded, overhanging houses, and the wharves and warehouses – it was like being assailed by those demons in Hell who so often crowded his dreams.

One thing, and one thing only, lifted his spirits: the sight of the lofty naves, and the massive square tower of Paul's, the spires of St Laurence Poultney and St Dunstan-in-the-East, and a whole plethora of lesser towers and spires, all lifting up the soul to God in this ant-heap of a capital.

Crossing London Bridge his companion eagerly pointed out the rotting heads of traitors on their bloody poles. With relish he drew Thomas' attention to a mass of grim walls and turrets rising out of the mists on the opposite bank of the river. 'The Tower,' he said. He crossed himself. 'God keep us out of there, Master Cranmer.'

'Amen,' Thomas said fervently. He too crossed himself.

'Not long now,' said the man. 'You'll soon be with his Majesty.'

Thomas' heart fluttered. He licked his dry lips. 'What is he like, his Majesty?'

The man considered. 'As pleasant a gentleman as you could wish to meet,' he said at last. 'If you catch him in the right mood, that is,' he added thoughtfully.

'And if you don't catch him in the right mood?' asked Thomas.

'Then he could have the head off your shoulders and the skin off your back,' said the man. But after a few more minutes of thoughtful silence they came over the brow of a slight hill and saw before them a palace reaching down to the great river itself. 'Greenwich Palace,' said the man. 'Loves it, he does. I reckon if anyone can find him in a good mood they're as likely to here as anywhere.'

But the magnificence! Not only had Thomas never seen anything like it, he'd never imagined anything like it. Such beauty uplifted him.

Courteous, friendly servants led him through waiting rooms and corridors glittering with gold and silver and precious stones, hung with superb tapestries, peopled by men brilliant as peacocks, by women all, it seemed, of a surpassing loveliness.

Then, they were in a great gold-ceilinged chamber of which the focal point was a canopy of cloth of gold above two cushioned and bejewelled chairs, both empty. Thomas' escort opened a small door in the panelling, and held it for Thomas, who stood in the doorway feeling lonelier than he had ever felt in his life. 'Dr Thomas Cranmer, your Majesty,' the man announced, and retired. Thomas was alone with his Sovereign.

Henry was standing beside a crimson and gold chair. Silks and satins, feathers, velvets, precious stones had all played a part in his appearance. Yet these were only settings for those fresh-complexioned cheeks, that silky fringe of auburn hair and beard, those curiously brilliant blue eyes, that massive, kingly frame. Before Thomas could fall on his knees Henry was across the room and huge hands had grasped his visitor's upper arms and held him for a moment against a great oak bole of a chest. 'Doctor Cranmer!' There was an infinity of friendship and welcome in the four syllables. Thomas knelt, his eyes filling with tears. Weariness, relief, *love* for this noble being had unarmed him.

'Ah, you have ridden fast and far I hear.' Henry gave Thomas a friendly, but searching, look. 'You have studied the King's Great Matter, I understand.' Then, with a sudden, impatient gesture, 'Don't kneel there, man.' And he virtually hauled Thomas to his feet.

The King flopped into his chair, tugged violently at a velvet rope. A bowing servant appeared. 'Bring wine,' the King said, with the impulsive generosity of Princes who forget that what their subjects often want more than anything is food.

All this time his astute eyes had never left Cranmer's face.

He saw a weary, travel-worn cleric, indistinguishable from a thousand others.

What else did he see? The pleasant, anxious face of a man whose eyes, though used to smiling, yet carried a weight of anxieties; he saw, he thought, an honest man, a man who, once he had given his loyalty, would never waver; a pliant man, as Gardiner had said? Probably, though Henry would not have wagered on it. But a man who would fear death.

Then a strange thought came into Henry's mind: a man I could love. What nonsense! Men were his tools.

But this man? He had a simplicity, a vulnerability about him, so different from the power-seekers who surrounded Henry that despite the man's fears he seemed to emanate peace.

The King said, 'Doctor Cranmer, if you serve me you will have many enemies, ruthless enemies. Does this trouble you?'

'Yes, your Majesty.'

As he thought, an honest man. 'While I live you will also have a powerful friend, Doctor. Does that comfort you?'

'Your Majesty is most gracious.'

'I said, "does it comfort you?"' It was an impatient shout.

'Yes, your Majesty.'

'Then remember it. However dark the house.'

The wine was brought. Thomas sipped. The wine was sweet and strong. And he had not eaten since breakfast. Already the room was beginning to swim.

Henry gave him an understanding, but slightly impatient smile. 'Come, Doctor Cranmer, why should you be ill at ease in the presence of your Sovereign? Cheer up, man.'

Thomas felt better. How unnecessary all the fears of his long journey had been! Why, Henry was infinitely the most charming man he had ever met. Already the bond that was to hold these two men together, through storms and tempests and quiet waters, was forged.

Henry said, 'Doctor, you have studied the matter of my marriage to my beloved Queen Katherine, I understand?'

'I have, your Majesty.'

'And you have reached certain conclusions?'

'Yes, Sire.'

'My dear Cranmer, I will not ask what those conclusions are. That would be most improper. Because, Doctor Cranmer, I want you to write a book on this matter. And I need not tell you that I want it to be completely impartial.'

'Of course, your Majesty.'

The King sat back sideways in his chair. 'You understand, Thomas, what a sad and indeed terrible decision this is for me: to reject, after twenty years of married happiness, a woman I love.'

His voice became slow and measured, almost as though he were reciting an oft-repeated speech (as, indeed, he was):

'For never, Thomas, was there Prince had a more gentle and obedient and loving companion and wife than the Queen is, nor did I ever fancy woman in all respects better, if this doubt had not risen.' He sighed very deeply.

Thomas was silent. This was not quite the story he had heard from Gardiner. But the King was speaking again. 'And yet, Thomas, she is my brother's wife.' He gave what was almost a wail. 'I have uncovered my dead brother's nakedness. And the Lord has cursed my marriage that it be childless.'

'The Princess Mary – ?' began Thomas.

It was as though shutters came down for a moment over those friendly eyes. Then the face was smiling again. 'A Prince must always consider the Succession. A puling girl would be a constant temptation to some of my Council.' He lowered his voice. 'I can trust no one, Cranmer, no one.'

Thomas said, 'Who am I, to write a book about so great a matter?'

'A man who has the sow by the right ear,' the King said jovially. He sprang up from his chair. 'All is arranged. You will stay at the house of Sir Thomas Boleyn while you write the book, and you will be given every comfort and facility.

Thomas could not hide his astonishment. 'Your Majesty! Is not Sir Thomas the father of Mistress Anne Boleyn?'

There was no doubt about it now. The shutters were down again, fastened tight. Then again mercifully they opened. A reproachful voice said, 'Thomas, Thomas, surely a learned doctor of Cambridge does not listen to the tattle of the market place? As God is my judge, Thomas, Mistress Anne has no place in this matter.'

Thomas inclined his head. Simple cleric he might, or might not, be. But he knew that men, even Princes, lusted after women, and were prepared to do far more than lie to gain their ends. Yet he believed what in his heart he feared were Henry Tudor's lies; believed them and accepted them out of loyalty to a Prince he wished to serve all his days. It was illogical, perhaps muddled. But it was not unprincipled. He allowed himself to be taken to Durham House, home of the father of Anne Boleyn, to study the Great Matter.

Yes. He had found here on earth the Master he wished to serve as devotedly as he served his Master in Heaven. A Master of overwhelming graciousness and charm. Yet as he left the luxurious Privy Chamber he felt like a man leaving the cage he had just shared with the lion and was thankful to be still alive and unmauled.

It seemed to Thomas Cranmer that Durham House was only a little less grand than the Royal Palace of Greenwich. It was a magnificent place, its formal gardens running down to London's noble river. And Thomas was welcomed like royalty. Sir Thomas Boleyn received him in person, took him to his room, begged him to make known any requests to himself personally; installed him in the great library with a vaseful of quills, with paper by the ream, with sand and ink and a penknife; consulted him earnestly about his devotional requirements and his meals, and then respectfully withdrew.

Thomas was intrigued, and decidedly embarrassed, by this treatment: knowing in his heart yet not admitting that while most of the Council wanted a settlement to the Divorce situation so that their heads might sit more comfortably on their shoulders, Sir Thomas Boleyn hoped that one might eventually set him among the highest in the land. (Mistaken ambition, of course. As Cranmer well knew, and that from the King's own lips, Mistress Anne had no place in this matter.)

So none of this concerned Thomas Cranmer. His one duty was to decide on the truth of the matter, and then put it in a book to help the King throw off his burden of sin.

And he had *already* decided – long ago. It was all in Leviticus. Henry had uncovered his brother's nakedness; and God's anger was plain for all to see. All those miscarriages!

Thomas worked on diligently, to a rigid timetable. Boleyn let it be known that any member of the household who disturbed him would incur the gravest displeasure.

But one member of the household was above such restrictions. You couldn't expect someone who spent all her time at Court to be bound on her rare visits home. Thomas, writing away at his desk, at first took little notice when the library door was flung open and a young woman flitted into the room and began moving round the shelves, stopping every now and then to peer without interest at some of the titles, and at other times to look at Cranmer himself with considerable interest. But he was not a man to be unaware of a woman in the same room as himself. He looked up and saw a pair of dark, almond-shaped eyes regarding him with amusement.

'Who are you, sir?' She was direct, imperious, but still amused.

He rose, bowed. 'I am Thomas Cranmer, Ma'am, of Cambridge University.'

'Ah. The fellow who is to get my Henry untethered from that Spanish cow. Do your work well, Master Priest.'

She was never still, jigging about, smiling, now shifting away, now moving provocatively close. He watched her, appalled by her cruel words, yet fascinated by her vitality. She was as restless as the sea. Her hair hung down below her waist, and with her constant movement it rippled like a brook. But it was her eyes! All her life seemed to be in her almond eyes, which now slid sideways to smile at him, now away to look unashamedly at what he had been writing.

He wished she would not come so close. He, a priest, felt his arms might move of their own accord to take her to him if she got too near.

'And how do you like sudden fame, Master Priest? It is said you were quite a nonentity. Then suddenly – pouf! All the world is talking of you and your cleverness.' She came very close, smiled up into his eyes. Her breast was almost touching his. Her teeth, between her long lips, had a sharp and cruel look, like a cat's.

He said, uncomfortably, 'I think you exaggerate, Mistress. I am still a nonentity, always will be, I believe.'

She twisted away. 'Oh, you are over-modest, sir. You will do what that fat fool Wolsey has failed to do.' She came close again, gave a deep and evil chuckle. 'You will bring the King and me – honourably – to bed. And for that worthy service the King will give you half of his Kingdom.' She laughed mockingly. 'And if you fail, he will cut off your head,' she added, smacking her hands together and laughing delightedly.

Cranmer was shocked and horrified. 'Madam, such is not my warrant. My warrant is to discover and express the truth of the matter. Nothing more.'

She said "And the King intends to use that truth to make Cambridge speak for him, then Oxford, then the foreign Universities. And in all this, Doctor – ' she used his title for the first time – 'in all this you are to be the lead horse. The King speaks of little else. So fail him at your peril, Master Priest.' And she was gone, sudden as a summer breeze.

Thomas sank back on to his chair. He was trembling. All the world talking of *him*? His book to be used to impress the Universities? And, worst of all, to what end? To help the King ease his conscience, to rescue him from living in sin? That was what the King wanted. But this lovely, fascinating, yet – he thought – somehow evil woman and her father seemed to have other plans.

What ought he to do? He felt sick with worry. He needed to see the King, to ask for reassurance that what he was doing had but one aim – the annulment (if that was God's will) of Henry's marriage to Katherine.

But what could he say to the King? 'I will continue with the book, Majesty, only if you assure me that the aim of this matter is not the marriage of yourself with Mistress Anne Boleyn?'

But he broke into a sweat at the very thought of so addressing the King. Besides, had not Henry already told him, and with a solemn oath, that 'Mistress Anne had no place in this matter'?

It was at this troubled moment that Sir Thomas Boleyn bustled into the room. 'Now, Doctor, things are going well with your great task?'

Thomas heard himself say, 'I would like an audience of the King, Sir Thomas.'

Boleyn froze. His stare was hard and hostile. 'Why?' He almost spat out the word. 'Things are not to your satisfaction, Doctor Cranmer?'

Thomas said, 'You have been most accommodating, sir. But the King himself assured me that this matter did not concern Mistress Anne.'

The stare had become even more hostile. 'So?'

Thomas looked down at the floor. His voice was almost a whisper. 'Mistress Anne appears to think otherwise, Sir Thomas.'

Boleyn stared at him in amazement. 'And you would broach this matter with the King? By God, Doctor, you are a braver man than I.'

Thomas swallowed, 'I am not brave. Yet I would approach the King, sir.'

Boleyn looked at him hard and long. At last: 'Very well,' he snapped. 'It shall be arranged. And may the Lord have mercy on your soul, Cranmer.

King Henry VIII was always a good stage manager. This time the audience was not in the sumptuous Privy Chamber. It was in a small room whose unadorned stone walls and pillars suggested a dungeon. And this time the door was guarded by two men-at-arms, who let Thomas pass only with a great clanking and clashing of halberds and armour.

Thomas knelt. The King glowered at him in silence. And when at last he spoke that high-pitched voice was sharper and higher than usual. 'So, Doctor Cranmer, you would call your Sovereign a liar, would you? And a blaspheming liar at that.'

Thomas, staring piteously at the floor, murmured, 'No, your Majesty.'

'Did I not tell you, did I not say to you, "As God is my judge, the Lady Anne has no place in this matter"?'

'Yes, your Majesty.'

'And now, I am told, you want me to say it again before you can believe me. Or perhaps you want to hear it a thousand times.' He began to speak more and more quickly. 'I tell you, Cranmer, *that* could be done. I have pinned men down in the Tower before now, and voices have screamed my message into their ears until they believed it – or went raving mad. It mattered little.'

Thomas said, 'I believed your Majesty. But – am I then to call Mistress Anne a liar?'

Henry said abruptly, 'How goes the book?'

'Well, your Majesty.'

'And you have found the truth?'

'Yes.'

'Which is?'

'That your marriage to the Lady Katherine is accursed of God. Only by putting her away can you hope for salvation, and a male heir.'

'And your book will persuade the Universities of this?' Henry was eager, now, his stage anger fading.

'Almost certainly, your Grace.'

He became wheedling. 'My dear Thomas, you would not really let a young girl's foolish chatter stop this noble work? She is not, after all, the first lady of the Court to imagine herself in love with the Sovereign.' Thomas continued to look unhappy. 'Oh come, Thomas. Not many Englishmen can sulk before their Sovereign and keep their heads on their shoulders and their guts in their bellies.'

'I am not sulking, Sire. I am cast down because I have angered your Majesty.'

'You are wise to be cast down. *Indignatio Principis Mors Est*. But – you have a strange, appealing innocence. Only – ' his voice hardened, 'do not tempt me too far.'

'Your Grace.' Cranmer bowed his head.

Henry's face clouded, with a brooding evil. Clearly his visitor was quite forgotten. Thomas bowed deeply, and withdrew in something approaching terror. He had obeyed his conscience. And the result had been a buffeting that took him straight back to the school bench. Perhaps, if it had been possible, he would have escaped then into some forgotten corner of Henry's England. But it was too late. Henry had found a man who could be useful to him. Thomas knew he would never let go.

Chapter 5

The book *was* good. It said everything Henry wanted it to say. And suddenly Thomas Cranmer, Doctor of Divinity, was moving in Court circles, feeling admiring eyes upon him wherever he went. The King sent him to his own tailor, insisting he give up his old black robe for one of rich grey velvet. Courtiers even began to approach him when they wanted a favour from the King, a sure sign of royal approval.

So Thomas finished the book, and the King's blessing was again upon him, warm as the mellow October sunlight. And Henry and Anne rode lovingly together in the flaming woodlands, knowing that thanks to this 'wonderful and grave wise man' their towering desire one for the other was nearing fulfilment.

But each autumn day grew shorter, until the dry and gentle warmth had changed almost imperceptibly to chill and dampness. And all the richness and luxury of the Court could not hide the sweating stones, the damp tapestries, the howling draughts and whistling winds that invaded even a royal palace.

Yet, even in this chill discomfort, the Court was merry. The Court was merry because the King was merry. The King was merry because Thomas Cranmer had given him hope of soon pleasing God by annulling his marriage to Katherine; hope of thereby easing his burden of sin; hope of at last taking his sweet Anne into a *lawful* marriage bed (for the dear infuriatingly virtuous creature, unlike her sister Mary, would have no other); hope of getting strong Tudor princes, vigorous and cunning and powerful as himself, on her body, to maintain the peace and prosperity he himself had brought to this land.

On New Year's morning Henry was as happy and excited as a child. As was the custom he sat at the foot of his bed, swathed in so many furs that he looked like a large and genial bear, and received his gifts with exuberant delight. 'Sire, here is a gift coming from the Queen. Let it come in, Sire.' The usher of the Chamber was growing hoarse by the time he called, 'Sire, here is a gift coming from Mistress Anne Boleyn. Let it come in, Sire.' Ah, this was the one that really mattered.

It was a tiny, but most lovely, thing: an alabaster Cupid, plump and naked, setting a very determined arrow to his bow. Rich jewels were everywhere: his eyes, his mouth, his navel, his arrow heads, all were of jewels. It was not perhaps the most tactful gift. But by God he loved her for it. 'How the poor wench does dote on me,' he muttered, and his eyes filled with tears. He hated this Pope, and his gouty minion, Cardinal Campeggio, for refusing to untie him from Katherine, thereby not only keeping Anne from his bed but also exacerbating her not too easy temper, the sweet little vixen.

On this happy New Year's morning, the Master of the Revels was all ready to introduce a fellow with a dancing dog. But he was too late. Henry was already walking over to a thoughtful, lonely-looking cleric standing somewhat apart. 'My dear Thomas, why so thoughtful? Do you foresee aught in this brave new year to give you concern?'

'I see nothing, your Majesty. God does not share His secrets with a poor sinner like me.' He smiled shyly.

'But I do, Thomas.' He threw an arm, thick as a pillow in its massive furs, about Thomas' shoulders. He said, with more than a little archness, 'Now hear me prophesy, Priest.' He paused. Then said with slow deliberation, 'I, Henry, prophesy that before Spring you will be in Bologna, Dr Cranmer.'

Bologna? The King must be jesting. All the world knew that Charles V was to be crowned Holy Roman Emperor at Bologna. But there could be no connection between that earth-shaking event and a poor Cambridge divine.

The King began to stroll through one beautiful room after another, his arm still about Thomas' shoulders. Thomas perforce strolled with him. 'My Lord of Wiltshire, he that was Thomas Boleyn, is leading an Embassy to attend the Coronation of the Emperor. You will be part of that Embassy. But – would you be prepared to defend the arguments put forward in your book before Pope Clement himself? In Rome?'

They strolled on. And now they were in a less ornate part of the Palace: a vast area of stone, its roof supported by pillars more massive than oaks, a place where the killing cold of out-of-doors could no longer be held at bay.

The Pope himself? This *must* be a dream. He heard himself say, 'If it is your Majesty's will – I would certainly try.'

'Could you also persuade the Italian Universities to your views?'

Thomas said, with a sudden rush of feeling, 'I would do anything that would serve your Grace.'

'So. So.' Suddenly the King seemed to weary of the subject. 'Gardiner tells me you are a good judge of horses.'

'Thank you, your Majesty.'

'Come and see my old Barbary.' They stepped out into a stable yard sharp and brilliant with morning sunlight, cold sunlight that seemed to do no more than spread a lacquer on the ice and the snow and the frozen stone.

The King, in his furs, seemed impervious. And Thomas, dazed by the revelations of what this New Year held for him, felt nothing of the cold.

They entered the stables. Horses by the dozen, exquisite, beautiful, noble, proud horses. 'And here's old Barbary,' said the King fondly. He slapped the whinnying delighted creature fondly, passed on. 'Now Thomas, which of these is the best?'

Cranmer examined them carefully. They were all superb beasts. Yet to his eyes there was one stood out among these aristocrats: a Welsh pony sturdy, small-headed, with a golden mane and a golden tail that almost touched the ground: a gentle-looking friendly mare. 'She is my choice,' said Thomas.

'Hannibal,' bellowed the King. A groom came running. '*Beauty* belongs to Doctor Cranmer whenever he is at Court.' He turned back to Thomas. 'Welsh, like myself, Thomas. Good stock. You have chosen well.'

'But – your Majesty?' cried Thomas.

The King laughed delightedly. Then said, with mock severity, '"But" is not a word to use to Princes, my reverend friend. Come, let us ride.' So Beauty was saddled and a great roan was quickly saddled for the King, and they were off, in the bright morning of a new year that was to prove more eventful than simple Thomas could possibly have imagined.

He had ridden with the King! And he was to visit Bologna, and Rome, and the Italian Universities. He was to meet the Pope! Surely it was time he began to have a better opinion of himself!

But he couldn't. Despite what other people seemed suddenly to be thinking of him, he couldn't. *He* could see the doubts and fears and indecisions that led slowly and painfully to his every action. *He* knew his night fears, his gnawing reluctance to face each dawning day. He already felt himself crushed between the upper and lower millstones of King and conscience.

And now, suddenly there was to be no shutting himself away in a quiet Cambridge study, like a timorous mouse in a nest of leaves. He had been flushed out, into a brilliantly lit world, to expound the truth (as he alone knew it) to the leaders of that world, to support a Monarch who would put him down like a lame horse the moment he failed, or was no longer needed.

He did not see the King again before he sailed. All his instructions (and they were many) came from Thomas Boleyn, now Earl of Wiltshire.

Any man of honour whose daughter has got him a title must feel that in return he ought to do his best for his daughter, so it speaks well, both for Wiltshire's honour and for his sense of fatherly duty, that the bulk of Thomas' instructions concerned his handling of the Pope and of the Italian Universities. There was of course no question of bribing the Holy Father. A few threats as a last resort, perhaps, provided they were made with the appropriate pious humility. But no bribes.

The Universities, however, were a very different matter. Thomas was surprised to learn that the doctors at the different Universities would require a 'retainer' before they could deliver an official opinion. In other words bribes were not only possible: they were *sine qua non*.

Thomas' English soul was outraged. 'I will not pay these so-called retainers.' He said firmly.

Wiltshire gave him a sideways look. He wasn't having this damned cleric spoiling his daughter's chances. But he started quietly. 'My dear Doctor Cranmer! Of course, you've never been abroad, have you.' (Never outside Cambridge, if you ask me.) 'Well, of course the first thing you have to remember is that Italy isn't England. They think differently from us; they're dark-skinned, you know, it's with their blood being curdled, I've been told.'

Thomas said, 'I will not pay these retainers.'

'Then you will not get a single opinion in favour of the King,' Wiltshire said flatly.

Thomas stared at him. 'You cannot mean that, my Lord?'

'I mean every word of it. Doctor, Europe is not England. They do not have our ideas of honour and fair dealing. After all, how can they have? They're not English.'

'But *we* are.'

Wiltshire tut-tutted. 'Cranmer, do you wish to serve your King?'

'From the bottom of my heart, my Lord.'

'Then you must pay the retainers. *Si fueris Romae, Romano vivito more.*'

'St Ambrose,' sighed Thomas. A writer he respected deeply.

'Exactly.'

The two men looked at each other. Wiltshire sighed. 'My dear Cranmer, I sometimes think that self-interest is a better guide than principle in these degenerate days.'

Thomas said hotly, 'I cannot agree, my Lord.'

Wiltshire said musingly, 'Thomas More is a man of principle. And he will lose his head as sure as night follows day.'

Thomas was silent. But he had paled.

It was some time before Wiltshire spoke. Then he said silkily, 'I shall not lose *my* head, Cranmer.'

CHAPTER 6

The Embassy left London in the small hours of January 21st. Men, horses, carriages, baggage milling together in the pitiless dark of five in the morning, with eighty miles to go to Dover, and then the unknown terrors of the ocean. And the vast, unimaginable forests and plains and mountains of Europe.

And not only the perils of nature. They faced a continent in upheaval: man in his first mass struggles against his master; Emperor against Pope, Lutheran against Rome. The clash of arms was everywhere. Europe was a maelstrom of death and festering wounds.

But on that January morning the first enemy was the cold. Thomas had known cold in the vast hall at Aslockton, in the stone cells of a Cambridge College. But this cold was something malevolent, spiteful, all-embracing. Comfort was a forgotten thing. To sit your horse, to shield when you could your face from wind and snow, to repeat the Offices of the Church through each long day, this Thomas Cranmer had already accepted as his life. Soon, he knew, it must end; to be replaced by even worse discomforts.

He found only one thing to lift his heart. On the fourth day they came to a little snugly-walled town, with a vast honey-coloured cathedral towering unbelievably above ramparts and walls and keeps. Canterbury, thought Thomas.

It was unlikely he would ever see this place again. He must seize this opportunity, make his hurried pilgrimage to England's noblest shrine and Becket's tomb.

But it was not to be. It was still mid-morning. With only fifteen miles left to Dover there could be no stopping now. To lose the long straggle of horses and baggage-wagons was unthinkable. He would never reach Dover on his own. Highway robbers or bands of Abraham-men would see to that. Sadly, he rode on.

Now they were on a wide plateau. Before them, in the far distance, the vast and shimmering cloth of gold which they told each other excitedly must be the sea. And the pace quickened.

But Thomas Cranmer saw nothing of this. He had reined his horse, and was staring back the way they had come, lost in wonder.

A vast black pelt of forest, stretching as far as the eye could see! And, lifting from it, lit brilliantly by the morning sunlight, the great Cathedral of Canterbury, soaring, pointing the way to Heaven.

His eyes filled with tears. 'Lord, now lettest Thou Thy servant depart in peace… For mine eyes have seen… '

What had his eyes seen? They had seen a brilliant powerful giant of a man who was indeed England. They had seen a cathedral of incredible power and beauty that went back, through English history, to Saint Augustine.

And what had his inner eye seen, on this sharp and beautiful morning? A vision, perhaps, of England, sea-encircled, united, peaceful, under its own King and its own Church, free of the dogma and the stranglehold of Rome?

Perhaps? Perhaps not. But now voices were calling, angry and impatient voices. He turned his horse and cantered forward, to Dover and the sea.

Rome! He was going to Rome! Rome, where Peter and Paul had walked, and suffered. The seat of Christendom. Even a reformer like Cranmer was filled with awe and eager anticipation by the name of this ancient city. Surely every street, every building, must glow with an aura of sanctity.

They arrived on a misty, blue and silver morning. Waiting for the veils of mist to part and reveal the golden city was like waiting to tear the wrappings from a rich gift.

But, as the mists cleared, Thomas stared in disbelief. The city walls were a jumble of broken stone. The vast buildings were crumbling ruins. Noble statues lay in the dust, broken and headless. Great areas of the city were a wilderness of coarse grass and weeds. Apart from a few newly-built and beautiful churches, Rome was a ruin and a desolation.

If the thought of Rome had perhaps weakened his reforming zeal, its actuality gave it fresh life. He began again to see the old religion as something crumbling and decaying like this ancient city.

But, yet again, the reformer in him was challenged when he was shown into the presence of His Holiness, Pope Clement VII.

The approach to this earthly Godhead, past the upheaval and mess of the rebuilding of St Peter's, was not encouraging. But once inside the Papal Apartments, he was enfolded in a beauty and an elegance that made Henry's Court look brash and tawdry. Before him he saw a magnificent creature seated in a great chair, clad in a crimson, sweeping robe: a creature who held out a white-gloved hand bedecked with jewelled rings; a creature whose voice was low and sweet, whose oval face smiled with a most welcoming warmth.

'My dear Thomas, I have longed so much for this meeting.'

Thomas bowed low and kissed the extended hand.

'I, too, your Holiness.'

'And I look forward so much to our Disputation. Your King describes you as a grave and wonderful wise man!'

'His Majesty is too kind, Your Holiness.'

'Shall we say Thursday, at eleven in the morning?'

Thomas was overcome. Such promptness delighted him. He had feared that there might be delays.

Thursday morning. Thomas was apprehensive, but he was already learning to have some faith in his own powers of argument, especially when he was arguing for his master the King. So he was a little relieved but also very disappointed when the Disputation was put off for a week.

Still, what was a week in this long and wearisome business? He re-read his notes, and settled down to wait.

But after six more postponements (all announced with overwhelming courtesy and regret) Thomas realized that he was not the man to deal with Pope Clement. Pope Clement VII needed someone who would bully him into acquiescence. And when it came to bullying, both his gentle nature and his upbringing put Thomas firmly on the side of the bullied.

So he remembered his second commission: to obtain favourable verdicts from the Italian Universities. He left Rome and began his travels again; and despite the fascination of the cities he visited, he was an anxious man. He had failed humiliatingly in his first commission to serve his revered King. He must not fail a second time. His head might depend on success. But there was more to it than that. *Le Roi le veult.*

For these reasons he forgot his principles about 'retainers': either because of this or of his powers of argument he soon had obtained a favourable verdict from Bologna, Ferrara, Padua and Pavia. At which point Clement prohibited the Universities from discussing the matter. Thomas, defeated a second time, set off for home, fearful of his reception. But there was no criticism. During Thomas' absence, Henry's mind had taken a great leap forward: the Pope of twenty years ago, he had decided, had had no power to grant the dispensation, which therefore was quite ineffective to make his marriage lawful.

This revolutionary idea opened up even more exciting vistas in Henry's subtle mind; if the Pope had no power to dispense, what *had* he power to do? In what other ways could this weak and vacillating pontiff be challenged? If Thomas Cranmer had had his vision of an England free of the yoke of Rome, perhaps Henry had the same vision; and knew, with his brilliant instinct, that to make this vision reality he must bind Cranmer to him with hoops of steel.

To insist on a wedding ring in exchange for one's virginity may be a commendable, clever, even virtuous ploy.

But – and especially when it means fending off a man like Henry – it is a ploy that can be maintained only for so long. And the cunning and skill of the game is knowing when to capitulate.

Anne Boleyn knew the game backwards. She held out for years: teasing, tormenting, nagging, mocking.

Then, suddenly and joyously, she surrendered and took Great Harry into her bed.

Everyone breathed a vast sigh of relief. Now, at last, the King would be able to think of something other than his Great Matter. His interest in it would quickly wane. He had already banished Katherine from Court to the Moor in Hertfordshire (and this was probably why Anne had suddenly become so accommodating). So the Great Matter could be forgotten, and the Council could actually give its mind to government.

But they were wrong. Henry went on hounding his once-dear Katherine, his daughter, Mary, and his Council and his divines, even though he was now happily bedded with her whose 'maidenly and womanly pudicity' had been so warmly recommended to His Holiness. So. Had the Court been mistaken? Were his efforts *really* all for a male heir and a settled succession, and the ending of all cause for strife and civil war?

Thomas Cranmer heard the rumours and the gossip but it was not until he saw Henry and Anne laughing together and saw the knowing look on the girl's face, that he let himself believe.

He crept away to his own chamber, fell on his knees, and prayed for guidance and help. He was convinced that God thoroughly approved of Henry's putting away Katherine. But to live openly with Anne while still officially married! That was mortal sin. And he, Thomas Cranmer, was now one of the King's Chaplains. For him to let mortal sin go unrebuked was unthinkable.

In the end he rose to his feet. Two courses lay open to him: to feign ignorance (and, after all, he had no proof), or to ask the King to explain himself.

The latter course was hazardous, unpleasant, and highly dangerous. But his duty was to the King; in this case the duty to save him from everlasting damnation. He did not flinch.

As Chaplain, he was received in the Privy Chamber.

Henry greeted him warmly. 'Thomas! Or should I say "Father" to my reverend Chaplain? How found you Clement? Devious, vacillating?'

'Both, your Majesty.' Cranmer was cold and unbending. 'And dilatory in the extreme.'

'Pah! A man of water.' He sighed. 'But water can drown a man, Thomas.' Then: 'What is it you want?' the question was sharp, the glance suddenly wary.

Thomas said heavily, 'Your Majesty, the Court says you are living in sin with the Lady Anne.'

'Who says? Who says? I'll have the tongue out of his throat.' Henry's face had become suffused with blood.

Thomas said, 'The whole Court. You cannot silence the whole Court, your Majesty.' He was amazed to hear the authority in his voice.

The King sat back in his chair. He spoke more quietly. Reproachfully. 'I thought *you* would have understood, Father.' Then he jerked up again and banged his fist on the chair arm. 'Can't you see that I must get a son? Can't you see that *God wants me* to get a son?'

Thomas said woodenly, 'Your Majesty already has a son: the bastard Fitzroy.'

'Do not call my son a bastard, Priest.' Henry was smouldering.

Thomas' mouth was dry, and his bowels quaked. But he said, 'Fitzroy *is* a bastard, and his accession would be the signal for immediate strife. And a son by the Lady Anne would be in the same case.'

Henry said, in wonder, 'You *dare* to speak to your Prince thus?'

Thomas stood silent and pale. He inclined his head.

Henry went on staring. Then, in a whisper, 'Little man, do you *really* think yourself fitted to meddle in great affairs of state?'

Thomas took a deep breath. 'Only when they concern your Majesty's immortal soul, Sire.'

'The Devil roast my immortal soul,' shouted Henry; then looked abashed and frightened. 'Intercede for me, Father. I should not have spoken thus. But believe me, Katherine is no longer my wife, by bed or board. And the Lady Anne *shall* be my wife.'

'Until she is, your Grace, you lie with her at your mortal peril.'

Henry's face was pale, and those blue eyes had the coldness of ice. His voice had a hard rasp. 'Now listen to me, Thomas. I shall lie with any woman I please. God's Body, man, I am King of England. Other Kings have lain with their subjects and not been prated at by sickly clerics. So. What do you intend to do about that, Doctor Cranmer?'

Thomas said in a flat voice, 'Only leave you in the shadow of my reproach, Your Majesty.'

'*Your* reproach! Who are you, man?'

'Your Father in God, my son.'

Suddenly the King gave a great laugh. He stepped down from his chair, embraced Thomas in those bear-like arms. 'You are more than that, Thomas. You are our Ambassador to the Court of Charles the Fifth.

The change was too sudden. Thomas could not find words. At last: 'The Emperor?' he gasped.

'Yes,' Henry said with relish. He always enjoyed the bewilderment he so often created. 'And you will also carry instructions to visit the Lutheran Princes.'

Thomas swallowed. 'Sire, am I banished to Europe because of my reproach?'

Henry said scornfully, 'I do not work that way, Thomas. If it were for your reproach I should not banish you to Ratisbon. I should banish you to Hell.' His brows came down again. 'Remember that, Priest,' he added viciously.

CHAPTER 7

It was another winter journey, starting in January, ending in March. But this time Thomas was carried and guarded like some precious treasure. A litter piled high with rugs and furs was at his disposal and he had cooks and vintners all demanding his personal instructions as to what they should cook and serve.

Dressed in silks and velvets, half smothered in furs, he made his progress across frozen Europe, receiving almost as much adulation as the King he represented. And it was as they were nearing the end of that long journey that Thomas, for the first time in his life, showed something of his Master's wilfulness. 'I wish to visit Nuremberg,' he announced. 'Send riders on to announce our coming.'

Consternation! 'But sir, our arrival at Ratisbon will be delayed.' 'Sir, Nuremberg is no fit place for such as yourself. They say the Lutherans – ' ''Tis said –' and here eyes grew wide with horror, and the more devout crossed themselves, ' – 'tis said the priests marry.'

'Then maybe I will marry one of their wenches,' Thomas said, pleasantly but unwisely. He was strangely excited. The Lutherans had taken over the city seven years ago. And Thomas Cranmer, who had spent so many dusty years trying to decide between the Pope and Martin Luther (and moving more and more towards the latter) was eager to see what they had made of it.

His grumbling retinue brought him to the western gate of the city towards sunset, when the red sandstone of the castle rock glowed like a dying ember below the ash grey of the castle walls. And there, waiting to greet him, was a group of the city's notables from which one man stepped forth, a thick-set, heavily bearded man in his middle thirties, who cried in Latin, 'Which is Thomas Cranmer, he who bids his King defy the Pope of Rome?'

'I am he,' said Thomas cheerfully, descending from his horse.

The German looked at the velvet gown and cap with amusement. 'You dress well for a priest, Master.' Then, taking any sting out of the words, he dropped two heavy hands on Thomas' shoulders and kissed him first on one cheek, then on the other. 'I am Andreas Osiander. *You* will lodge at my house. Your retinue will be well provided for.'

The warmth of his brisk welcome, after the rigours of the journey, moved Thomas deeply. And he was flattered to be welcomed by someone whose name he knew well from his reading. Why, this was the blacksmith's son who even now was helping to write the new Brandenburg–Nuremberg Church Order. In the house of Osiander, he told himself, he would be at the beating heart of the new religion that so interested and – yes – attracted him.

So, with Osiander's arm about his shoulders, Thomas walked a few yards to a house that crouched over a narrow street, and he was shown into a dark hall crammed with intricately-carved black furniture.

'Wife!' bellowed Osiander in German. A plump smiling woman appeared carrying a candle. She curtseyed to

Thomas, relieved him of his furs, and led him into a room where a heavy oak table was laid with pewter plates, spoons, bread, and a great bowl of stew which made him suddenly aware of a ravenous hunger.

Osiander held a chair for him. Thomas, not knowing the ways of Lutherans, hoped the Grace would not take too long.

Osiander said, 'We have prepared fish for you, brother Thomas.' And at that moment a girl came into the room and put a plate of steamed fish before Cranmer.

Two emotions swept Thomas: a deep, urgent awareness of the young femininity that actually brushed his sleeve. And a veritable lust for that bowl of stew. 'Fish?'

'Is it not Friday today, man? We Lutherans respect other religions even if – ' Andreas chuckled quietly – 'others do not always respect ours.'

Thomas bowed to Frau Osiander, smiled. 'I thank you, Madam. But tonight, if I may, I will be a Lutheran.'

Osiander's great laugh filled the room. He slapped Thomas on the back. It was like a blow from a sledgehammer. 'And not only tonight, if we had our way. We need men like you, brother Cranmer.'

Thomas shook his head sadly. 'I am a weak vessel. I am pulled both ways.'

'Nonsense! All Europe is talking of you. And disagreeing with you, many of them. Here's the Turk at the gates of Christendom, and all your King can do is fret about marrying his whore.'

'That is not the way of it at all,' began Thomas, eager to defend his King. But at the moment the girl, who had carried his fish back to the kitchen, returned to the room and, to Thomas' surprise, took her place at table, facing him.

Osiander said, 'Sir, this is Margarete, niece to my wife. Margarete, this is the learned and eminent Doctor Cranmer, of London.'

To Thomas' surprise, Osiander did not change from Latin to German when he addressed Margarete. Thomas looked at her with interest. Evidently a girl of some learning.

Under her white linen cap he saw a sweetly pretty face. And thought that his own stillborn daughter might now have been of this age and looked thus. The thought of that forgotten little ghost moved him deeply. He smiled. 'Mistress Margarete, I would you were my daughter.'

She coloured, her eyes still lowered. Osiander said mockingly, 'You will never have a daughter, Priest, unless you become a Lutheran.' He seized Cranmer's wrist, and banged his arm on the table in friendly emphasis of his point. 'Think of it man: a warm little wife, a strong son, a pretty daughter. And a good meat stew every Friday. Do I not tempt you into our fold?'

Thomas smiled. 'These are earthly arguments, Brother Andreas.'

'And are not we children of God also of the earth? And are not these earthly things gifts from a loving God? Meat for a man's belly, a helpmeet to share his joys and afflictions – and his bed.' Then he looked lovingly at Margarete, 'And creatures as exquisite as Margarete, blending such beauty of spirit with such beauty of face?'

Margarete looked up at Andreas, and smiled. 'Thank you, Uncle Osiander,' she said with composure.

When she smiled her eyes became brilliant slits between their long lashes. Her teeth were white and even, her cheeks dimpled prettily. Yet, did her smile show an inner self-contained amusement, rather than a fondness and gratitude towards her uncle? He put the thought quickly from him. His mind would accept no criticism of this desirable creature. She was young. And youth was entitled to its laughter.

He knew that he would give much that he possessed for Margarete to smile so on him. He said clumsily, 'Your uncle speaks truly, Mistress Margarete. I – ' he lost his words.

But, he did not win a smile. Staring down at the table she said flatly, 'You are very kind, Reverend Sir.'

He felt rebuffed. In his embarrassment he turned back to Osiander. 'I am interested to hear you speak so of happiness. I had expected – '

'Joylessness? Long faces?' Osiander drew down his lips, frowned, while at the same time bubbling with inner laughter. 'Tomorrow I will show you our City; show you our people walking with laughter on their lips, now that we have freed them from the stranglehold of Rome.'

But Thomas said, 'Alas! I am awaited in Ratisbon. Yet – perhaps I may one day return, Brother Andreas?'

'With all my heart. Eh, wife? Eh, Margarete?'

Thomas looked quickly at the girl. 'Of course, Uncle,' she said dutifully, without feeling.

That night, Thomas slept not at all.

He was in a Lutheran stronghold, in a cramped, heavily over-furnished house, where Lutherans had not only made him feel happier and more welcome than he had felt since Joan died, but had also shown him the joys of simplicity as against the pleasures of his own growing worldliness. Yet in a few days' riding he would be at the Court of His Most Catholic Majesty, at the hub of Christendom: *he*, a man learned in the Scriptures but in little else; certainly not in any deviousness or cunning. And, once at that Court, he had to represent his unpredictable (yet strangely loved) Sovereign, Henry of England. Henry, five hundred miles away, yet with a long reach, shared Cranmer's bedchamber that night. So did others, as yet unmet and unknown: the Emperor Charles, Martin Luther, Katherine of Aragon. And, almost certainly, at this very moment, Henry and Anne Boleyn were romping merrily in Harry's great bed, to the peril of their immortal souls and, he felt in his bones, of Thomas Cranmer's future.

And, as if all this were not sufficient cause for sleeplessness he had another cause that was both sweet and bitter: Margarete! Meeting her, after all the years of celibacy, had brought back the memory of so much that womankind had to offer. Suddenly, appallingly, as though he hadn't enough troubles, he had discovered a shameful truth: he, Doctor Cranmer, ordained Priest, desired to have a wife: for company, for comfort; to ease the insistent yearnings of the flesh. Margarete! A lovely name! A lovely face! From what he had seen, a demure and gentle nature!

And he was forty-three, perhaps ten years older than her guardian even. And she was – what? Twenty? It was a madness. He tumbled out of bed, flung himself on to his knees, prayed long and fervently. To no avail. God wasn't going to help a priest in this wickedness. He had made his vows of celibacy. He must keep them. He was a man for whom marriage was, literally, death and damnation.

To his relief, two earth-shattering events overshadowed Thomas' arrival at the Imperial Court: Soleiman and his Turks were obviously on the point of invading Austria; and the Emperor Charles was stricken with gout.

The first meant that everyone was too busy and frightened to pay much attention to an unassertive envoy from England. The second meant that Charles had taken himself off to the health resort of Abbach, and so wasn't there to have his hands kissed. As a result, Thomas was able to spend some time on his second commission: making contact with the Lutheran Princes.

This was more to his taste. Before March was out he was riding back unobtrusively, with a single attendant, to Nuremberg.

And, despite his vows, despite his high office, he was obsessed with one emotion: he was going to see Margarete! He, a man in his forties, an Ambassador and a man of God, lusted after a simple provincial girl to make her his wife.

After the pomp and ritual of the Imperial Court, the cheerful simplicity of Osiander's hot, stifling little house was wonderful. And what a welcome! 'Brother Cranmer! I knew you would return. Oh, this is good. You can tell me how my new Church Order strikes a Catholic. And you can justify to me, if you can, the way your King has treated your poor Queen. And – ' he looked at Thomas shrewdly, 'and why a man like you should have stooped to help him do so.

Thomas said, 'The marriage was invalid. The King uncovered his brother's nakedness.'

'Quite happily, for twenty years. Until suddenly he saw a sweeter apple on the tree.'

'And there you are wrong,' said Thomas sharply. 'The King has two reasons only for seeking an annulment: his desire for a male heir, for the sake of the Kingdom. And his constant fear that he is incurring God's anger by living in sin with his brother's wife.'

Osiander said quietly, 'Some say he is already living in sin with his latest whore.'

Thomas was both shocked and angry. 'Sir, you have shown me great kindness. We have broken bread together. But I cannot let you speak so of my Lord.'

Osiander lolled in his chair, stroking his great red beard, regarding Thomas quizzically. 'So. It is not true.'

Loyalty to the truth? Or to his Sovereign? Thomas made his choice. 'It is not true,' he whispered with dry lips.

Osiander jumped to his feet. 'You are a loyal servant, Thomas,' he said wryly. 'Come. Let me show you our Church Order.' From a drawer he produced a pile of manuscripts.

Thomas read. It was revolutionary. *Thou art Peter, and upon this rock I will build My Church.* A Church, built by Christ upon a rock? *Could* this thing be changed?

He read on. When at last he looked up his eyes were filled with tears. 'You will work much good, and much ill, with this, Brother. Yet I think the good will prevail.'

The two men looked at each other. Each knew that he had found a friend in a dangerous world. Thomas said hesitatingly, 'I have not met the poor Queen, her they call Katherine of Aragon. I hope I may never do so. Yet – she haunts my night-thoughts, Brother Andreas.' He hoped desperately that his friend would give him some kind of absolution.

But Osiander said nothing.

The liking grew between Thomas and Osiander. And there were pleasant evenings before the fire, in the little house in Nuremberg, when the strict solemnity of the Imperial Court was forgotten. Here he was loved for himself, not because he walked with the King or was the envoy of a powerful monarch.

Margarete and her aunt worked quietly at their embroidery, sometimes murmuring in conversation, sometimes smiling fondly. The men talked – Lutheranism, Catholicism, Henry and Katherine – and sometimes the chessmen were brought out, and while Thomas and Andreas thought out their moves, they still polished their arguments.

So that in the end Osiander was more in favour of the King, and Thomas was made to face the fact that he could help his King only by mortally wounding the Queen; and that the simple piety of Nuremberg was coming to appeal to him far more than the bigotry and sacerdotalism of the Emperor's Court.

And Margarete? There were many times now when she would look up from her embroidery to glance quickly at the fresh-complexioned face of a hard-riding sturdy Englishman that was also the thoughtful, kindly face of a learned scholar.

The nearest thing to a father that she had ever known was Andreas Osiander: a powerful, noisy, figure who terrified a little girl by brisk teasing, by impulsive embraces that knocked the breath out of her small body; an irascible, impatient teacher who yet gave the adolescent girl a love of Latin; a man who tried to teach her to fear God and walk in His ways; a man who loved her deeply, yet, sadly, inspired in her aloofness rather than love.

And here was another man: gentle, quiet, a man whose features broke so easily into a smile, a man whose courtesy and thoughtfulness were part of his very nature. Such a man, she felt, her unremembered father could have been.

Sometimes, when she looked up, their eyes would meet. Sometimes he would smile, then look away, guiltily. Sometimes he would continue to stare at her, apparently unseeing, as though he sought the answer to some question too deep for understanding.

And one evening, when the fire was low in the hearth, and the women had retired, and the candles burned low, Cranmer took Osiander's queen with one of his pawns.

Osiander grunted.

Cranmer said, 'Brother Andreas, I am deeply and honourably in love with your niece. I wish to marry her.'

Osiander took the presumptuous pawn. Then he said, 'Are you mad? You are a priest. You could bring her nothing but persecution and misery. And *you* would fry in Hell.' He heaved himself up in his chair. 'Anyway, how do you *know* you love her?'

Cranmer said, 'We have never touched. We have only smiled across the room. I am old enough to be her father, and she deserves a lad of her own age. Yet I love her.'

Osiander said, 'You would be facing death. The hangman, the fire even.'

'I want no one but her,' he said.

'But what would you do with your Lutheran bride, man? Take her to Catholic England? Show her to Junker Harry? "Behold, Sire, your Royal Chaplain has achieved a new wife faster than you." Why, he'd have the skin off your backs.' He shuddered. '*Both* your backs.'

Cranmer said dully, 'I want no one but her.'

Osiander banged the table. 'But you're vowed to celibacy.'

'The world is changing. *You* have a wife. Martin Luther has a wife.'

Osiander was silent. Then he said. 'You are a surprising man, Thomas. You often appear anxious and fearful.'

Thomas laughed ruefully. 'I *am* anxious and fearful.'

'Yet somewhere inside you is a core of steel.'

'I wish what you say were true,' Thomas said sadly.

'It is true. Me, I roar and shout and quarrel. But I have not your inner strengths, Thomas.'

Thomas laughed, unbelieving.

Osiander rose. 'It is late. We will talk again, on your next visit. You are a good man, Thomas. There is no one I would like better for a nephew-in-law. But – ' he pointed to the unfinished chess game, 'that is how the world is. Peasant against master, Lutheran against Catholic. You, Thomas, are a pawn in that game, and pawns soon finish up in the box. I cannot hand over my niece for safe-keeping to such a one.'

'Are you not also a pawn, Andreas?'

Suddenly Andreas gave his great laugh. Then he was immediately grave again. 'How old are you, Thomas?'

'Forty-three.'

'Margare the is nineteen. And – I must say this. I do not know her, Thomas. I know she is honourable and chaste, but could a man of forty-three keep her so in the English Court? Honest wives are not as plentiful as herring, there, I understand.'

Thomas said stiffly, 'You malign your niece, sir.'

'My dear Thomas, now I have offended you.' He flung a friendly arm round his visitor's shoulders. 'Let us discuss this on another visit. It is too late for such a grave matter.'

The following morning Thomas rode off to Ratisbon.

Margarete wept.

Her uncle kissed her on the forehead. 'Why are you weeping, child?'

'Because Doctor Cranmer has ridden away,' she said simply.

Here was a new development. It had not occurred to either men to wonder what Margarete's feelings were in the matter. 'But – you have scarcely spoken to Doctor Cranmer.'

'Oh, but we have exchanged glances, sir. And his eyes hold such kindness.'

He laughed. 'Love and marriage are about more than glances, niece.' He pulled her closer to him. 'Are you telling me you think yourself in love with this man old enough to be your father?'

She said, 'I know little of such matters. I only know that he is like a gentle bird released from the trap. And – I would save him from the fowler, sir.'

He said roughly, 'With you as his wife, I do not see how he could escape the fowler. Or you either,' he added.

She looked fearful. 'Are men so cruel? To punish the love of a man for a woman?'

'They are so cruel,' he said heavily. 'Especially when the man is a priest.'

She wept silently.

His heart bled for her. Yet such things had to be said. Now he tried to soften his harshness. 'Come! Dry your tears. Doctor Cranmer will not let the Emperor of the World keep him long from your side.'

And, sure enough, Thomas was soon back in Nuremberg, ostensibly to see Spalatin, adviser to John Frederick of Saxony; but also eager to see Margarete. And having assured Spalatin that Henry would help his master if he were attacked by the Emperor, he hurried back to the house of Osiander. Where he found, to his surprise (and delight), the door being opened to him by Margarete, who curtseyed with downcast eyes and said, 'My aunt is at market, sir, and my uncle bade me say he is called away. But I am to give you wine and meat after your journey.'

Already it was summer, the high, baking, windless summer of Central Europe, before the great mountains had started brewing up their daily storms, and the tiny gardens, crowded with geraniums and herbs, were heavy with scents and sunlight and the drowsiness of noonday. He said, with a dry mouth. 'No. No wine. Mistress Margarete, I would talk with you.'

'If that is your wish, sir. It will be pleasant in the garden.' She opened a door. They passed through.

There was a small arbour, hung with vines. They sat down. And he, who could argue and persuade so cogently for his King, was speechless. He stared down at this young and lovely creature in her plain gown and linen cap, and could not even smile.

It was she who came to his rescue. 'You wished to speak to me, sir?' And now she lifted her eyes to his. And they were bright and brilliant and – he dared to think – loving.

'No. Yes. I – When I was a little older than you I – married a wife,' he stammered. 'I – was not then a priest.'

'Where is she, this wife?'

'She died, bearing our child.'

'Alas! Poor lady,' she said quietly.

'Yes.'

'I often wondered why you looked so very sad.'

'You have a kind heart,' he said. Suddenly he took her hand. She did not withdraw it. 'Pray for me in my loneliness,' he said. 'I think your prayers will be heard sooner than the prayers of mitred bishops.'

'I will pray for you,' she said.

He was very moved. This was no frail windflower. She was composed, self-contained, a woman of character. Now she said, 'And you must pray for me. We both need prayer, you and I.'

Firmly, she took away her hand. A moment later the little garden was filled and overflowing with Andreas Osiander. 'Why, there you are, niece. And you, Thomas, old friend.' He grinned down at Thomas. 'Not hearing her Confession, I trust?'

Thomas smiled. Andreas said, 'Into the kitchen with you, girl. Doctor Cranmer and I would eat an ox.'

'There is no ox,' she said laughing. 'Only a hare.'

Margarete curtseyed, and disappeared into the house. Osiander lowered himself on to the stone seat. Thomas said, 'Andreas, here, in the peace of this garden, I wish to confess.'

Osainder looked at him sharply. 'I do not hear Confessions.'

'No. I mean about my wayward thoughts.'

'Proceed, friend.'

'I am confused and distressed. The ritual of the Mass at Charles' Court is unending. Yet, one might say, a necessary reminder of the glory of God and the unworthiness of man. But, Andreas, those priests remove their piety with their vestments. Outside the Church all is spite and licentiousness.'

'And it is not so in England?'

'No. I know you think our King has many faults. But he would not allow this. He is both devout and God fearing.'

'Are you telling me, friend Thomas, that you prefer *our* simple ways?'

Thomas sat in silence for a long time. At last: 'I am attracted, yes. Why should the power of Rome still weigh so heavily on faraway England? *You* have thrown it off.'

'So far, my friend. But the stake and the fire are never distant from our night fears.' He added, gravely, 'Be careful, Cranmer. You wade in deep waters. Rome has a long arm; and a longer memory.'

Thomas said sternly, 'The question is, how can God, and my King, be best served? That Imperial Court-backbiting, lechery, frivolity! The ceremonial is like a rich crust on a pie of corruption.'

Andreas gave a short bark of laughter. 'You have a gift for simile, friend.' Then he was serious again. 'So. You would become a Lutheran? Then you could prise the Bishop of

Rome off your King's back. And you could marry my niece and live happy every after.'

Thomas rose. 'I had hoped, Andreas, that you know me better than that.'

'Oh, sit down, Thomas. I know men. And I know you: a man of shining sincerity. Such a man as I would wish my niece to marry. But – I repeat – do not wade out of your depth, Brother. I mean – marriage. The Pope has sharp ears. And a young bride is a heavy burden for a priest.'

Thomas said impulsively, 'If she were willing, would *you* marry me to Margarete?'

'Me, Thomas? Are you determined to put your head in a noose?'

Thomas said, with great and heavy weight, 'To marry Margarete, yes. And to save myself from the corruption I see in Rome.'

'Rome is stronger, and colder-hearted, than you, Brother.' He sat, thoughtful. 'Nevertheless – in this great turmoil and turning of the world, the name of Cranmer would cheer our friends and dismay our enemies. You tempt me, Brother.' He smiled, sadly. 'Yes, I would sacrifice you, Thomas. But I will not sacrifice my niece. Unless, silly wench, she thinks marriage to you makes up for all. Margarete!' he suddenly bellowed.

She came running. 'Yes, Uncle?' But her smile, full and open now, was all for Thomas.

Osiander said, 'Doctor Cranmer, foolish man, wants to make you his wife.'

Thomas watched her face as a prisoner watches a sentencing judge. He saw shock, alarm, and then a smile dawning like a summer sun. She ran forward, seized his hands. 'Doctor Cranmer,' she cried, covering his hands with kisses.

Thomas released his hands, placed them on her head. 'God bless you, my child,' he said in a choking voice.

Osiander said, 'And now, my girl, have you thought what kind of life the wife of a priest will have in a Catholic country like England?'

Thomas knew he must confirm what Osiander was saying. Honour demanded it. He said, 'There will be great dangers, Margarete. At best, you will be humiliated, insulted. At worst, your life could be at risk. I should not ask you to share these tribulations. Only the fact that I love you so deeply, and see in you a woman of strength and character – only thus would I ask you to share my perils.'

When he spoke about great dangers, she had paled, and carried a hand up to her mouth. But now, she had pulled herself together. She said, lifting her chin, 'No. I am not strong. I am a fearful person. Yet – God forbid that you should think I could not suffer tribulations with a stout heart, provided only I was by your side.'

Thomas stooped, and kissed her on the lips. 'You will be the braver of us two,' he said admiringly. He turned to Osiander, clasped his hands. 'I shall guard her well, friend,' he said. 'No more high office for me. A small benefice in the country, or a study in a Cambridge backwater. There need be no scandal.'

But as he cantered back to Ratisbon his thoughts were in turmoil. No more high office, he had said. But suppose the mercurial King would not let him go, kept him at Court, or sent him on other missions where a wife could not be hidden? He, Thomas Cranmer, would not only be that misshapen monster, a married priest, he would be a priest married by a Lutheran to a Lutheran, surely a fit subject for burning both in this world and in the world to come.

Then he thought of his sweet, composed Margarete. Surely having her by his side would make up for any torment, any humiliation. Besides, he wanted to devote his life to protecting her, to giving her happiness. Was he learning, slowly, something of that rare virtue, courage?

But then, as he rode into Ratisbon, he saw the black-robed priests padding two by two about the streets. He saw the glitter of eyes taking in the latest scandal, he heard the sniggers over the latest tale of bawdy, and was sickened. He could not bring his young bride here. And would the English clergy really be so much less censorious? No. They would not. But he had taken his stand against the celibacy of the priesthood in the most definite way possible.

For a normally cautious weigher-up of pros and cons, Thomas could at times be surprisingly impulsive.

Thomas, though impulsive, was not one to shout his defiance from the housetops. Nor was Andreas Osiander the kind of friend who would let him. So the wedding was a quiet and secret, even conspiratorial, affair. And after the ceremony the food and wine were shared almost sacramentally. Then the young bride took her husband up to her tiny room beneath the eaves, and stood before him, white, virginal, her hands half raised towards him in a gesture of surrender and love. He staggered forward, weeping, and took her in his arms: the mystery and sweetness of a loving wife, the bride he longed to protect all his days.

The following day he travelled back to Ratisbon, bearing the memory of a tearfully smiling Margarete, while the enormity of the step he had taken slowly took possession of his mind.

And it was as though the marriage had been the signal for chaos to enter his life. A messenger had arrived in Ratisbon bringing Henry's reply to Charles' request for help against the Infidel. And it was not a reply that would endear Cranmer to the Emperor. Henry would have been delighted to help with thirty thousand men. But the soldiers were untrained, would be exhausted by the time they reached Austria, and English soldiers preferred to be led by their Sovereign in person. Still, Henry said cheerfully, he was sure Charles could manage perfectly well on his own.

Charles replied forcefully, mustered his army at Linz, and demanded that his ambassadors should meet him there. So the newly-married Cranmer set off down the Danube, and hoped his bride would get his secret instructions to stay where she was in Nuremberg.

Moves continued in the chess game. Charles marched against Soleiman, Soleiman retreated into Hungary. Charles went to Vienna, then to Mantua. Cranmer followed. And it was on this journey that chaos turned into nightmare.

October had come again. The snows were down in the mountain passes, the winds shrieked in the high corries, the streams were already leaping and tumbling over the stony, wandering roads between Vienna and the Italian border.

But though nature did her best, it takes men to create the real horrors. And so it was here. Charles' army had mutinied; and, denied their true enemy, the Infidel, they had replaced him with an enemy of their own choice: the Austrian people. Thomas now learnt, for the first time, what the human heart is capable of. Among these wild hills were ravaged towns and villages, their houses burnt, their churches desecrated, their inhabitants left grotesque and bloody corpses. Everything that could be useful had been stolen. Everything that moved, slain.

Village after village. Thomas stared, almost unbelieving. Had not He made man in His own image? And had man done this? In one place he saw a crucified peasant, nailed to the church wall, his body hideously contorted by its long agony. He thought of Charles' priests, in their laundered white, kneeling devoutly before some smooth-cheeked, painted Christ on the Cross, while their thoughts ran on white thighs and naked breasts. Henceforth, he thought savagely, *this* shall be *my* Crucifix. This picture shall go with me all my days. To the astonishment of his small retinue he walked forward, reached up, and kissed the dead foot of the peasant. Then he knelt in the filth and prayed from an anguished heart.

There was another thing that was to stay with him as a constant memory all his days. One night, cold and starving, unable to sleep, he wandered away from the small camp. He was almost distracted. He, a cautious, responsible man had impulsively married an innocent girl, and then immediately left her for the near-certainty of his death in the mountains. And even if he did eventually get back to civilization, what hope was there for her criminally married to a priest? He beat his breast, and lifted up his eyes to the hills.

He had come round a bend in the track, and now the dying camp fire was hidden from him. He might have been the only living soul left on earth. The cold was a live thing, tearing at throat and eyes and fingers.

But the stars! They were not like any stars he had seen in an English heaven. They were needle-sharp, beautiful and brilliant, diamonds on black velvet, they were the thousand thousand eyes of a hostile and malevolent Being, watching one poor ant of a mortal, solitary in the wilderness.

Then something happened that made him cry out in terror. One of those fixed and everlasting stars fell from its place and tumbled across the heavens, and was gone.

Thomas had seen falling stars before. But the clarity of the sky, and the brilliance and nearness of the stars, and his own desperate circumstances, all made of this something new and terrifying. Obviously God was sending him a message. But what? Was it an assurance of hope, like Noah's rainbow? Or was it a warning of God's anger? In accordance with his nature he assumed the latter. Bowed with despair and self-loathing, he returned to his cold and sleepless bed of stone. There were also more practical difficulties: it seemed that in all this vast and tumbled wilderness of mountain and ravine there was not a loaf, not a blanket, not one thing of solace or comfort for the body of man. Thomas reached the safety of the Italian border half-starved, half-frozen, shocked and horrified.

It was November before he reached Mantua. But even here there was to be little respite. Scarcely had he changed into dry clothes than Nicholas Hawkins arrived from England to replace him in his post.

Why? Nicholas Hawkins did not know. Or would not tell. All he would say was that Cranmer was to return immediately to London, travelling in post; adding, sourly and laconically, that the King had need of him.

He set out on one more winter journey in a state almost of shock. *Why* did Henry want him? Was he in disgrace? Or did the King wish to promote him still further?

Disgrace, or promotion? He did not know which was the more dangerous. Either way, the small country benefice, with Margarete discreetly hidden behind the church wall, now seemed more and more unlikely.

And then he had a thought so horrifying that he reined in his horse and sat silent, his chin on his breast. In the dispatches from London he had read that William Warham,

Archbishop of Canterbury, had died in August. Surely, *surely* Henry did not intend to raise him, Thomas Cranmer, to those heights! No. It was unthinkable. There were far better men than he: Gardiner, Lee, Stokesley, all had better claims than he. Why, he wasn't even a bishop.

But then, he thought wretchedly, none of *them* would be acceptable to my Lord of Wiltshire; or, even more important, to my Lord of Wiltshire's daughter, Anne.

In deep perplexity he urged his horse into a trot. Before he left England, Henry and Anne had been living in mortal sin. He had remonstrated with Henry, and had been relieved to get away from England before he could judge whether his remonstrance had had any effect (though, knowing Henry and Anne, he thought it most unlikely).

No. He wanted nothing more to do with it. He was a man of God. He served God, not the King. In the unlikely, *most* unlikely, event of the King offering him Canterbury, he would refuse. It would be better both for his own conscience and for his wife's safety.

And yet, and yet? Walking with the King, being made much of by the highest in the land, being at the *heart* of things: none of this had been as disagreeable as he had imagined. In fact, he had acquired rather a taste for it. And as Canterbury he could introduce into the Church of England some of the ideas that had fired his imagination in Nuremberg.

But he was too steeped in scripture not to recognize the dulcet tones of the Devil. No. He would have none of it. The weather gave him every excuse to travel slowly. Even if the King *had* had this quite preposterous idea, Cranmer would give him time to have second thoughts before his Archbishop-elect returned to England.

But Thomas had underestimated his Sovereign. Henry wanted Cranmer home. And he wanted him home *now*. Here he was, without an Archbishop of Canterbury, just when he needed an Archbishop of Canterbury most.

For Henry had made a cosy little arrangement with the French King, whereby Francis would stand by him if he defied the Pope by repudiating Katherine and marrying Anne.

And Henry knew that for this bold move he needed the seemingly unlikely Cranmer. And where *was* Cranmer?

When Henry wanted something, December's ice and snow became irrelevant. Distances, oceans became irrelevant. A messenger was despatched to Europe with instructions to drag the fellow home by his bridle if necessary.

CHAPTER 8

Thomas' reception at Court took his breath away. Five minutes after his arrival (filthy, weary, famished after nearly two months of winter travelling) he was being rushed by panting servants along corridors, up and down steps, through formal gardens.

And now Thomas heard strange noises: the shouts of men, angry or jubilant; high screams and squeals of pain; and, louder than all, a deep and terrible and despairing roar.

Before them now stood a large pavilion, and it was from this that the noises came. And Thomas realized where he was being taken in such haste: the bear pit.

He arrived at an unfortunate moment. One of the King's favourite dogs had just been disembowelled: a dog, moreover, on whom Henry had placed a large stake.

Squealing and screaming, the dog dragged himself blindly round the arena, leaving a trail of blood and entrails. Normally this would have caused a good deal of amusement. But not today, not with this dog.

Henry was in a towering rage. God's Body, he'd have the bear killed, the bearmaster whipped. *And* this fellow trembling and grovelling before him. 'Well, what do you want?' he demanded, glaring.

'Your Majesty. Doctor Thomas Cranmer.'

The glare was transferred from the servant to Thomas, who fell on his knees. 'God's Death, Canterbury. You have incurred our gravest displeasure. Dallying with German whores when you should have been here, at Court, about *our* business.'

To the kneeling Thomas, the words that fell about his ears were like an axe falling upon his neck. 'Gravest displeasure.' 'German whores.' (Had some malevolent and garbled rumour about Margarete reached him?) But, most alarming of all, confirming his darkest fears, that one word 'Canterbury'.

Despite this angry giant towering over him, he owed it to God, whose servant he was, to say, 'Your Majesty, I am a Royal Chaplain and an ordained priest. I do not consort with whores.'

'I've never yet met a priest who didn't,' grumbled Henry. 'Oh, get on your feet, man.' Cranmer rose, and stood trembling before his King.

The heart had gone out of the baiting for that day. The torn and bleeding bear was being led away until tomorrow. A few courtiers stood in chastened groups not daring to leave in case they were needed.

It was always dangerous to question Majesty. Yet the King seemed to have nothing further to say. Thomas said, humbly, 'Your Grace called me "Canterbury".'

The cloud that hung over Henry did not lift. 'You *are* Canterbury – my Lord,' he added sardonically.

Thomas swallowed. 'I am not a fit person for such an honour, Your Majesty.'

Henry slowly lifted his eyes and glared long and hard at Cranmer. He almost spat out the words. 'Do you *dare* to question my judgement, Cranmer?'

Thomas took a deep breath. He was fighting against faintness, so powerfully did the King's presence dominate him. He said, 'I am questioning only my inadequacies, Sire.'

The King put out a great hand and seized Thomas by the shoulder. He even shook him. 'Listen, Thomas. Don't be a fool. I'm offering you power. Unbelievable power. More power even than that decrepit ass in Rome.' He looked at Thomas keenly. 'Ah! You do not pale at that description of the Holy Father?'

Thomas said, 'I am no lover of Rome. Or of the Holy Father. Yet – he is our spiritual lord.'

'Why is he? Is he spiritual lord of your friends in Saxony? Is he spiritual lord of Doctor Luther?'

'No,' Thomas said quietly, wondering how much the King knew of his secret visits to Nuremberg.

'And why isn't he? Because they have had the courage to throw off his yoke. And you and I, Thomas, could do the same.'

Thomas said humbly, 'I have no taste for power, your Majesty.'

'You've never tasted it. It is a heady wine, my lord of Canterbury.' The King seized Thomas' arm, began strolling about the arena. 'You and I, Thomas,' he said again. 'Myself, the supreme head of the Church in England; yourself, my loyal servant. We could build such a Church as would make Rome a thing of tinsel and tawdry.'

Walking thus, with the King's arm in his once more, watched enviously by the few remaining courtiers, and with the English Church put into his hands to mould as he would, Thomas was tempted. He remembered the simple sincerity of life in Nuremberg. He remembered something else from Nuremberg, something he had never for a moment forgotten. He went down on his knees. He said, 'Your

Majesty, be merciful to your servant. I can never be Archbishop. I – have married a wife.'

'You *fool*!' Then the King was silent for so long that at last Thomas dared to peer upward, and saw Henry biting his lower lip in what looked like indecision. But if it was, it did not last long. Henry said: 'Then that is your folly and your misfortune. Do with her what you will: hide her, lose her, carry her around in a trunk. But you are still Archbishop of Canterbury, Doctor Cranmer.' He had an afterthought. 'Who is she?'

'A Lutheran maid. Niece to Andreas Osiander.'

'A Lutheran? By the Bones of Christ, Cranmer, you do not do things by halves. Anyway, she is your problem.' Impatiently he pulled Thomas to his feet. 'Now listen. You will be consecrated at the end of March. Before your consecration you will read out a protestation which nullifies any oaths to the Pope which may occur in your consecration. You will repeat this protestation at your consecration and again after. Then in May you will rule on the validity or otherwise of my marriage to my dear sweet Katherine. By which time the canonists will have decided that she and Arthur did consummate their marriage, which makes mine even more of an abomination to the Lord, and should make it easier for you to reach a clear-cut decision.'

Thomas said, as he rose slowly to his feet, 'Your Grace, if I am to give such a ruling, I must have absolute freedom of conscience.'

Henry sounded reproachful now, sadly reproachful: 'My dear Thomas, do you think that I – I of all monarchs, would expect anything else?'

Thomas tried to tell himself he was reassured. 'I thank your Grace.' But he shook his head sorrowfully. 'Indeed, your Majesty, I am neither worthy nor capable of this great office.'

'I say you are,' the King said harshly. 'And now, leave me.'

So. The die was cast. If Thomas Cranmer had ever been in a position to refuse the Archbishopric, he was so no longer. When the King pressed on him the poisoned chalice, he had shrunk away; but he had not said no. All his instincts, his very conscience, has said no. But he himself had not said no, for he feared for his life if he did.

Events were rushing on, turbulent as a millstream. Anne Boleyn had opened the sluice-gates by whispering to the joyful Henry that she was pregnant. So there wasn't a moment to be lost. Conception could come before the marriage, and not much harm done. But if the *birth* came before the marriage the whole weary business of securing the Succession would be put at risk. Henry made sure of things by marrying Anne secretly, regardless of the fact that he was still married to Katherine. After all, arrangements were well in hand for Cranmer to sort out that little difficulty.

But if events moved turbulently, the matter of Cranmer's consecration moved on well-oiled wheels. Thomas was disturbed to find that all arrangements had been made even before he knew he was to be Archbishop. And he found the way that Tudor Governments slid into action alarming and sinister.

Before he had recovered from the announcement at the bear pit, the Master of Jewels arrived with a loan of a thousand pounds to help him with his expenses.

Thomas was horrified. 'But I could never repay such a sum.'

'Then how will you pay for your vestments? Or do you intend to be consecrated in a monk's habit? How will you pay your servants? Believe me, Doctor Cranmer, before this matter is done you will be trying to wheedle another thousand out of me.'

Thomas said, 'I do not wheedle, Master Cromwell.'

A flash of anger passed over Cromwell's porcine face and was gone. His features immobile, his voice flat, he said, 'I have no time to waste on quibbles. Sign here, Doctor Cranmer.' And he stubbed a blunt forefinger on a form of receipt.

Thomas signed, and bowed coldly. Cromwell nodded, and waddled out; like, Thomas thought uncharitably, an overfed porker. A mild and courteous man himself, rudeness was one of the few things that brought him to sudden anger.

A thousand pounds! But before he could absorb the thought of so vast a sum he was besieged by tailors, seamstresses, shoemakers; he was being shown silks and velvets, rings and jewels, and croziers, some flashing with diamonds, some of gold, some inlaid with the wood of the True Cross. There were carpets and furniture for his Palace at Canterbury, his Palace at Lambeth, his various manor houses.

Messengers were riding post through the filthy February weather, bringing Papal Bulls from Rome authorizing the consecration, eleven Bulls altogether. Henry was making sure that, whatever this heretic Archbishop might do to the Pope in the future, he would start his archiepiscopal life with the Pope's full, and written, approval.

So, at that gorgeous and solemn and godly ceremony in the Chapter House of Westminster, Thomas Cranmer swore to be faithful and obedient to the Holy Roman Church and to the Pope, and to persecute and denounce all heretics, schismatics and rebels against the Pope. He then read out the protestation that Henry had prepared for him, and that he had previously read in a private room: that he did not intend to be binding any oath to the Pope that was against the King or the laws of England, or that bound him not to advise and agree to the reformation of the Church of England in any way which furthered the prerogative of the King.

It was a typical Tudor arrangement, and gave satisfaction all round. It did not even greatly offend Cranmer's watchful conscience: which means that it was either an honourable compromise, or that the conscience was already developing a few callouses on that tender skin.

Thomas was not a tall man. But he carried himself well, and with authority. In his gorgeous vestments, and with the mitre to give him height, and with his thoughtful, kindly face, he looked noble.

And if he looked noble, he felt noble. He had put on nobility with these rich vestments. He felt power and wisdom pouring into him. He had been a focal point of a vast concourse, every one of whom had prayed and sung for him. He remembered his omen of the falling star. But now he had no doubt as to its meaning: it was a sign from God calling him to rid England of the power of Rome.

Two days later, Convocation decided that if the marriage between Arthur and Katherine of Aragon had been consummated, then the marriage of Henry and Katherine must be void. The canonists then gave their opinion that the marriage *had* been consummated. It was then the logical conclusion for Cranmer to petition the King to be allowed to sit in judgement on his marriage to Katherine: a series of events that had been decided upon long before Cranmer had the Archbishopric thrust upon him.

Thomas had never met Katherine of Aragon. Nor did he wish to do so. He had convinced himself that her marriage to

Henry was sinful and invalid. He was now called upon, as Archbishop of Canterbury, to state this view in a public trial of the marriage. Yet, a humane man, he knew that to meet the poor Queen would be painful in the extreme.

So it was a great relief to him when she refused utterly to attend his court at Dunstable. This way, he could speak the truth, as he saw it, *and* serve the King, without actually watching the pain he was causing.

Yes. He spoke the truth as he had seen it years ago at Cambridge. As Papal Legate he forbade Henry and Katherine to cohabit and annulled their marriage, thus making their daughter Mary a bastard. There was nothing for his conscience to cavil at in that, surely?

But he still hoped he would never come face to face with Katherine of Aragon, or with her newly bastardized daughter.

Yet, even before Thomas had given this judgement, he was hearing the most appalling rumours: London was in a ferment because, it was widely reported, the King had secretly married the Great Whore, as the common people now brutally referred to Anne Boleyn. Worse, he received letters in the King's name instructing him to be prepared to declare this secret marriage valid. And he was given eight days in which to do it.

He hurried back to London, sought an immediate audience of the King. It was a monstrous instruction. Nothing would make him obey it.

The audience was granted. But when Thomas was shown into the presence he found, to his great discomfiture, the King closeted with Anne Boleyn. They were in a small, sumptuously appointed chamber, both half buried in a great heap of pillows.

They ignored him. They were in a merry mood, playing chess for kisses. Henry had just taken a pawn, and was demanding his forfeit, which Anne was laughingly refusing: the sort of romp that Henry loved. But before it could develop into more aggressive lovemaking, the King suddenly broke off and said, 'Well, my Lord of Canterbury? What is it?'

The lady pouted, struggling out of her nest of pillows. 'Harry, do we have to listen to prelates *now*?'

'Yes, my chicken, we do. If you are to be crowned next week.'

'But why now? All arrangements are made: my litter, my golden canopy, my gowns?'

'None of these would be possible without the help of Cranmer, chuck. First he must declare our marriage valid.'

Anne flounced back into her pillows. 'Our marriage? It was performed by a priest. Why should it not be valid?'

Thomas said, boldly, 'Because, Madam, the King was already married at the time.'

She laughed unpleasantly.

'Silence!' It was a roar from Henry. She looked up at his red, suffused face. Her laughter ceased. She looked suddenly weary, and coarse. Pregnancy did not suit her. She was a far cry from the mocking, willowy creature Thomas had first met in the library of Durham House.

Henry's roar had the deep, earth-shaking male defiance of the rutting stage. 'Am I not the King? Am I to stand on one side while my wife and my Archbishop *prattle* to each other?' His furious gaze fixed itself on Cranmer. 'Are you so puffed up by my patronage, my Lord, that you think you can ignore me?'

Thomas went down on his knees. 'Your Majesty, I cannot declare your marriage to the Lady Anne valid. Have mercy on your servant. But I cannot.'

'Mercy? Mercy? I raise you up out of the gutter. And at my first request you *dare* to come here and, ignoring me, tell my Queen that, so far as you are concerned, or care, she can remain a whore.'

At this insult Anne flounced furiously out of the room, leaving the door open.

Henry went to the door and bellowed, 'Cromwell! Cromwell!', setting the courtiers scurrying like ants in a disturbed nest.

Thomas Cranmer was no Sir Thomas More. He was not the stuff of martyrs. Such gales of royal anger terrified him; as indeed they terrified all who saw them. Yet he fought bravely against being cowed. 'Your Grace, the marriage was bigamous.'

'Then search the Scriptures, man. Did none of the old kings marry bigamously?'

Thomas said, 'There is no warrant for bigamy in Scripture, your Majesty.'

Henry rocked slightly on the balls of his feet, beringed hands on those powerful hips, like an athlete preparing for action. 'Then find another answer. Take a leaf out of Rome's book. Popes have given Princes dispensations for bigamy before now.' He went on fuming. 'Why, even that oaf Luther kindly gives me permission to have two wives.'

Thomas rose from his knees; and stood and faced his terrible Sovereign who held absolute power of life and death over him. He said, bravely, 'Sire, I am no Pope. I am the loyal subject you made your Archbishop, and to whom you promised freedom of conscience.'

The little eyes narrowed. 'Are you accusing me of bad faith?'

Thomas' voice was a whisper. 'No. I crave your Grace's mercy.'

The King said, 'An Archbishop who defies his Sovereign? What do we do with him? The Tower? The block? The stake? What is good enough for such treason, eh, Master Cromwell?'

Thomas saw that Cromwell had slipped silently into the room; and that those porcine features were regarding him with – could it be? – relish.

Cromwell said, 'What is the trouble, Your Majesty?'

Henry said, 'He refuses to validate my marriage to my loved and virtuous Anne.' They might have been discussing some servant who stood before them accused of stealing a mutton bone. Thomas was oppressed by a fearful loneliness.

Cromwell's voice was harsh and rough: 'Then hang him, Sire. There are plenty of clerics would know better their duty to their King, given such a high office.'

The King said, 'Not so quick, Master Cromwell. Perhaps my Lord of Canterbury has not considered fully what he will be doing if he defies me.' He turned to Cranmer. His manner was ice-cold. 'If this my son in my sweet Anne's belly is born a bastard – and that is in your hands, Master Archbishop – then at my death the Kingdom will be plunged into strife greater than the Wars of the Roses. And one man will be wholly responsible for all that carnage and suffering. Are you prepared to take that on your shoulders, my Lord?'

Thomas was silent.

Cromwell said, 'I say hang him, your Grace. God clearly wishes you to have a legitimate heir, now that you have been freed from your sinful ties. He would not be pleased, surely, if you allowed one meddling priest to destroy His, and your, efforts?'

Henry turned to Thomas. He picked up a bishop from the chessboard, flung it into the fire. There was a moment's pause. Then the tiny manikin began to blaze. Henry said, 'I could destroy you, Cranmer, as easily as that.'

There was silence in the room. Cromwell's white, coarse pig's-flesh did not move. Only his eyes glittered with life as they rested unblinking on Cranmer. Henry walked over slowly to his chair and sat down. He too never took his baleful eyes off Thomas. Thomas stood white as death, face to face with martyrdom.

If he died, another would step straight into his shoes, the marriage would be made valid, and history would rumble on. But then, England would be the poorer, because men in high places had broken a principle.

Yet whatever *he* did, men in high places would still break that principle. And few would know that Thomas Cranmer had died for that principle, because the State would take care to degrade him and vilify his name. And Margarete? He was determined she should be brought secretly to England. Dangerous though this was, he must have her by his side. Yet, by destroying himself, he would also destroy her. And the Church? What would happen to his dawning plans for a liberated English Church?

What value is there in a death, as opposed to a life?

Henry said, 'I have treated you as a friend, Cranmer. But do not be misled by that. A friend turned traitor I would kill as I kill this flea.' And he plucked a flea from his rich fur collar and squeezed it between finger and thumb.

Thomas said heavily, 'I am no traitor, Your Majesty.'

Cromwell said, 'What else is a man who would defy his Sovereign and bring his country to ruin?'

Thomas said angrily. 'What is a man who would defy his conscience to satisfy his Prince's lusts?'

The silence in the room seemed to last for minutes. And when at last the King spoke it was in almost a whisper. 'Cranmer, I command you to declare my marriage to the Lady Anne lawful. Only then shall I forget the awful folly of the words you have just spoken.'

They waited. Henry knowing that for all his threats he was dependent on Cranmer. Cromwell fearing this cleric might ruin everything for a principle (Cromwell had never understood the importance some people attached to principles).

And Thomas Cranmer? He said, formally, slowly, in a flat voice, 'Your Majesty, since your Grace's marriage to Queen Katherine has been declared unlawful, then in the sight of God your Majesty had never been married. I therefore pronounce your marriage to the Lady Anne, Marquess of Pembroke, valid and lawful.'

King and Archbishop looked at each other hard. Then the King turned and walked from the room without a word.

What value is there in a death, when it is set against a life?

The King knew, and Cranmer knew, that the long, level look that had passed between them was a summing up of their future relationship. Henceforth there might be disagreements, occasional stands on principle. But the King would always win. And Cranmer knew that he was trapped in a world, brutal and rapacious, that must, ultimately and inevitably, destroy him.

But now, the servant must have his reward. On Anne's procession from the Tower to Westminster for her coronation, Thomas rode in a place of honour. The next day he crowned her Queen in the Abbey. And, a signal honour, at the great banquet in Westminster Hall he was seated with Anne at her table, and had two future Dukes as his carver and cupbearer, while some of the most powerful men in England sat at lower tables.

What value is there in a death, when it is set against the abundance of life?

Yet, despite all this joy and merrymaking (Anne was borne through London in a litter of cloth of gold under a canopy hung with silver bells. She wore white robes and ermine, and a circlet of priceless jewels in her black hair, and there was music and pageantry everywhere, and fountains cascading wine), men's hearts were full of dread. How should they not be when, as they saw it, their beloved Monarch had put aside his true wife of twenty years and married a common stewed whore? (A whore, incidentally, with six fingers on one hand and the Devil's mark on her neck!) Should they not fear when both earth and heaven were suddenly full of dire omens and warnings: a monstrous fish beached on a northern shore; a ball of fire over Greenwich, a comet with a silvery beard heralding each dawn for weeks on end, a flaming cross seen in the sky over Beccles, to say nothing of an abstruse but very disturbing prophecy about the coming of the Dreadful Dragon and the Bare-legged Hens? Dark days were coming.

And the simple, honest people of England were right as usual. Dark days *were* coming; though from a direction they did not altogether expect.

King Henry VIII of England was now in his forties. He had a new young wife, with the promise of a male heir kicking lustily in her womb. He had, among all the plotters and place-seekers and back-biters of his Court, found an honest, guileless man of God who was moved, not by ambition but by an absolute dedication to his earthly Prince. And with this wise and clever man at his command, and with Anne changed from an impatient and querulous mistress into a grateful (for the time being) Queen, there was, he decided, nothing in this Realm of England he could not do. Power was already his. *Supreme* power, both in Church and State, should be his. There would be a ruthless and bloody end for any who denied him.

King Henry fell on his knees and thanked God mightily for all His loving kindness to him, a royal sinner.

Chapter 9

So the man who less than four years ago had been a humble Fellow of Jesus, was now one of the most powerful men in England, head of an army of chaplains, chamberlains, secretaries; the target for every cleric seeking preferment, for every place-seeker.

He discovered very soon that his preferment brought with it another and terrible power: one which, in his innocence, he had not bargained for: the power of life and death over his fellow man.

Thomas, working in his study, was startled by the noisy irruption of an officer, followed by two armed men roughly handling a man in a monk's habit.

The officer saluted, and gave Thomas a sealed letter.

Thomas, angered by this unmannerly entrance, ignored the letter. He said, 'Sir, let your prisoner be seated.'

They pushed their prisoner towards a stool, on to which he half fell. Thomas saw now he was a young, pleasant-faced man. He gave him a tentative smile. The young man did not smile back.

He kept the officer standing while he read the letter.

It was from Gardiner. And it was one of the most extraordinary letters that Thomas had ever read.

It said that the prisoner Frith, a Cambridge student, denied both the Real Presence and Purgatory: damnable heresies for which he had been sent to the Tower and was now brought before the Archbishop.

But Gardiner continued (and this was what made the letter so extraordinary): 'Frith claims it is not necessary for salvation either to believe or disbelieve these points.'

Not necessary for salvation! No theologian had ever heard, far less made, so outrageous a statement. Thomas dismissed the officer and his men. Then he looked at this remarkable young man almost with disbelief. He said, 'You *really* think that – one may believe as one wishes – and not risk Hell fire?'

'My God is a God of love. I cannot believe he would condemn to everlasting torment on a question of belief.'

Thomas said, 'My son, you are in deep and grievous error. Believe me, unless you repent the Church will burn you for your heresy; and God will condemn you. There is but one Truth. He who does not believe that Truth is damned.'

Frith smiled wearily. 'I still say, reverend sir, *it does not matter*.'

Such blasphemy was too much for Thomas. He said, 'You will stay here, under instruction, as my prisoner. And I do command you, here and now, to consider the fearful danger in which you stand, both physical and spiritual.'

That night, he slept little. Anger, with him, was a rare emotion, one he had not learnt to cope with. It left him troubled, irritable, twitching with a nervous intensity. That a student of Cambridge should blaspheme against God by saying that His presence or otherwise in the Host *did not matter*! 'He looketh to go unto the fire,' he muttered as he tossed and turned in his bed.

Unto the fire! And suddenly he realized that, if this pleasant but misguided young man did go to the fire he had so thoroughly deserved, he, Thomas Cranmer, would be instrumental in sending him there.

A week later, after hours of exhortation and prayer, he found Frith as set in his monstrous beliefs as ever. He sent him to his Bishop for sentence, knowing it meant the fire. He had done his rather unpleasant duty. He had done what any sixteenth-century prelate would have done, faced with such monstrous and wicked heresy. Yet he accused himself bitterly of squeamishness because, the night before Frith burned, he heard the watch cry every leaden hour, and heard in the darkness the cock greet the coming day; and wondered whether John Frith was hearing him too.

There remained one awful dilemma: Margarete! It was over six months now since they had married. Six months, with her in Nuremberg and himself in England. She would think herself deserted and forsaken, she would think he no longer loved her, he who yearned and longed for her sweet beauty through the long night hours. He *must* bring her to England, whatever the danger: for *her* sake, for both their sakes!

He wrote, an urgent, impassioned letter, telling her of his love, his longing, begging her to come to England.

But a letter required a messenger. A bride required an escort across Europe. And both messenger and escort needed to be utterly trustworthy.

Had he one friend he could trust in all this rabble of a Court, or among the obsequious staff at Lambeth Palace?

No.

In the end he sent for his secretary, Ralph Morice: a likeable and seemingly honest young man.

Ralph entered, bowed and smiled. 'Your Grace?'

Cranmer too smiled. Unused to dealing with inferiors, he had already adopted the manner he would keep to all his life: courteous, thoughtful, treating them as equals. And he had already warmed to this Morice. He said, 'Now, Ralph, I want you to do something for me.'

'Of course, your Grace.'

Thomas, watching him keenly, said, 'I want you to deliver a letter for me.'

Ralph bowed. 'Certainly.'

'To Nuremberg,' Thomas said calmly.

Ralph had been expecting Greenwich, or Hampton Court. But he recovered himself quickly. 'Very well, your Grace.'

'When you are there, I want you to arrange carriages in relay to bring a lady to Calais, then to find a ship, and bring her at last to Knoll, my house in West Kent.'

He sat, enjoying the sight of Morice struggling to hide his surprise.

And Ralph Morice *was* surprised. Not because an Archbishop of Canterbury had a harlot. There was nothing remarkable in that. But because *this* Archbishop of Canterbury had.

For the secretary had formed a great devotion to his new master: a kind, austere and godly man he thought him: a man aloof from, and above, the lechery and triviality of the Court. Well, he realized now, he had expected too much of human nature. He would know better next time.

Thomas rose. He gave the letter to Ralph. 'I think you will not have any difficulty in finding the lady.'

Ralph Morice read the address. *Frau Margarete Cranmer, at the house of Osiander, Nuremberg.*

He stared at the letter. Then, slowly, his eyes came up and he stared at Thomas in horror and disbelief. A wife? A concubine was one thing. But a wife was another.

Thomas was smiling. 'What are you thinking, Ralph? That there are three possibilities? The lady could be my mother.

She could be a sister-in-law. Or – she could be my wife.' He even chuckled. 'Now which do you think she is, Ralph?'

Ralph said, awkwardly, 'She cannot be your wife, your Grace.'

'No.' Thomas looked suddenly sad. 'She cannot. But she *is*, and a wife should be by her husband's side. Will you do this service for me, Ralph?'

Ralph Morice stood, flushed and silent.

Thomas was filled with a great disappointment. He said, 'There is a danger, I know. I should not have asked you, Ralph.'

'Your Grace!' The young man was shocked out of his silence. 'It is not *my* danger. It is for you that I am fearful.'

Thomas said, 'You are a faithful servant, Ralph. You know that in giving you this letter I also give you the head off my shoulders.'

'I do, your Grace. And I am the more honoured.' He went down on his knees. 'Bless me, Father in God.'

Knoll was an ideal place to hide a concubine, or even a wife. Small (compared with his other properties), remote, buried among trees, it could have kept a harem secret from the world.

Even the wagging tongues of servants did not give Thomas' secret away. Because the arrival of a woman, shrouded in black, at midnight; her ensconcing in a meticulously prepared bedroom (adjacent to the Archbishop's); the arrival, six hours later, of his Grace, his features anxious and at the same time ecstatic and exultant; the lady's door closing behind him, not to be opened for another six hours: all this meant but one thing: the Archbishop hadn't wasted much time in installing his harlot.

He was saved (for the present at least) by the prurience of the public imagination.

After dinner they walked in the grounds. Already the day was turning towards evening. A time of infinite sadness, infinite thought. All nature brooding and silent, as the sun went golden down to his setting, to die in flames like the phoenix.

And Thomas, with this loved and loving creature by his side, was no longer exultant. At almost every step she smiled up lovingly into his face, and he smiled down at her. But he was troubled. What life could he possibly give her? The only possible hope for this virtuous wife lay in acting the courtesan.

The hour was too solemn, the future too forbidding, for unthinking happiness. On a high elm a thrush, its breast reaching to the sun, mourned the passing day. Thomas remembered the tiny, high-walled garden in Nuremberg. She had been safe there, among friends and well-wishers. She would find no well-wishers in England, he thought bitterly, and no safety.

The red ball of the sun went down, and the western sky flamed in glory. But a cold breeze of evening came and troubled the leaves, and he shivered and felt the shiver pass to his beloved. And they turned and were glad to be back in the shelter of the house and the doors locked, and the candles bright against the Tudor dark.

Chapter 10

In later life he could never see a calm evening, with the birds flying to their roosts across an azure sky, without remembering that evening at Knoll. And he could never remember that moment of peace without his eyes filling with tears. Swept along by the turbulence of life in Tudor England, he was to know little of such times. Serving a man as boisterous and wilful as Henry might have its rewards: wealth, power; but peace of mind was not on the list.

Especially now. Henry was beginning to think that his thanks to God for all His blessings had been a little premature. His old friend and companion Thomas More was less than enthusiastic about Henry's claims to supreme power. And More would be as powerful as an adversary as he was faithful as a friend.

And Anne! Her devotion and gratitude to him for making her Queen and Consort had proved very short-lived indeed. As a mistress she had often been shrill and nagging to her besotted lover. Now, as a wife, and with the husband decidedly less besotted than the lover, she was impossible.

She disrupted Court life, threatening old and trusted servants with dismissal, quarrelling with high Officers of State, treating with venom any lady who caught the King's eye. And though the King was no longer besotted she knew she could go to any lengths with impunity, simply because of what she carried in her belly: the seed and the fruit of English Kings.

And Pope Clement had chosen this depressing time to take positive action at last: he announced that if Henry did not return to his lawful wife Katherine, he would suffer excommunication and its terrifying concomitant: everlasting damnation (and so, incidentally, would the Queen and Archbishop Cranmer).

But, for Henry, there was one shining lantern in all this gloom: his son and heir. Once let this babe be delivered into the world, and Henry's strength would be doubled. With the Succession assured he could defy the Pope, he could defy Christendom. And, thanks be to God, he could get rid of Anne!

The dramatic moment was approaching. Yet again the astrologers and the physicians gave their unanimous verdict: the child would be a strong and healthy boy.

And now the time had come for the Queen to 'take to her chambers'. The nobility of England escorted her to and from High Mass. Then she stood under her cloth of estate while her chamberlain bade all pray that God would send her 'the good hour'.

She entered the inner chamber and they left her alone with her women. Now no man would see her until she was delivered.

And delivered she was on September 7th. And King Henry at last realized that God was *not* on his side. The King's decision to call the child either Edward or Henry had to be abandoned.

Instead they called her Elizabeth.

Everybody suffered. The King raged: a torrent, a surge, a spate, a veritable tidal wave of frustrated anger.

Everybody suffered: the astrologers and soothsayers, the doctors and the midwives, anyone who was even remotely connected with the birth was lashed with the royal tongue. Even God had a few reproachful remarks thrown at Him.

But the person who suffered most, of course, was Queen Anne. Even while she was carrying her precious and vital burden, Henry had turned on her in fury with the threat that he 'could at any time lower her as much as he had raised her'. Under that threat she had carried and borne her child; nourishing it with her body; yet unable to do one thing, one little thing, to influence its sex; and in the awful knowledge that the wrong sex could spell her doom.

So, while the common sort drank from the fountains of wine, and were deafened by the bells of every church in London; and while the Princes and Prelates of Europe rocked and roared with laughter at the joke – the Queen lay in her magnificent bed, clinging to the scorned child in her arms, and wept in a dark misery of loneliness and fear.

Well, Elizabeth might be only a girl. But since Katherine's daughter Mary had been declared bastard, she was the only legitimate heir to the Throne. So Henry, with typical exuberance, gave her a christening worthy of such a one. The 'right high, right noble, and right excellent Princess Elizabeth, Princess of England' was christened in a mantle of heavy purple velvet, and had for godparents a Dowager Duchess, a Marchioness and an Archbishop.

But Cranmer was seeing far beyond the silver font, and the gold hangings and the rich tapestries of the church. He was seeing Knoll; and Margarete, lovely and neglected but uncomplaining, in what had become for him a rare and longed for haven of refuge. And beyond that he was seeing

Rome, and the threat of excommunication that still hung over his head, as well as over the heads of his King and Queen.

And he understood the King's temper. This elaborate and splendid christening had nothing to do with any possible love for his new daughter. It was purely an act of defiance from England to Rome. So. Henry and the Pope were like two jousting knights, rushing full tilt at each other. And he, Thomas, was wearing the King's colours. But this was no sport. This was battle, with judgement and death and everlasting damnation the lot of the loser.

And against the might of Rome, who could ever, finally, be the winner?

Henry had made his decision. As a monarch he had rightly thought himself responsible for the bodily needs of his subjects. Now, he decided with superb Tudor confidence, he would also make himself responsible for their souls.

It was an awesome burden he laid on himself. But he would be supreme, spiritually as well as temporally. Two men, Cromwell and Cranmer, would help him to this end: Cromwell, because he lusted for power; Cranmer, because he was already a Lutheran at heart.

One day Thomas escaped to Knoll. A guilty conscience led him to fear reproaches. But Margarete greeted him as though nothing could be more delightful than living alone with a very occasional visit from her lord to make all well.

He enfolded both her hands in his, smiled gravely down at her eager face. 'I am sorry to have been away so long. You should hate me for abandoning you in this way.'

'Hate you, my husband? Hate you, because you are about the Lord's business? Set against that, I am nothing. To say otherwise would be very blasphemy.

He was silent, ashamed. How much, he was asking himself, had been the Lord's business, and how much the King's. And how much Thomas Cranmer's?

He put his arm about her, deeply protective. Together they strolled through stone corridors to a small room where a great fire burned in a carved fireplace. (Oh, to be here, winter and summer, with his dear Margarete, and his books.)

He saw the well-stacked logs, the gleaming brass, the polished furniture. They were things he would never normally have noticed. Now he saw them through her eyes.

They sat, on an oak settle, and gazed at the fire and at the dying November day outside. A servant offered wine and sweetmeats. Thomas stretched out his legs to the blaze. He was tired, and cold from riding. And infinitely content. He said, 'Your household? They are good, and loyal?'

'Thomas, they are wonderful. So kind. I have to ask for nothing.'

'Good. Good.' But she must never know what a drain on his resources this household was. He had already realized that as Archbishop he would inevitably be impoverished. Entertaining almost every day, maintaining his establishments, giving alms to a veritable army of beggars – there was no provision for a wife in the finances of an Archbishop. And Cromwell was already hinting that he would like his thousand pound loan repaid.

Yet even all this paled before the cost of his coming enthronement. He said, 'Next month, I am to be enthroned. In Canterbury Cathedral.'

Already they were conversing in a mixture of Latin, English and German. But 'enthroned' was too much for her. 'What is this "enthroned"?'

He explained. How he would walk to the Cathedral in gorgeous vestments, yet barefoot through sanded streets, as signs of both humility and spiritual power. How he would be brought to his Throne in that great Cathedral by all the spiritual and temporal power of the Realm; how afterwards there would be a splendid banquet which bade fair to impoverish the City, the monks of Christchurch, and Cranmer himself; and how for him all this splendour and pomp would mean nothing because she could not be beside him because he would be thinking of her alone among the dripping trees of Knoll.

And so it was. When all was done – the sweet singing lost among the aspiring roofs of the Cathedral, the missals and the Bibles closed, the candles quenched, the last words spoken; the swans and nightingales and partridges and boars all eaten, the wine all drunk – then Thomas walked alone, in the brown habit of a monk, the aisles of that vast Cathedral. Around him the pillars soared vertiginously, almost as high as the vault of heaven itself, to be lost in the darkness and the shadows of night. A votive light glowed before the High Altar. Canterbury! Only two winters ago he had seen, and loved, and been deeply moved by, that Cathedral bathed in morning sunlight. And now he was in its dark, sleeping heart. More incredibly he *was* Canterbury. The spiritual power that this magnificent, soaring building generated was his to channel into the souls of his countrymen: souls that, freed from the yoke of Rome, could soar and aspire heavenwards as did even these pillars of stone.

He had come to the steps of the great High Altar. Deep in inchoate thought, in a highly charged emotional state, he went down slowly on one knee, then on both. He was, he knew, in the presence of the Hosts of God: apostles, archangels, angels, cherubim and seraphim, saints and martyrs. High above him the Altar glowed mysteriously in the gloom. Suddenly, terribly, he saw again the crucified peasant, for him the awful symbol of government overthrown. Government must be strong, the King must be strong. There, in the dimness of that superb shrine, he offered himself anew to the service of his King, the reformation of his Church, the unity of the Realm, and the peace and happiness of his young bride.

Chapter 11

With the consecration and enthronement of this gentle, learned Archbishop, England entered upon a new phase, of which Thomas Cromwell was architect and builder, and Thomas Cranmer the willing figurehead. No sooner was Cranmer enthroned than the Council announced that the Pope had no authority in England, and within a few months all his powers in this country were tranferred to Thomas Cranmer.

It would have been an almost insupportable burden, even for one of the senior Bishops. England was still a Catholic country, but now lacking a Pope. Thomas had to learn the tangled intricacies of his Archbishopric, while delicately feeling his way in his assumption of the Papal powers. Well, he had a good brain, and now he discovered a gift for administration. Only he (and perhaps his Monarch) knew of the doubts and fears that still troubled him.

Yet he trod a sure path. The ease with which he and Cromwell brought about this deliverance from the power of Rome astonished everyone.

England felt like a poor swordsman who, facing a renowned opponent, suddenly finds he has struck to the heart. The very swiftness of the change alarmed some. It had been too easy. And Thomas, knowing that Rome would regard him as the scapegoat for this treachery, remembered

Osiander's warning, and shuddered. 'Rome has a long arm, and an even longer memory.'

But he had a more immediate peril. King Henry had found that being an absolute monarch was not as easy as it looked: that torture, imprisonment and death, terrible weapons though they were, were not strong enough to subdue the human spirit; that the spirit of a people was like an incoming tide.

In this case the tide was not running strongly against the break with Rome, but against the Great Whore and her bastard (as many of the people still saw it) Elizabeth.

Henry was filled with a monstrous self-pity. Not for him the easy comforts of the fireside, the leisure and simple pleasures of his meanest subjects. No. For him the unending wrestle with Pope and Emperor, the fearful struggle to give his loved people a male heir for their comfort when he was gone.

And how did they repay him? By calling his Queen whore, by calling his darling daughter bastard.

Well, he would shake them out of their ingratitude, by God! By spring, he had got an Act of Succession out of Parliament, naming savage penalties for anyone who refused to swear an oath of loyalty to the succession resulting from the divorce.

So. The new Archbishop found himself (together with three others) responsible for ensuring that the oath was administered to every man and woman throughout the length and breadth of England.

It was a stupendous task. Yet, with a furious and impatient King behind them, the four commissioners achieved wonders. Within weeks they were congratulating themselves that every swineherd and ploughman in the land had signed or made his mark on the great lists compiled by JPs and squires. And Thomas, relieved, set off on a leisurely visitation of his Diocese, interspersed with golden hours at Knoll.

Such peace did not last long. He was called peremptorily to London.

He was taken straight to the Council Chamber, where the Lords of the Council were already gathered at a great table. They looked round hurriedly at his entrance, like a group of schoolboys dreading the arrival of a stern teacher; but when they saw who it was they resumed their anxious conversations.

Thomas scarcely knew most of these people. Master Secretary Cromwell was at one end of the table, his papers and quills before him. The Dukes of Norfolk and Suffolk crouched, heads together, over the table. One man did give him a hostile, unsmiling look: Stephen Gardiner, now Bishop of Winchester.

But there were no smiles in that assembly. An assembly of the hardest and most ruthless men in England; and they cowered as they awaited the coming of their King.

Shouts of command, the clatter of halberds, the flinging open of the great double doors; and King Henry entered like a thunderbolt.

The most powerful men in England sprang to their feet; and, after one look at the King's face, decided this was an occasion when it would be wise to be on their knees.

Henry flung himself into his chair, and glowered. 'Well, gentlemen, have we no business today? Off your knees, or I'll have you lopped so that ye travel on 'em in future.' He glared at Thomas. 'Prayers, my Lord Archbishop, prayers.'

Thomas offered up a short prayer for wise counsels and divine guidance. When he finished, Henry stared at him long and hard, as though waiting for another prayer. When none came he said, 'A poor pennyworth, my Lord. More worthy of a mendicant friar than of a man I have made my Archbishop.'

Thomas bowed low. The King roared, 'Come, Master Secretary, announce the business. Do not expect more scraps from Canterbury. He considers he has earned his stipend for one day.'

There were sycophantic titters from some, grave silence from others. To laugh or not to laugh could be almost a hanging matter.

Thomas quaked inwardly. He had seen something of the King's anger before. But then they had been alone. Now he was seeing how Henry's rage could reduce great officers of state to trembling serfs. Could generate in a council chamber something akin to thunder and lightning.

Cromwell said, in his harsh, flat voice: 'Noble and puissant King, we wish only to hear your word.'

'Then by God you shall hear it,' said Henry. He gathered himself together in his chair, a tight, compact ball of royal menace. 'I will tell you, gentlemen. My people are traitorous, almost to a man. They call my Queen unutterable names. They call my dear child Elizabeth –' his voice suddenly broke, 'bastard.' He recovered quickly. 'And what do you do about it, my Lords?'

There was an appalled silence until Henry said, 'I'll tell you, gentlemen. Nothing.' His voice became silky. 'But I'll tell you what you *will* do about it. You will see to it that every man and woman in my Kingdom swears an oath of loyalty to me and to my Queen and to my Succession.'

'But your Majesty, this has been done.' Lord Chancellor Audley, one of the four commissioners, could not keep the indignation out of his voice. God's Teeth, had not he and Cranmer (and the Dukes of Norfolk and Suffolk) sweated blood making sure that every labourer and ploughboy and their stinking doxies had sworn allegiance to the King and his heirs?

'*Has* it been done, Lord Chancellor? *Has* it been done, Canterbury? Norfolk? Suffolk?'

Cranmer said, 'It has not been easy, your Majesty. A swineherd here, perhaps a – '

Henry's great fist crashed down on the table. 'I am not talking of swineherds, Canterbury. I am talking of John Fisher, of Sir Thomas More, of the Princess Dowager, of my bastard child Mary. Why have *they* not sworn?'

'They – would not, Sire.'

'*Would* not? *Would* not? Then where are they, man? In the Tower? The penalties and punishments are there, Archbishop. Both for those who refuse, and – ' again he became suddenly silky, 'for those who fail to enforce the law.'

Thomas said, 'Sir Thomas More and Fisher are in the Tower, your Majesty.'

Henry grunted.

'But Queen Katherine – ' he fortunately noticed the royal scowl and corrected himself, 'the Princess Dowager is vehement in her refusal. And we thought – it would not be seemly – '

'*I* say what is seemly, Archbishop. And the Lady Mary? What of her?'

'She too refuses, Sire.'

The King was silent. He seemed to be struggling with his emotions. To Cranmer's amazement tears appeared on his cheeks. 'All my people have sworn, from the highest in the land to the most humble – all except two old friends, and a once loyal wife, and a disobedient daughter. Oh, thankless generation.' He sat, pensive, mopping his cheeks with his plump, beringed hand.

The King spoke. 'Send the Lady Mary to the Tower. The rackmaster will soon handle her.'

There were gasps of horror. Not because the King was speaking of his own daughter, a royal princess. After all the rack was a highly regarded instrument for making folk see sense. But the Lady Mary was very popular with the common sort. Many would curse the King if he sent to the Tower someone most of them still thought of as Great Harry's daughter.

Someone must speak, must stop the King in this dangerous folly. Slowly Thomas Cranmer became aware that all eyes were on him; for already the feeling was growing that Thomas, like Somers the Fool, could say things that would earn anyone else the gravest displeasure. For them it was solely a matter of expediency that the Lady Mary should not suffer. But, for this new Archbishop, they sensed, it was an emotional matter.

Thomas knew that if anything *was* going to be said, he had got to say it. They were willing him to. He took it for granted that he was the least brave among all these leaders of England. But when it came to saving the King from himself something strong inside him compelled him to speak. He went down on his knees before the King. 'Dread Majesty, I beg mercy for the Lady Mary.'

Henry had spoken in the heat of anger. He was already regretting his wild words. Thank God one of his advisers had the courage to throw him a rope.

But he wasn't going to be seen grasping the rope. His voice was cold when he said, 'On what grounds, Priest?'

'On grounds of humanity, Sire. The Lady Mary is your daughter.'

'A wilful and disobedient daughter. Who must be brought to heel like a cur.'

To go further was dangerous. Cranmer knew that if he did he might well take Mary's place in the Tower. Yet, when he saw something as right, obstinacy gave him a kind of courage. He said, 'Mercy is the prerogative of Kings, your Majesty.'

'I will not be disobeyed,' screamed Henry.

He sat, fuming.

Thomas said, 'There is not a man in this room, your Majesty, who would not die to save your Majesty from being disobeyed. But – the Lady Mary was always a loving daughter to your Grace. She is young, and the young *are* sometimes wilful. May I humbly suggest that your Majesty give her a month to reconsider her hasty decision?'

Honour was satisfied. 'Very well. She shall not go to the Tower – yet. But if she remain recalcitrant – on your head be it, Priest.'

CHAPTER 12

Spring, at Knoll. Daffodils; silver birches; birdsong at dawn and in the evenings; Margarete, sweet and loving, teaching him the sad songs of her homeland.

He gazed at her, seated with her lute, in a simple white dress, and thought he had never seen so beautiful a picture. My wife, he thought, in *my* home. That I should have this gem, this pearl, gazing up at her, at her lips, her white teeth, the smile (the secret smile that was only for him) in her wonderful eyes. 'These songs,' he said, 'of your country. Do they not make you sad?'

'Sad, my Lord, when I have you?'

He laughed. 'You should not call me Lord.'

'But you are my Lord. I wish to honour you by calling you Lord. I *will* call you Lord.' And she struck a chord across the strings and laughed gaily.

He leaned forward, imprisoning her fingers, reaching to kiss her laughing lips.

There was an urgent knocking at the door. Thomas rose hurriedly. It was not seemly for an Archbishop to be seen kissing his wife, especially since he wasn't supposed to have one.

Ralph Morice came in. He handed Thomas a letter. 'Your Grace, a messenger has arrived from Master Cromwell. His business is urgent.'

Thomas sighed and took the letter. His friend Cromwell's business was always urgent. But then, he thought charitably, it was what Cromwell lived for. For Cromwell, each day was crammed with the King's business, with the acquisition of power, and with scheming to keep his head on his shoulders for as long as possible.

For a few moments Thomas held the letter in his hand. He didn't want to open it. He had, for once in these strenuous and turbulent years, been lapped in peace and contentment. And he sensed that a letter from Cromwell would shatter that as surely as a ball from a cannon.

With a feeling of dread Thomas broke the seal, carried the letter over to the light from the window.

The letter was terse. 'Your Grace, Return at once to Lambeth. Await instructions. Thomas Cromwell.'

Yes, a veritable cannon ball of a letter. It was three years now since Thomas Cranmer had been consecrated Archbishop. In those three difficult years he had grown greatly in stature and authority. Yet he retained his humility. He took no offence at the tone of Cromwell's letter. Even Archbishops must be commanded when it is the King's business.

Was Henry ill? Or Queen Anne? Was it rebellion or war? Either was possible. Was he himself in danger, either from his enemies or some whim of Majesty? The curtness and secrecy of the letter pointed to this last, he thought with a sudden clutch of fear at his bowels.

Anxious, sick at heart, he sought for explanations from his wide knowledge of Court. The King was becoming more and more autocratic. (The people were still shocked by the execution of his old friend and counsellor Sir Thomas More. And the aged and respected Cardinal Fisher had gone fearfully to the block in the same month.) The Queen was quite insufferable, and that was nothing new. But the rumour was that the King was weary of her insolence, and was seeking consolation from a lady of the Court, Jane Seymour.

Then he remembered two other facts: in January proud, ill-used Katherine of Aragon had died; and the new child that Queen Anne had been so desperately nurturing in her womb was stillborn (and, to heighten the King's rage, the foetus appeared to have been male).

Thomas' heart sank. In January the King's behaviour had been irrational: gloating horribly over the death of one wife; abusing and abandoning another because she had borne him a dead male child. Things boded ill for the Boleyn faction. And he, Thomas, was tied to the cart-tail of that faction. He reached Lambeth on May 2nd, a very worried man.

Cromwell wasted no time on greetings. 'Well? You have heard the news?'

Thomas braced himself. Now he was about to learn the worst: war, rebellion, a quarrel that could destroy all his moves to reform the Church?'

It was worse, far worse. Mark Smeaton, a mere court musician, had, incredibly, laid with the Queen. So, even more incredibly, had her own brother, George Boleyn. So, unbelievably, had various others of the royal household. These gentlemen had all been charged with high treason. And Queen Anne herself was today on her way to the Tower.

It was shattering. It was the end of all he had worked for. Take away the Protestant Queen (and, no doubt, the Protestant Archbishop) and the Papists would be back in power. Every reform that Cromwell and he had introduced would be reversed in no time.

And the Queen. During recent years he had come to know her well. She had grown tart, demanding, insolent. She inspired hatred and fear rather than love. Yet she still had a haunting beauty, and for men the fatal attraction of the lamp for the silly moths. But could she, would she, have lured these men to risk a hideous death and everlasting damnation?

Yes. He thought she could. And would the men be so persuaded? Yes. He himself, even as her chaplain, had been only too aware of her allure. *Would* she? That was what hurt. Because he feared that she, his loved daughter in God, *would* play the whore: either for her own lusts or to spite her unfaithful husband.

As soon as Cromwell had hurried off on further urgent business, Thomas sat down and wrote to the King: a letter so long that it was the following day before he finished it.

In it he commiserated with Henry, comparing his present sufferings with those of Job. He said he was 'clean amazed' that the Queen could be guilty of such things, as there was no woman of whom he had a better opinion; but, if she were, then she deserved no mercy.

(Yet, even as he wrote this, he pitied her. He, perhaps alone of all the Court, knew the lonely frightened woman behind the arrogant Queen.) Then he urged the King not to let this terrible thing change his views on church reform.

He read the letter through several times before sealing it. It was, he felt, a letter on which the whole future of the Church of England might rest.

And his own future? Yes. Once again the waking nightmare that was always a part of his mind (and of the minds of all those who served the King), oppressed him: the hammering on the door, the lapping of river water about

Traitors' Gate, the axe that had taken More and Fisher (both finer men than he, he told himself).

He read the letter again. What had he said about the Queen? 'Next unto your Grace I was most bound unto her of all creatures living.' He spoke of her kindness, and begged that 'I may with your Grace's favour wish and pray for her, that she may declare herself inculpable and innocent.'

Folly! No one else would have written that. If their situations had been reversed, she would have watched him go down without lifting a finger to save him. He knew that.

He looked at the letter again. No, he couldn't alter it. He sealed and despatched the letter. He could do no other.

He waited. But no hammering came on his door. Only, after nearly a fortnight of fearful waiting, a brief note informing him that the King had appointed him Anne's confessor, and that Anne had been convicted of high treason and sentenced to death, either by the fire or the axe at the King's pleasure.

'Morice,' he called. Poor girl, he thought. Never could woman have been in greater need of comfort. 'Morice!' His secretary came running. 'Ralph. Tell them to saddle a horse, quickly.' He saw Ralph's look of sudden concern, laughed. 'No, Ralph, I am not fleeing. Just visiting the Tower.'

The look of concern remained. 'Just get me a horse, there's a good fellow. I'll explain later.'

'Your Grace.' Morice was off, slightly chastened. Thomas went down to the door. A minute later Morice arrived from the side of the Palace, followed by a groom leading Beauty. 'Ah, thank you, Ralph. I am going to bring what comfort I can to the Queen, if such she still is.' He swung himself into the saddle and cantered off and was soon in the busy London streets.

People recognized him. Some touched their caps. Some crossed themselves. Many spat. Queen Katherine was not forgotten, nor would be for years to come.

Absently, he blessed them all. He had other things on his mind. How do you comfort a woman who already feels the flames about her thighs, the axe crashing onto her neck?

Now he was in sight of the grim fortress that was his goal. What had his escort said, that distant day when he first rode to meet his King? 'God keep us out of there, Master Cranmer.'

'Amen,' he had said on that occasion. And 'Amen' he said now. He clattered over a drawbridge, was challenged and was taken to Sir William Kingston, the Constable of the Tower. 'How is the Queen?' he asked urgently.

Sir William looked at him sardonically. 'Merry, your Grace.'

'Merry?' Thomas said sharply. Was the fool jesting or simply heartless?

Sir William said contemptuously, 'It takes little to make a condemned prisoner merry. When he expects to die tomorrow, and then his death is put off for two days, he feels he has been given all eternity.'

Thomas was silent. *He* knew why Anne's execution had been postponed: so that he could have time to declare her divorced before her death; and to give her time to watch the bloody, ritual slaughter of her alleged lovers. 'Take me to her,' he said coldly.

She was well housed, for the Tower. A windowless room, lit by a single candle. But she had a stool, table, crucifix, and a few feet for exercise.

Sir William said, 'Your father confessor, Madam.'

Madam! Thomas felt a surge of anger. He said, reproachfully, 'Is Majesty fallen so low, Sir William?'

Kingston looked sour. But now Anne had seen who this priest was. She jumped up, ran towards him and threw her arms about him, holding her head back so that she could smile up into his face. 'Thomas! It's you!' She turned to Sir William and said in the contemptuous insolent tone that had so infuriated the Court: 'Leave us.'

Grudgingly Sir William went and hovered outside the open door. Anne strode across and slammed it shut. Then she came back and once more threw her arms round her confessor. 'Thomas! I am reprieved until the nineteenth. That is good, isn't it? The King *is* relenting, isn't he?'

Gently Thomas unwound her arms. Even now, with her long black hair unkempt and streaked with grey, and her blemishes – the crooked tooth, the great mole on her neck, the devil's extra finger – no longer cunningly hidden, she was not a woman a man could hold unmoved in his arms. He said, his heart almost breaking with pity. 'I do not know the King's mind, my daughter. But – set *your* mind on the joys of Heaven, which far exceed any possible joys in this vale of wickedness.'

Her dark, wonderful eyes were never still: now on his face, now on the crucifix, now on the candle flame. Then she burst out: 'Oh, you were always a cautious old fool, Cranmer. I always despised you for it. I tell you, Henry won't kill me. Perhaps he'll send me to a nunnery.' She sat thinking, then suddenly laughed coarsely. 'God's body, I shall teach those sisters a thing or two.'

He smiled at her sadly. 'My daughter, that is no way to speak where you stand now.'

She said challengingly, 'And where do I stand now, Father in God?'

'On a precipice,' he said bleakly, 'between Heaven and Hell.'

Her mood frightened him. Her darting eyes were wild. Madness, it seemed to him, was not far away. He said, 'Do you wish me to shrive you, my daughter?'

She sat on the stool, shaking her head from side to side through ninety degrees, like a child.

He said, 'You will need to be shriven, if – '

She was mocking, now. 'If – ? If I go to a nunnery? No need, they will shrive me there, good Father.'

He persisted. 'And if – ?'

But her mind had slipped from the subject. She said, apparently with great satisfaction, 'I have sent to St Omer for a French swordsman. They say – ' and now her voice wavered, 'they say – it is quicker that way.'

'Good,' he said. 'Good.'

'They say the King is merry,' she said heavily.

Cranmer was silent.

'I should like to take out Jane Seymour's eyes with hot irons,' she said, flexing her claws like a cat. There was no doubt she meant exactly what she said.

He said, urgently, sternly, 'You must not speak like that, think like that, situated as you are. It is damnation.'

Quietly she began to weep. Soon the tears were a flood. He put his hands on the greying, bowed head and blessed her. Then he stole away, heavy-hearted. By eleven o'clock next morning he had declared her marriage a nullity and her daughter a bastard.

At the same time Anne was being forced to watch the ceremonious butchering of her lovers: the horror was approaching its climax.

On the evening of the following day, the 18th, Cranmer hurried to the Tower. Anne, beginning to accept that death might be only twelve hours away, had sent for her confessor.

The great bulwarks of the Tower glowed in the loveliest of evenings. The light of the setting sun lay on its stones like a blessing. But no sunlight blessed Anne's quarters. The evening's gentle warmth did not touch these dripping stones. A single candle was still the only light. It was a fitting antechamber to the tomb.

Thomas was fearful. Anne had been found guilty of high treason by the peers of England, including her own father and uncle. The King wished her found guilty. Therefore, by Tudor reckoning, she *was* guilty.

But suppose, at this late hour, Cranmer discovered in the secrecy of the confessional that she was indeed innocent? His lips must be forever sealed. His priestly vows saw to that. And even if he could speak, what would happen? Neither Henry nor Cromwell would tolerate a reversal of their plans. Anne had been doomed, whatever the truth, long before her trial.

Yet he was a man to whom the truth, as he saw it, was of supreme importance. If he, discovering her innocent, allowed her to die, he would know no peace in his life hereafter. Yet his vows permitted no other.

It was a sombre meeting. Her mood was different today. She had watched the hacking to death of five young bodies (bodies whose warmth and sweetness she perhaps knew only too well) knowing that without a miracle her own white body was about to suffer thus.

There were no embraces, no arrogance tonight. She knelt before him, addressing him humbly as Father, a woman broken at last by crude mental torture.

He too knelt. Her voice was little more than a whisper. When he came away his face was ashen. Outside, he gulped the night air like one who has been near drowning. The stars glinted coldly about the turrets of the White Tower. The Milky Way trailed above England like a tattered shroud.

Four o'clock on the morning of May 19th.

A small, silent procession of women approached the Tower in the misty dawn: the Queen's women, come to dress and adorn her for her last public appearance.

At Greenwich Palace the weary courtiers saw a grey light suffusing the windows. Morning! God! Would the King never tire? He – and therefore they – had been dancing all night. And *he* looked as though he could carry on until this time tomorrow. Never since the death of Queen Katherine had they seen him in such joyous spirits, so bursting with nervous energy.

Someone else had not slept all night; but for different reasons. Thomas Cranmer walked in his orchard, the hem of his gown soaked with dew, in an agony of doubt and indecision.

Suddenly there was a gleam of gold in the grey light. Day had come, and brought with it decision. He knew what he must do. Intercede with the King, desperately, forcefully, yet without breaking his vows. The King was no fool. He would know what his Archbishop was saying.

And then – farewell Archbishop, probably. But he could not think about that. Truth was what mattered. He hurried into the stables, woke the grooms who were still sleeping beside their charges. And if he was to seek an audience of the King, he must hide the effects of a sleepless night. He went to his room, peered into his mirror: a stubbled chin, a greasiness about his normally fresh complexion. He washed with a ball of scented soap, shaved, smeared a linen cloth with tooth-soap and rubbed his teeth, changed his gown. By the time he was ready it was five o'clock. Another hour, he thought, and the King would be rising.

But he was unaware of the nervous energy that was riding the King like a mad horseman. By the time he reached Greenwich the King had abruptly finished the dancing, called for a bath, his barber and his hunting clothes, sent instructions to the stables and an order to Thomas Cromwell to join him in the field, and Cranmer found Henry mounted and clattering with roaring, royal impatience about the forecourt.

Now Henry's cunning brain had not of course overlooked the following possible sequence of events. Anne might persuade her unworldly confessor of her innocence. Her confessor was a man who, though normally pliant, was a stickler for truth and justice. So it was always a possibility that Anne's father confessor would seek urgent audience before the execution.

And here, sure enough, came the Archbishop on a hard-driven horse. Henry put two and two together and made exactly four. 'Huntsman,' he called, 'sound for the chase.' He who was fearless in the lists, who had even led his armies into battle, was not above bolting to avoid a tiresome suitor.

The horn brayed. Henry wheeled his horse, urged it into a gallop. The assembled courtiers fell in behind him. The whole splendid cavalcade pounded away, out through the gates, a noble, colourful picture. Thomas watched them go.

A latecomer reined in his horse beside Thomas. 'Well, your Grace? What brings you to Court so early?'

Thomas said, bitterly, 'I came to intercede for the poor Queen. But the King has defeated me.'

Cromwell looked at him sardonically. 'You were better praying for her soul, man.'

Thomas said heavily, 'I tell you, Cromwell: she who was Queen upon earth will today become a Queen in Heaven.'

Cromwell was silent. The two men sat their horses. Only the clink of harness disturbed the stillness of the morning. Thomas Cranmer wept quietly.

A sound broke the silence of that summer morning: a distant, muffled roar. It sounded like a single cannot shot. It seemed to come from far up river.

Thomas crossed himself. He gave his companion a look of sheer, beseeching anguish. Then he slid from his horse, knelt upon the ground, and prayed fervently.

Thomas Cromwell stared down at him thoughtfully, contemptuously, critically. Then he spurred his horse, and went to join the hunting party.

And Thomas Cranmer returned to Lambeth and, as instructed, prepared a dispensation permitting Henry to marry Jane Seymour in spite of a distant relationship.

CHAPTER 13

Suddenly, the North was up! Henry was outraged to find a rebellion on his hands.

He had good reason to feel hurt. At no one knew what cost to himself he had got rid of Katherine and Anne, those producers of unwanted daughters and dead foetuses. And here he was, in his old age, settling down with a douce new wife. And those damned peasants in the north (aye, and some nobles) had chosen this time to revolt.

And why? During the summer Cranmer and Cromwell and the Bishops had produced Ten Articles which steered a tortuous middle course through theological rapids and shallows (the Articles approved of masses for souls, while being uncertain about Purgatory. They ignored Transubstantiation, but approved the Real Presence). And *this* cautious document had set England on fire.

There were other things, of course: the suppression of the monasteries, unbearable taxation; but above all the fact that they saw themselves as being governed by men no better than themselves: Cromwell the brewer's son and Cranmer the ostler (so rumour said) from Cambridge.

At Louth the rebels demanded that Cranmer, Cromwell and certain Bishops be handed over to them. The Yorkshire rebels demanded they should be burnt. All over England

Cranmer was denounced as either a heretic or an ostler. No one could have said which was the more damning charge.

Henry VIII treated all such demands with sublime contempt. He sent the Duke of Norfolk to put down the rebellion, with specific instructions to 'cause such dreadful execution – hanging the rebels on trees, setting their quarters in every town – as shall be a dreadful warning.'

Norfolk did as he was told. In every town he hung the rebels in chains and gibbets. And wives stole their husbands' corpses and hid them in their houses, awaiting decent burial, so that plague was added to the harvest of that fearful winter.

And Thomas Cranmer, who had been so horrified by the results of insurgent strife on the road to Mantua, was charged with keeping order in Kent. And this he did eagerly and willingly, remembering always his winter journey through the aftermath of mutiny and rebellion.

And, thanks to the Tudor sledgehammer, he survived. Henry defeated the northerners who were demanding Cranmer's blood. He trampled them into the ground. He slaughtered them without pity or compassion.

Slowly, the north came back to life. The bitter winter passed. The rebels crept back like whipped dogs to their ravaged farms, their smouldering barns, their stricken villages. They had learnt their lesson. And Great Harry was still on the throne, and Thomas Cranmer was still in power.

And gentle Thomas Cranmer, whom they hated more than all was still Archbishop of Canterbury.

Yet, though they never had the satisfaction of knowing it, they dealt him a blow that struck him to the heart. And, ironically, it was the result of Henry's half-pennyworth of appeasement to the rebels.

They demanded the restoration of the monasteries, and a return to the old religion.

The fools, thought Henry. The monasteries were now in the hands of greedy and rapacious worldlings. *No one* could restore them, not even an absolute monarch. And once having got rid of the Pope, Henry wasn't having *him* on his back again. But the very foolishness of the demands made Henry obliging. He could make a gesture that would hurt nobody. He wrote to the Bishops, stating that he had heard some priests had dared to marry. As a sop to the people, such priests were to be arrested by the Bishops. He sent a copy to the Archbishop of Canterbury.

Thomas had spent the late autumn and winter at Ford. He had not seen Margarete for weeks. He was desperate for her presence, yet he had not dared to remove her from Knoll. And now, the roads were clogged with snow. They were as far apart as if she were still in Nuremberg.

The room was lit, not from the leaden sky, but from the snowy lawn: a cold, white snowlight. By its suffused light he re-read the letter.

Personally it was a bitter blow. His constant dream was of a day when Margarete could stand by his side as his wife. That day, he had been convinced, was not far off. Now, suddenly, a few written words had set its dawning back for years, perhaps for ever.

He gazed out at the lying snow, a barrier of cold purity set (by God?) between this priest and his wife's bed.

But the danger in this arbitrary threat of Henry's was on a slow fuse. The snows melted, and that blood-soaked winter changed to dancing spring.

And with the North cowed and sullen in defeat, King and Court were dancing with the spring. Yet again a Queen was pregnant. And this time, surely, nothing *could* go wrong. For Henry, it was a brief period of hope and comfort in his turbulent life. To be married to the sweet and docile Jane Seymour, and to have planted a legitimate heir in her womb stripped away the terrible accretions of the years. He was a young man again, witty, brilliant, leading his Court in nightly revels and disguisings. What did it matter, in such careless days, if a priest or two was a bit forgetful of his vows?

And nothing did go wrong. Oh, Jane suffered in labour, but everyone knew that that was the way God punished the daughters of Eve for their mother's little lapse with the Serpent. But the child was not only comely and strong; it was a boy!

Bonfires, the shooting of cannon, the ringing of church bells, feasting and pageantry! Te Deums were sung in every church. And through all this uproar the gigantic splendid Monarch gloated over a babe so tightly swaddled that the flesh of his tiny face was redder and angrier that the flea bites on his fingers and toes.

But if Henry was beginning to wonder in his joy whether God was not perhaps on his side after all, he was soon disillusioned. God was not prepared to indulge Henry too much, it seemed. The Chapel at Hampton Court was no sooner stripped of its damask christening tapestries than it was hung with black cloth and rich images for the funeral of Queen Jane. Cranmer had been godfather when the child was christened Edward. Now he rode, with his cross borne before him, behind the mother's corpse on the sad journey from Hampton Court to Windsor.

Chapter 14

One of Mary Tudor's earliest memories was of a rough giant of a man who dandled her lovingly on his knee, who showed her off with foolish pride to courtiers and foreign ambassadors, whose jewels and rings scratched her painfully in his bear-like hugs; a man she adored with all the force of her passionate young nature.

Another memory was of a gentle, loving, pious mother.

As Mary grew up into girlhood, this picture of her mother did not change.

But, slowly and subtly, the father picture did change. Now he was proud and delighted to dance with his fair and lovely daughter, he revelled in her skills at music and languages. Yet he was being distanced from her, thanks (or so it seemed to her) to an upstart hanger-on of the Boleyns, a Thomas Cranmer. He it was who annulled her mother's marriage to the King, so that proud Queen Katherine became the Princess Dowager, and she herself (O God, forgive such wickedness) became the bastard Lady Mary.

Then, after her father had married the Boleyn woman (and the marriage had been validated by his creature Cranmer, whom he had bribed with an archbishopric) she, Princess Mary of England, had been sent by this once-loving father to act as servant to the Boleyn brat Elizabeth: a time of bitter humiliation and misery.

Her loved mother had died, worn out by suffering and ill usage. But she herself had survived – and would go on surviving. Now she was back at Court, having finally, under unbearable pressure, sworn the Oaths of Succession and Supremacy. Her still-adored father, and Jane Seymour, had both received her lovingly. But the years of humiliation had left a bitterness in her soul that neither the love of God nor the love of man could ever sweeten.

The ostentation of Elizabeth's christening had been a defiance to the Pope and to all the Princes of Europe.

The rich ceremonial of Edward's was a paeon of thankfulness to a God who appeared at last to have come round to Henry's way of thinking. Torches lit the way to the Chapel where stood the gilt and silver font, with the three Godfathers, Norfolk, Suffolk, and Canterbury, already assembled.

Two by two entered abbots and bishops, Lords of the Council, peers. Then Edward, under a canopy of estate, in fur-trimmed crimson and cloth of gold, carried by the Marchioness of Exeter. Then Mary, followed by the ladies of the Court.

For Mary, it was a moment of inward rejoicing. The years of harsh treatment, degradation and poverty had taught her to be thankful for any small blessing. And here she was suddenly lapped in blessing: Godmother to her half-brother, the future King of England.

The sacred music swelled louder. Now the head of the procession was in the Chapel, the courtiers were taking their appointed places. All eyes were fixed on that newcomer to the Court, the Lady Mary, approaching, proud and exultant, in her golden youth.

But suddenly Mary was no longer exultant. Her slow and solemn progress had brought her at last to within sight of the font, and of the three men who waited there: the gorgeously clad Dukes of Norfolk and Suffolk, both of whom she knew; and a stranger, whose magnificent vestments outshone even the richness of the Dukes' clothing. There he stood, the Stranger, the Enemy, Antichrist.

The colour drained from her face. For a moment she stopped, swaying slightly. Then, her thin lips pressed tight together, she called on her strong will to force her onward.

The Marchioness of Exeter reached the font and gave Edward to the Archbishop, who took him tenderly in his arms and smiled lovingly down upon him.

Mary was very close to hysteria. Her legs felt weak and uncontrolled, she was hot and cold. She wanted to cry out, to scream, yet her iron will controlled her. But Antichrist had possession of her helpless brother. He could dash him to the ground!

Walking like an automaton, she went to her appointed place. But she neither knelt nor sat. She stood, her eyes fixed intently and fervently on the incarnate devil who held not only the Prince but the future and the fate of English Catholicism in his arms.

Mary's mind was absorbed with dark thoughts of poison and hired murderers and silent night-deeds. Thomas Cranmer must die: not only because of the misery and degradation he had brought on her loved mother, but because he threatened the source of all her comfort, all her joy: the Catholic Church, under the fatherly guidance of Christ's Vicar here on earth.

Thomas enjoyed holding the babe in his arms. It made him think of homely, family joys that, it seemed, could never be his.

But after a time he became aware that he was being watched (as, he thought, Our Lord, pressed on all sides by the throng, asked, 'Who touched me?').

A hundred pairs of eyes were watching him. Yet one pair, he felt, was staring into his very soul.

He looked about him as the anthem droned on. And soon found what he sought: it was a slim, twenty-year-old girl, placed among the most honoured guests. And her green eyes were staring at him with passionate hatred.

Then he realized. This must be the Lady Mary whom, in order to serve his King, he had been forced to wrong. The Lady Mary, who he had long realized, must regard him as her bitterest enemy: the babe's Godmother, whom he must shortly beckon to come and stand at his side.

He looked away, sick at heart. For years, he thought, their lives had been bitterly intertwined. And now, for the first time, they were about to meet; and already there was hatred and contempt in her eyes.

The music ended. With his usual gentle smile he beckoned the Lady Mary forward.

She came, proud and stiff, her eyes still blazing. He studied her with a kind of wonder. She was not beautiful. Her most noticeable features were those angry eyes and the tight, determined mouth. But she had youth, and the loveliness and the arrogance and the menace of youth.

He was the Primate of All England. She should have curtseyed, with lowered eyes. She did not. She stood, stiff and unbending, and stared into his face as though she saw the lineaments of Satan there.

A stirring passed through the assembly, like a gust of wind through woodlands. This would give the court gossips something to mull over. They fairly itched with pleasure.

The ceremony began. For Thomas Cranmer, it was a nightmare. To a man who loved his fellow men, one of the hardest things had been to accept that as a reforming Archbishop he must inevitably have enemies. He deplored it, hated it, even though it was for his God and his King that he set men against him.

Mary would not see it like that, however. She would see only that by so doing he had served his father's lusts, and wounded her and her mother almost to death. And everything he was doing to reform the Church would in her eyes be the blackest heresy. He looked down at the child in his arms: and knew, with awful certainty, that the survival of this tiny, frail creature was all that stood between him and certain revenge.

The ceremony ended. Trumpeters played a fanfare, and a Te Deum was sung while the long procession was re-formed. The little Prince was escorted back to the royal apartments.

Queen Jane lay on a couch, supported by pillows and cushions. She looked defeated by illness. She fastened her eyes pathetically on her son, and held out her arms for him as though conscious of impatient death.

But the King was in the highest of spirits. He embraced Mary, who suddenly unfroze and kissed her father fondly. He even had a fatherly word for four-year-old Elizabeth who was clinging desperately to Mary's hand. Then he embraced Cranmer. 'Thomas! Why have we not met for so long? And you have brought our beloved son – ' he looked proudly down at the babe, now secure in his mother's arms ' – safely into our Church?'

Our Church? Was it the royal 'we'? Or did it signify 'yours and mine'? Either way, Thomas thought, it certainly wasn't the Pope's church any more.

But now Henry was looking quizzically, first at Mary then at Cranmer. For a moment he seemed undecided. Then, in a typical gesture he hung an arm about his daughter's shoulders and said, 'Mary, you have not met his Grace?'

Mary flushed. Then: 'Grace? *I* see no Grace,' she shouted in her deep, masculine voice. She turned on her heel, and walked angrily towards the door.

'God's Body,' whispered Henry in amazement. Then his voice became a bellow. 'Mary! Come back here, or by God I'll have you whipped, daughter or no daughter.'

Mary stopped, and stood, her head held high. But no one, not even one of Tudor blood, defied that voice.

'Here,' shouted Henry, jabbing a finger towards the floor in front of him, like one summoning a trained hound.

Mary took a few steps forward, and stood.

'Here!' barked Henry again, again pointing.

She moved one more pace, arrogantly, defiantly.

'I am content here, your Majesty.'

Henry growled, 'You will apologize to his Grace.'

Thomas, horribly embarrassed, murmured, 'If it please Your Majesty, it is not necessary.'

'*I* judge what is necessary,' roared Henry.

Mary said, in her clear, deep voice, 'But surely this is a disguising, Your Majesty. This fellow is an ostler. Does your Majesty really wish a Princess of England to apologize to an ostler, however well disguised?'

Henry's small mouth twitched. By Christ's blood, she was a Tudor. He looked at Canterbury, and actually smiled. It was true, these *were* the rumours. He said, 'You see, Thomas. I have to govern a country. Yet I cannot even govern my daughter.' He called Mary to him, whispered in her ear, 'Do not tempt me too hard, girl. Do you wish me to send you back to Hunsdon?'

She whispered, 'I had rather you sent me back to that vile prison, than bid me apologize to that imposter.'

'Damned ingrate,' snarled Henry, and cuffed her hard on the ear.

Mary stared at him, her face a vivid red. Then she curtseyed deeply, and ran from the room.

The King watched her go. Then he turned to Cranmer. 'The lion's cub would be as dangerous as the old lion,' he said thoughtfully. 'Mark her well, Thomas. Were you wise, do you think, when you saved her from the Tower?'

Thomas said, 'I think that to ask for mercy and justice is always right – and wise.'

'Then you are a fool,' Henry said.

Thomas said, 'Sire, the Lady Mary is your daughter.'

'And that is why you must fear her,' said Henry. 'Because she has me in her.' With great seriousness he said, 'One day, you may regret having interceded for her, Thomas. You would have had one enemy the less.'

Then, with April swiftness, his manner changed. He slapped his Archbishop painfully between the shoulder blades. 'Thomas. I want Knoll.'

Thomas was so appalled that he stared at the King in horror. Knoll! Had Henry discovered that this was where his criminally married Archbishop had hidden his wife? Was this the beginning of one of the King's cat and mouse games? Henry was quite capable of accepting for years his Archbishop's crime; and then, suddenly, pouncing. But, with a little tormenting of the victim first.

Even if there was no such sinister explanation, it still put Margarete and himself in a very dangerous situation. At Knoll, the servants accepted her, as wife or mistress, they neither knew nor cared. She was simply the Archbishop's whore. But if he had to take her to another house – other eyes, other tongues might be less charitable.

And Knoll was his refuge, his haven of peace in a tempestuous world.

Henry had been smiling. When he took a liking to someone's house, the owner was always only too delighted to give it him. But Thomas looked as though he was going to be difficult over a miserable little place like Knoll. Henry was rather hurt. He stopped smiling.

Thomas said, 'Your Majesty, I would beseech your Grace to leave me Knoll. To me, it is a home more than all my other houses.'

'Why is it?' It was a cold, sneering question. He knows about Margarete, Thomas thought miserably. But he said, 'It is small, your Majesty, and quiet. And – ' he managed to keep the break out of his voice ' – I have grown to love it.'

Henry said, 'And you would grudge your Sovereign the peace and comfort you have found there?' He sank on to his chair. 'Thomas, Thomas.' He spread his arms wide. 'Do you not think I have deserved some ease of soul and body in the few years that remain to me?'

Thomas said miserably, 'Of course, your Majesty. But – '

'But – ?' The word was like a bolt from a crossbow.

'But – ' stammered Thomas, 'the house is small and unassuming. It is not worthy of your Grace. Sire, take my house at Otford. It is large, more suited to your Grace's dignity.'

'And set in a marsh. Do you wish your King to spend his last years plagued with Otford's rheums and agues?' But Thomas saw those eyes, grown small and crafty with the years, grow smaller and craftier. 'But if you were to give me Otford as well, my dear Thomas, then my retinue could lodge there while I lived at Knoll. And you would not need to be anxious at the thought of your King being discomforted.' He smiled expansively.

There was no escape. He said, 'Your Majesty, I humbly beg your Grace to accept my houses at Knoll and Otford.'

The King nodded. 'Tell Cromwell to prepare the legalities,' he said.

Where now was he to hide his dear Margarete?

Lambeth was out of the question. Too near London and the Court. At the vast palace at Canterbury there were too many gossiping monks in the neighbourhood.

He said to Morice, 'Ralph, I have heavy news. The King has taken both Knoll and Otford.

Morice looked alarmed. 'Your Grace, may I speak roundly?'

Cranmer nodded.

'Then it seems to me, your Grace, that Mistress Cranmer is in great danger. There is only one place where she would be safe.'

'And that is – ?' Thomas asked eagerly.

'Nuremberg, your Grace.'

'No.' It was a cry of pain, uttered without thought or reason.

Morice said, 'Perhaps, after a time, she could return. But at present we do not know the King's mind. This could be a trap, your Grace. His Majesty is not averse to such – games.'

This last sentence was treasonable. The fact that Morice used it to Thomas showed how much he trusted his master the Archbishop. Thomas was deeply moved. 'You are a loyal servant, Ralph. And your advice is sensible and wise. But – if Mistress Cranmer once went to Nuremberg it might prove impossible ever to bring her back. And –' his eyes were full of tears ' – that would break my heart and, I think, hers.'

The two men were silent; until at last Thomas said, 'No, Ralph. He has known for years that I am married and has taken no action. Why should he do so now?'

Morice said, 'As well ask why an old bull, docile for years, suddenly gores the farmer.'

Thomas had accepted (and agreed with) one treasonable remark about the King he revered. He could not accept two. He said sternly, 'Watch your words, Master Morice, lest evil befall you both in this life and the next.'

Morice said, 'I beg your Grace's pardon, most humbly. I should not have spoken such foolish and evil words.'

'Nor even thought them,' said Thomas.

'Nor even thought them,' echoed Morice. He had gone very pale. 'Your Grace, Mistress Cranmer cannot be wholly safe anywhere.'

Thomas said sadly, 'Do you think I am not aware of that, Ralph? In fact, the only place where there is any possibility of safety is Ford, to my mind.'

'I would agree, your Grace,' Ralph said doubtfully.

Thomas seized both his hands. 'You are a true friend, Ralph. And now, I must take the heavy news to Mistress Cranmer.

He said heavily; 'You love this house, I think.'

'Oh, I do. I do.'

'The King has taken it from me.'

She looked at him in disbelief. 'Why? Has he found out about me?'

He shook his head. 'I do not think so. But there is always danger. I know only one place where you would be safe.'

'If you mean Nuremberg,' she said. 'No. Unless – ' she asked in sudden hope, 'you could come too.'

One look at his face killed that hope. 'Where then?' she asked wretchedly.

'Ford.'

'Then, husband, we will be happy at Ford, she cried in sudden gaiety. 'We will be happy anywhere, so long as – ' her voice suddenly broke ' – so long as we are together.'

He put out his hands. With the tips of his fingers he lovingly and wonderingly touched her brow, as a man might touch a statue of finest alabaster.

CHAPTER 15

So. With a male heir at last achieved, and the sweet young mother laid to rest, Henry vowed he had had enough of matrimony, and enthusiastically gave himself up to old age.

He had run the race, won the victor's crown, and now he could rest. England had cast off the Pope, and men like Cranmer and Cromwell were groping their way towards a Church built on compromise and even a little tolerance. And Queens had died. But England had an heir and a settled succession. And it was all Great Harry's doing. Vivat Henricus!

Now he passed his days in theological disputation, in burning a few heretics and quartering a few Papists, in fussing over the health of Prince Edward, and in trying to find a husband for his daughter Mary (a difficult task, since he was mean over the dowry, and the word 'bastard' stuck in the craw of the Catholic princes, while Mary vowed that rather than marry a Lutheran she would die).

With the King so quietly occupied, Cranmer eagerly began the work he longed so much to do: the revision of the Church service books in a great new Liturgy. And he found that the work gave him tremendous joy and delight.

Most of this work he did at his house at Ford, with Margarete apparently safe by his side. And the snows, when winter came, built a snug wall around them. Ford was cut off from Canterbury, cut off from London. And the clouds that had brought the snow lifted, and the clouds of conscience and anxiety and fear that so often darkened Thomas' skies also lifted. No one could get at him here. The snow hid him as it hid the snowdrops and the tangled grass.

It was a winter idyll. He and Margarete played and laughed and walked in the snow. He taught her the mysteries and the jargon of falconry. And sometimes they rode, brushing with their shoulders the powdery snow from the branches. For him it was a reminder of the innocence of life. He gulped the sharp, clean air and started at the azure sky like one who beheld angels and archangels there.

And she taught him something else he had almost forgotten: the sweetness of a nature untouched by self-seeking. He longed to be able to show her to the world as his wife, and he felt once again that this day was fast approaching. He was well-informed about events in Europe and as a good chess player he was used to seeing several moves ahead. Emperor Charles V and Francis King of France had grown tired of fighting each other. Once let those two bury the hatchet, and one or both of them was likely to turn on England. So England would need allies. And where could she find them except among the Lutheran Princes, who would no doubt demand in return that England take a few more steps down the Lutheran road? And one of the most convincing steps she could take would be to allow her clergy to marry.

So the days passed in sweetness. And in hope. But as the snows melted; and Margarete, singing, adorned the house with the spring flowers, hopes once again began to seem as doomed as the melting snow, and fears as menacing as the great storm clouds of April.

Thomas, however, lacked the cunning to foresee the workings of his Sovereign's mind. The attempts to make allies of the Lutheran Princes failed; largely because the capricious Henry flatly refused to countenance the marriage of the clergy, to forbid private masses, and to forbid the administration of the Lord's Supper in one kind. Instead he announced that the Bishop of Rome had moved, excited and stirred great princes and potentates to invade England and exterminate the whole nation.

The nation panicked. Troops were levied, defence works were dug, Henry personally supervised the fortifications on the coast. Citizens formed themselves into armed bands, and cheered Great Harry wherever he went. He felt young once more, virile. Harry of England's name would strike terror into Europe yet again.

Charles and Francis recalled their ambassadors in England. A vast invasion fleet gathered in The Netherlands.

Thomas Cranmer watched things with a sorrowing heart. If a Papist force seized England, both he and Margarete would be doomed. Not only that. All his work to reform the Church would be undone overnight. The Pope's heel would be on England for a thousand years.

Preparations for war continued. A watch was set at all the coastal beacons. In villages, in towns and cities, recruiting went on feverishly. On Good Friday Thomas, prostrate before the Cross, heard a strange sound: the thin high-pitched wailing of the fife, the rattle of drums, the shuffle of many feet.

He left the chapel, and went out to watch: fresh-faced lads, fathers of families, old men of fifty even, marching raggedly to their own individual crucifixions. Sadly, he blessed them as they passed.

A voice spoke quietly at his side. 'Your Grace?'

He turned. Ralph Morice. Despite his heavy mood he smiled.

Morice said, 'Ill news, your Grace. Half a hundred great ships are preparing to leave Marsdiep. They could reach Dover by Sunday.'

Sunday. Easter Sunday. The great day of thanksgiving and rejoicing. Canterbury Cathedral alight with flowers and candles and the joy of the people. And the Holy Roman Emperor could be at the gates of Dover! 'It is a blasphemy,' he said with deep anger.

He returned to the chapel, and prayed long and earnestly for peace in our time (the utmost that one could expect even Omnipotence to provide). Then he went into the house.

Normally her smile of welcome lifted his heart like sunlight. But today it cut him to the quick, reminding him of all he must lose. He took her hands in both of his, looked down at her gravely, said, 'War is coming to England, my dear. The Emperor could be in Kent by Sunday.'

She paled. 'Then you are in mortal danger, my beloved.'

He said, 'So are we all. And you especially.' And he thought: again, I know I should send her back to the safety of Osiander's house in Nuremberg. Yet again he could not.

But the war fever abated as suddenly as it had started. It was found that the half a hundred ships, instead of bearing down on Dover, were bound for Spain, and carried more merchandise than guns. The fresh-faced lads, the family men, the old men of fifty, shuffled back to their ploughs or their chimney corners. And England forgot its panic, and tried to pretend, rather unconvincingly, that it had given the Frenchman or the Spaniard, it wasn't sure which, a bloody nose.

Yet, with the coming of this year's blossom on cherry and pear and apple, with the lightening of skies and the singing of birds, for Thomas the real threat came: he was summoned to the House of Lords.

Henry, it seemed, had decided that as head of the Church he should tell the people exactly what they must think and believe.

To this end he told the Peers to decide on six Articles of Doctrine, so that their findings could be enforced by an Act of Parliament.

The King himself joined in this discussion, supporting the old orthodoxy. Despite this, Thomas strongly and loyally defended the reformist views, especially on the marriage of the clergy.

But the House of Lords were deeply attached to the old Catholic doctrines, and bitterly opposed to the views of the reformers. And Henry, now that he had got the Pope off his back, was quite content to slip back into the old ways, and was a stout opponent of the reformist bishops.

Before the six Articles of doctrine could be enshrined in an Act of Parliament, punishments for transgressors had to be decided. Two committees were set up to devise punishments: one, of three conservative bishops, one, of three reforming bishops.

Thanks to Cranmer's influence, the punishment for denial of five of the Articles was reduced from heresy to felony, lacking even a death sentence for a first offence. But on the sixth, the marriage of clergy, the conservative bishops insisted on death by hanging for both the married priest and his wife.

By Tudor standards, it was not a particularly savage penalty; and this made it all the more difficult for Thomas to oppose it with vigour.

Yet oppose it he must, and did. Christ had never said a priest could not marry, there was nothing against it in Scripture. The Lutherans allowed their priests to marry...

It was at this point that the orthodox bishops shouted him down. Was England a Lutheran country, now, with a Lutheran Archbishop? The fact that the King, in his infinite wisdom, had delivered us from the power of the Pope did not mean that he wished to turn England topsy-turvy. On the contrary. It seemed that the Archbishop of Canterbury was out of touch with the laity, the clergy, the nobility and (the most sinister of all) the King himself.

But it was the old enemy, Gardiner of Winchester, who struck the most fear. For once, his manner was silky as he said, 'His Grace of Canterbury was most fervent, in the disputation, that all priests should be allowed to stew and copulate in the marriage bed. Now he is even more fervent that they should do it without penalty. If we were not so sure of his Grace's integrity, we might suspect he had a personal reason for his ardour.' He stared at Thomas with eyes as hard as marbles, his mantrap of a mouth quite belying the silkiness of his voice.

Did Gardiner, of all people, know? Or even suspect? Thomas' behaviour gave nothing away. In his Cambridge days he would have flushed, stammered. But a few years in this sophisticated Court had taught him poise, self-control, even a quickness of mind. He said, 'At a time when the whole country knows that my Lord of Winchester has two lewd women in his retinue, it ill behoves him to accuse his superior of wanton copulation.'

There was a sharp intake of breath from the assembled bishops. Gentle, anxious Cantuar, suddenly showing his teeth like that? They wouldn't have believed it. And especially to a redoubtable enemy like Gardiner.

Gardiner looked venomous. He rearranged himself and his robes in his chair; and only then did he say grumblingly: 'I had not expected the Primate of All England to soil his ears with listening to such foul gossip.'

Thomas said, 'I had not expected my Lord of Winchester to give cause for such foul gossip.'

The two committees took a few minutes to savour this confrontation. They then gave their verdicts. Death by hanging. Thomas Cranmer was the only dissenter.

Like any slow-thinking, unassertive man, Thomas was elated by his little victory over the blustering Gardiner. But as he rode back to Ford he grew more and more depressed and anxious. He *had* to make a decision about Margarete. It was now June. The new Act was being rushed through Parliament. And if he was discovered living with Margarete after July 12th, they both risked hanging.

Both! The coarse rope, round that white, soft throat that had known only scented linen and silk and the caresses of his hands. The very thought filled him with horror. Both! Two figures, hanging side by side in the melancholy fellowship of death; two withering fruits of the gallows tree.

And, more important, worse than all this: he was now partly responsible for an Act that decreed death for something he was doing himself: cohabiting with a wife. Worse still he, under the King, was head of a Church that forbade the marriage of priests. It was a terrible, impossible position for a man of honour.

There was only one answer: he must get her away; away before the Act was made law and all the ports became a hunting-ground for spies.

But first he had to persuade her. And, in the process, break that loving heart.

Again, her smile was like summer sunshine. He scarcely noticed it. He said, 'A law has been passed under which you and I could both be hanged.'

To his amazement she was still smiling. 'I have heard this before, husband. Years ago. And see – I am still here. And no one has tried to hang me, dear Thomas.'

He said, 'Then, they threatened the arrest of married priests. Now they will hang both priest and wife.'

She came into his arms, then. 'But who has passed this wicked law?'

'I – among others,' he said bitterly.

'You? You could not do anything so stupid. Unless – ' she looked at him in sudden horror – 'Unless they – forced you, my love.'

'They did not force me, Margarete,' he said.

'Then why – ?'

'Because if I had not they would have dispossessed you and – sent you wandering to beg your bread.'

'So. What are we to do? I shall not leave you, of course, whatever happens.'

He said, sternly, 'You will go back to Osiander. It is our only chance. Then, when the King dies, or – '

'Or the moon turns blue – no, Thomas, I stay here, at Ford. You go to Lambeth. Then no one can say you are not celibate.'

'They can. And will.'

She put her arms about him. He was fighting back the tears. 'Dear love,' he said brokenly. 'You must go to Nuremberg.'

'I will not leave you,' she said.

He sounded angry now. 'Then we shall both hang.'

'Oh, no.' It was a cry of alarm.

'Can't you see? You hold my life in your hands. Besides – I cannot keep you by my side. I am Archbishop. Would you have me do that which I must forbid my every priest to do? Would you have your husband a liar and a dissembler?'

She was silent, weeping quietly in his arms. At last she said, 'If I leave you, my beloved, I think I shall die.'

'You will not die,' he said brusquely.

'I think we shall never meet again,' she wailed. 'Not in this life.'

'We shall,' he said. 'Joy cometh in the morning, remember. Heaviness endureth but for a night.'

She was a woman of character. She smiled bravely up at him. But then she saddened again. 'I fear it will be a long night, Thomas,' she said.

There was plenty to do, and little time to do it: letters to dispatch, and receive; packing; a sea passage and relays of horses across Europe to arrange. And, on Margarete's part, detailed arrangements for the comfort and well-being of her lord during her absence.

Yet, as time crept pitilessly by, all was prepared. And Thomas and Margarete stood at last on the cold shingle at Dover, while the pebbles ground and groaned at the everlasting pounding of the sea. Not an Archbishop and his lady. But a man and a woman facing the tearing apart of flesh that had been made one; gazing into loved eyes, trying desperately and unsuccessfully to imprint on the memory a loved and loving face; speaking last words that should have been noble and memorable, but were broken and trite; lips clinging to lips already salt and bitter from the sea spray.

Then: one last clasp of loving hands as he helped her into the boat, and the amputation was done. Thomas watched as the boat bobbed out to the ship, as the sails filled and the ship turned for France. He watched till it was hull down on the horizon. Only then did he turn away.

And the waves crashed on to the grey stones on that grey June day. And surged, and crashed, and surged again. And it seemed to him that their cold tongues had but one message for him, one cry: forever!

Chapter 16

The house had died. Oh, there was a bustle of secretaries and chaplains, manservants and maidservants. But one woman had sailed away. And left the house, it seemed to him, a house of the dead.

But before he could even take off his riding boots, there was a clatter of hooves in the courtyard, and Thomas Cromwell was shown in.

As usual, Cromwell did not beat about the bush. 'Good day to your Grace. Have you heard the latest whim of his Majesty?'

Thomas said hurriedly, 'Not here,' and led the way into his study. He feared Cromwell's forthrightness. There were too many ears in the hall.

He shut the door, and poured wine, waved his visitor to a chair. He smiled anxiously. Any whim of the King's especially when it brought Cromwell in person, meant trouble.

Cromwell said, 'He wants another wife, Thomas.'

'Why?' Thomas said bleakly.

'The usual reasons: no point in hiring horses when you can have one in your own stable. Besides – another heir. Edward is only mortal.'

Yet another Queen! And on her might depend the future course of the whole reform movement in England. If the ageing Henry came under the influence of a Catholic Queen, then all Cranmer had worked for might be swept away like trees in a flood. He said, 'Has he anyone in mind?'

'Half the pretty mopsies in Europe.' He helped himself to more wine. 'The Duchess of Milan, for one.'

Thomas sighed. 'Niece to the Emperor. Great-niece to his Majesty's first wife. A dispensation would be needed.'

'Which you would supply,' Cromwell said, very matter-of-fact.

Thomas was silent. Cromwell said, 'For another, the French King's daughter Marguerite.'

'Another Papist,' sighed Thomas.

Cromwell gave him a sharp look. 'And we do not want a Papist, do we Thomas?'

After a long silence, Thomas said quietly, 'No. We do not.'

The two men sipped their wine. Thomas, after a sorrowful parting was weary, exhausted almost light-headed. And now he was being made to brace himself for another disaster, both for himself and his Church: a Papist as Queen Consort!

Cromwell said, 'The King seems prepared to welcome anyone to his marriage bed, Papist or Lutheran.' He showed his teeth in what his friends recognized as amusement. 'Our revered Monarch even asked the French Ambassador to assemble eight of the loveliest women of the French Court for his inspection at Calais.'

'No!'

Cromwell said, 'Francis told him it was not the custom in France to present such noble ladies in review like hackneys for sale.'

Thomas chuckled. Cromwell said enviously, 'How wonderful to be a King, and to be able to rebuff Henry so.' Then he became businesslike again. 'There is,' he said, 'another candidate.'

'Who?'

'Anne, sister of William, Duke of Cleves.' He sat back looking pleased with himself.

'Ah. The Duke of Cleves,' Thomas said thoughtfully. 'Brother-in-law to John Frederick of Saxony.'

'Just so.' He drew up his chair excitedly. 'In one stroke we should gain allies among the Lutherans and help from the German mercenaries of Cleves, and – ' he banged his fist down on the table – 'set up a great rampart against the King of France, the Emperor and the Pope himself.'

Though Thomas had only been sipping his wine, he felt as though he had taken a great draught. His tiredness fell from him. Not only would he be back in the world of his old friends Spalatin and Osiander, it would mean, surely, that his Lutheran wife could soon return to him. And he would be able to strip yet further his Church of the ancient accretions and superstitions of Rome.

Yet he was too cautious a man to take anything for granted where Henry was concerned. He said, 'And the lady? She is comely, and pleasant of person? She would grace the royal bed?'

His heart sank at Cromwell's slight pause before he said, 'Our envoy at Cleves says that both for the face and the whole body she is above all ladies excellent.'

'But – ?' said Thomas.

'There are no buts, man' Cromwell said irritably. 'Oh, she has little English or Latin, and she wears quite ridiculous clothes. But a dressmaker and a teacher will soon cure all that.'

'And Master Holbein has made a portrait?'

'It is not yet ready. But it will bear out what our envoy says. No. There is only one slight difficulty. At one time the

Lady Anne was promised to a son of the Duke of Lorraine. But that will be no impediment.'

Thomas said, with unusual cynicism for him, 'It may prove useful when his Majesty tires of his fourth bride.'

Thomas Cromwell looked shocked. *He* had already thought of that. But he didn't expect his simple friend to have such thoughts. He said, 'I propose to urge the Lady Anne on his Majesty. I came to tell you of this because I need your support. You must seek the ear of the King. And persuade him. Otherwise, he may plump for the dimpled beauty of Milan. In which case, my dear Thomas, I may bleed and you may burn. See to it.' And he heaved his vigorous, powerful body out of his chair, and departed with a clatter of spurs.

And things went just as Thomas had imagined. Holbein finished the portrait, Henry saw it and declared himself enamoured. Within weeks Thomas was dragged away from his work on a new English Bible in order to negotiate the marriage treaty with delegates from Cleves and Saxony. In foul December weather he was sent to greet the new Queen and escort her to London. But the eager Henry took one shocked look at Anne's uncomely face; and then, with great presence of mind, remembered the precontract to Francis of Lorraine; and his ever-faithful conscience told him he must not marry unless this doubt was cleared up.

Cranmer, perhaps acting in his own interests for once, ruled that there had been no precontract. Henry, foiled, let himself be married to Anne on January 6th. But he had only glares on this occasion for the officiating Archbishop. And when at last, reluctantly, he took his amiable bride to bed he was so revolted by her 'slack breasts and unmaidenly belly' that he 'left her as good a maid as he found her.'

Give him his due, Henry persevered for six months; by which time the situation had changed. The Emperor and Francis were falling out once more, so Henry's need of the Lutherans lessened. And, perhaps most important of all, Henry had spotted a little beauty at Court named Catherine Howard. Thomas Cranmer was called in to take another look at that precontract, and was able to show that the precontract had, after all, been a binding union. This, plus Henry's delicate statement that 'if Anne brought maidenhead with her to England, then so far as he was concerned anyway, she was still a maid,' this made a nullity suit possible without straining anyone's conscience. So Anne was pensioned off. And Cromwell and Cranmer knew that they would face heavy retribution for causing the King so much embarrassment.

Retribution was indeed swift: a lovely June morning, the yellow sunlight slanting down from the windows of the Council Chamber, on Thomas Cranmer in his sombre black and white robes and velvet cap, on Thomas Cromwell scribbling away at the head of the table, on the Duke of Norfolk in blue and gold: a noble scene, worthy of Master Holbein's canvas.

Then, suddenly, the white pig's flesh of Cromwell's face distorted with fear as Norfolk dragged him to his feet and held him struggling while armed men rushed in and dragged him from the Chamber and to the Tower. But not before Norfolk had torn the Cross of St George from his breast, and a crowd of Councillors had surrounded him with blows and insults and howls of 'traitor'.

And Thomas Cranmer had stood, still as a statue, and watched, sick at heart, knowing that this was more than retribution. That Cromwell's (and his!) hope of alliance with the Lutherans was dead and buried. And that he and Cromwell would very soon be the same.

The following day he wrote to the King a brave letter, eulogizing Cromwell's service to, and love for, the King, and expressing his amazement to hear him called traitor.

Yes, a brave letter, but to no avail. Despite his abject pleas for mercy, Cromwell was beheaded on July 28th. On the same day, Henry married Catherine Howard, his rose without a thorn. He was besotted with a Catholic bride once more.

And Thomas Cranmer waited, in fear and trepidation, during those long, hot summer days: for the mailed fist hammering at the door; for the peremptory summons to Court. In the streets the people had been shouting odds of a thousand pounds to a hundred that Cranmer would join Cromwell in the Tower. Yet the long, lonely, fearful days passed, and Henry made no move. Thomas, with much prayer and meditation, and despite his fears, worked long hours on his Bible, finding an increasing joy in the delight of moulding the English language.

Such peaceful, lonely days did not last. Henry decided, five years after the Pilgrimage of Grace, to visit the north of England and see for himself the bleak setting of 'the commotion time'.

Before leaving his capital he appointed Cranmer, Audley and Edward Seymour to govern London.

It was an awesome appointment. With the approach of fifty Henry was becoming totally unpredictable, wrathful and murderous. Quite obviously, anything his delegates did without reference to him would be wrong. Yet when you were in London and he in York or Durham, how *could* you refer to him? The only thing was to pray that no crises would arise while the King was away; and trust in God's goodness.

But God clearly was not listening. For the most difficult, painful and dangerous crisis blew up.

At first it seemed innocuous enough. A courteous letter from a John Lassells, requesting an interview, which was granted.

The visitor was lean, pale, ascetic-looking. His clothes, for that peacock age, were drab and homespun. He inclined his head to Thomas, but did not treat him with the deference shown by most visitors. He lowered himself on to the chair Thomas indicated for him, and sat silent, staring before him. His only movement was in his long, yellow fingers, which he incessantly clasped and unclasped.

Thomas sat down facing him. 'How can I help you, sir?' he enquired courteously.

John Lassells swallowed. He said, 'If I tell you what I know, I risk death. If I remain silent, I could be guilty of misprision of treason.'

Treason! If there *was* treason, it was vital for Cranmer to know about it. With Cromwell dead, and the King away, the safety of the Realm was in his hands. He said sternly, 'If you know of treason, sir, it is your solemn duty, both to your God and your King, to declare it.'

John Lassells said, 'I – dare not.'

Thomas said, 'You can tell me now. Or I can commit you to prison. In which case, I think you will wish that you had told me.'

John Lassells looked pleadingly at that stern face. He said, 'The matter does not concern me personally. But – the reward for the bringer of ill-tidings can be death. If your Grace could assure me of your protection – ?'

Thomas said, 'I can offer you no safety. Remember your duty to your God and King. Speak.'

John Lassells' lips moved. Thomas had to lean forward to hear the hoarse whisper. 'I have proof that Queen Catherine is guilty of wantonness and fornication.'

The room seemed to shift, as in an earthquake. Thomas said, 'Do you know what you are saying?'

'Yes.'

'If you fail to prove this, Master Lassells, you are already yourself guilty of the most heinous treason, and will suffer accordingly.' And in his heart he was praying, 'Oh God, let it not be true.'

Lassells said, 'My sister Mary Hall lived in the maidens' chamber with Catherine Howard at the Duchess of Norfolk's house. A lutenist, Manox, was privy to the person of Catherine at that time. My sister will take her oath on it.'

Thomas felt a great surge of relief. 'And this – this kitchen gossip is the molehill out of which you made your mountain?'

'By no means.' Master Lassells was beginning to sound a little more confident. 'Her cousin, Francis Dereham, lay with her on divers occasions.'

Thomas felt sick at heart. Since her marriage to Henry, Catherine had insisted on taking Dereham as her Secretary. He said, with most unusual sharpness for him, '*When* did he lie with her? *Where*?'

'In the maidens' chamber. When she served her Grace of Norfolk.'

So. It was not another royal adultery. Yet it was treason for an unchaste woman to marry the King. He said, 'You spoke of proof, Master Lassells.'

'The Duchess' household knew all that was happening. And both Manox and Dereham have boasted of their knowledge of her.'

Thomas thought of the bloated, ageing Henry setting off so joyfully with his vivacious young bride; thought of the love and happiness in those close little eyes as they gazed on his pretty 'rose without a thorn'. It will kill him, he thought. He said harshly, 'This could still be backstairs gossip. So far,

Master Lassells, you have incriminated one person only – yourself. Unless these facts *are* proved, you have doomed yourself to a fearful end.'

John Lassells looked drained of blood. Then, with a great effort, he seemed to dredge up some spirit. In a sullen voice he said, 'I think your Grace has overlooked some of the implications of this matter.'

Thomas saw, to his surprise, a sly look steal into that ashen face. Lassells said, 'It could be, your Grace, that this foul business could assist God's holy word.'

Thomas froze. 'What do you mean?'

Lassells actually smiled. 'I am sure your Grace does not enjoy seeing the Catholic Howards so greatly in the ascendant. Surely your Grace would not be unhappy to see my Lord Gardiner brought low?'

It was true. The great family of Howard was gaining tremendously in power almost daily. With a Queen in the family they were begging, wheedling, demanding her to give them place and position. And she was doing so. And Stephen Gardiner, his old enemy, was once again a threat to all Cranmer was working for.

And this Lassells had put in his hand a weapon that would undoubtedly destroy these enemies like a forest fire.

And all he felt was an almost disabling loathing of the white, sanctimonious face before him. Yet he said, quietly, 'And you would destroy a young Queen, and the happiness of a King's old age, to this end?'

'For such lewdness to go unpunished would bring God's anger down on the whole nation. But when punishment destroys at the same time the enemies of the Lord – *and* your Grace's enemies and mine – then – ?' he shrugged.

'Leave me,' Thomas said quietly.

Lassells had been looking quite pleased with himself. 'You – do not wish to speak further?' he asked, surprised.

'I am not interested in destroying my enemies, Master Lassells. God will decide between them and me. I serve the King. And I hate you for bringing sorrow upon his head.'

Lassells said, eagerly, 'But your Grace, we have in our hands a weapon to destroy the Papists.'

Thomas felt, and sounded, weary. 'Is this why you brought your story to me?'

'I brought it for the Lord's sake.'

Thomas said, 'You brought it in hatred and malice. That is not the way to serve the Lord.'

Lassells jumped to his feet. ' "I called thee to curse mine enemies. And, behold, thou hast altogether blessed them these three times." The Lord will not hold you guiltless, your Grace.'

Thomas looked up at the lean face, and saw only evil. He said, 'Leave me, Master Lassells, before you anger me further. And do not stray from your house, lest the interrogators cannot find you. And say nothing, tell no one.'

Thomas sat on at his desk. He was trembling. He would do anything to save his King from this new sorrow. But to say nothing now would be misprision of treason on his part. Besides, he *must* speak. The matter must be probed. And that could not be done without the King's knowledge.

He took up a pen. He wrote bald accounts of the interview to his two fellow commissioners for governing London, Audley and Seymour. He sanded, and sealed, the letters. Then he sat and looked at his still-trembling fingers.

From what he had seen of the Queen, the accusations could be true. She seemed to him shallow and silly, a wilful child who must have everything she wanted. She lacked the evil and malice of Anne Boleyn. Yet even her good points, her vivacity and love of life, might well have led her into dangerous and illicit wantonness.

He had but one duty in this matter: to serve his King and his God. And if, doing this duty, he brought down his enemies and, as he saw it, God's enemies, then there would be no exultation on his part. Power's corrupting influence had no part in him. All he felt was dread and a deep, sorrowing love for his grossly deceived Sovereign.

In London, he found Audley and Seymour in a state of shock. 'Your Grace! First, your dreadful news about the Queen. And now this. And the King, they say, less than fifty miles from London.' Lord Chancellor Audley literally wrung his hands.

'*And now this?*' said Thomas brusquely. '*What* this?'

Seymour said, scornfully, 'You mean to say that you, of all people, have not heard?'

'I have heard nothing.'

Seymour said impatiently, 'Prince Edward is sick, and like to die. What do you say to that, Master Archbishop?'

Audley said, 'If the King were to return and find the Prince dead, and his wife a wanton – ' Words failed him.

Seymour said, 'The Tower would not hold all those the King would blame.'

Thomas said, 'Are prayers being said for the young Prince?'

'Night and day. In every church in London.' Said Audley.

'And meanwhile the Prince's fever worsens daily. Perhaps,' said Seymour nastily, 'my Lord Archbishop will now see what *his* prayers can do.'

Thomas, apparently calm, said, 'Prayers will be made. And God will manifest His will in due time.' Yet he knew that the Prince's life was more vital to him even than to the others. If Edward died, Mary would become heir to the throne. And from that moment he, Cranmer, would be doomed.

'And what of this matter of the Queen?' he asked.

'Bedchamber gossip,' snorted Seymour. Audley swallowed nervously, but said nothing.

Thomas said, 'Gossip maybe. But if there were even a grain of truth, and the King had not been informed – we should die, Gentlemen.'

They stared at him in silence: Audley, white and fearful, Seymour red and angry.

Seymour said, 'And what does your Grace propose? That a rider be sent to meet the King with a message, 'Sire, your wife is a whore?'

Thomas ignored the sarcasm. He said, 'Clearly the King must be allowed to return to London. Then the news must be broken to him, carefully and gently.'

Audley shuddered. 'He will kill the messenger. With his bare hands.'

Seymour said, slyly, 'Not if the messenger were his dear friend Canterbury. Thomas has a smooth way of speaking to his Prince. Perhaps it springs from an aptitude for survival.'

Thomas ignored the sneer, though it hurt. He said, 'If you wish, *I* will inform his Majesty. But I must be allowed to choose my moment.'

But it was a hard task that Thomas had so nobly accepted. The King and Queen returned triumphantly from the North; and a Mass was celebrated in thanksgiving for their safe return and for Prince Edward's miraculous recovery due, it was said, to the prayers of Doctor Cranmer.

But Thomas was distressed to see how besotted the ageing bridegroom was with his young bride, fondling and kissing her in public, quite unable to keep his hands off her for a moment. It was not until All Souls Day that Thomas could bring himself to destroy the old man's happiness for ever.

Even then, he could not bring himself to witness the despair and rage with which Henry would learn of his beloved's wantonness. He slipped a paper into Henry's hand during the Mass. Henry put it in his doublet.

The Service ended. Thomas went to his room, to await the summons, bracing himself for the tempest, knowing that he himself would be in the very eye of the storm.

The summons came. Thomas was escorted to the Privy Chamber. He entered, prepared for a whole range of emotions: anger, reproach, tears, self-pity. He might even, he knew, be summarily executed for treasonably impugning the honour of an English Queen.

But Henry, unpredictable as always, was smiling.

'My dear Thomas, I missed you on my long progress. I missed your wise and gentle counsel.'

Thomas bowed low. 'Your Majesty is kind.' But he had to know, at the risk of royal reprimand. 'Your Majesty read the letter I put into your Majesty's hand?'

'I read it, and Lassells and his sister are being examined, and a reason is being found to arrest Dereham, which should not be difficult. But it's all a formality, Thomas. You only have to look at my sweet young Catherine to know she could never be unchaste.

Thomas bowed deeply again.

Henry said, 'I want you and Wriothesley to interrogate Manox. You will find nothing; but these people who have dared to impugn my Queen's honour must be shown to be malicious traitors. The Council will meet on Sunday morning. I want your report available then.'

But when the King attended the Council meeting on that Sunday morning, a shadow had stolen across the sun. Manox had not only inculpated himself. Partly through sexual jealously, partly through an attempt to save himself, he inculpated Dereham.

And, for much the same reasons, Dereham revealed that a Thomas Culpepper, a young courtier dear to the King, had lain frequently with the Queen even while she was on her triumphal progress with the King.

Now the full horror burst.

Deep in the Tower the rackmaster and his helpers were hard at work. And gentle Thomas Cranmer was there taking statements and confessions, for the sake of his God, his King and his Christian duty. (Yet, despite all this zeal, neither Dereham nor Culpepper would confess to adultery with the married Queen.) And when he came up into the sweet sunlight to visit Catherine (a prisoner and no longer a Queen) he found her 'in such lamentation and heaviness as I never saw in no creature'. She alternated between hysteria, a vicious determination to put all the blame on her lovers; and bitter self-reproach. He feared she would lose her wits.

Anyone named Howard was also quaking. It was not likely that a Howard Queen would be allowed to die without taking half her great family with her.

And Henry himself? As soon as Culpepper entered the drama Henry forgot his uncharacteristic calm. He cursed, he raged; he terrified his Council by calling for a sword to kill Catherine with. He wept, he stormed.

Through the bleak winter months the sickening tale of interrogations, trials and executions went on; while Henry, cuckolded before all Europe, humiliated and venomous, assuaged his grief in revelry and pastimes. Until, on February 13th, Catherine was brought to the place of execution. And, to everyone's surprise, this rather silly girl made a good and dignified exit.

Now Thomas Cranmer had a new set of enemies: the reformers felt he had deliberately thrown away a wonderful opportunity to bring down Stephen Gardiner and others of the conservative faction. Lassells had put the weapon into his hand. And he had refused to use it.

But though Thomas had behaved honourably in this aspect of the matter he was still sick at heart. On the instructions of the Council he had suppressed evidence of a precontract between Catherine and Dereham – a precontract which, if followed by sexual intercourse, would have made them legally man and wife, and thus invalidated her marriage to the King.

Another burden for his conscience! In order to serve his King he had robbed three Queens of their honour, and helped to bring two of them to their deaths. He had helped to bring men to the rack, and to the fire. For the first time he had seen men brought to the extremities of pain; he had seen the bloody, ruthless wrenching out of confessions. And though his hands were white and unstained, yet he could not forget those murky stone chambers, and the smell of blood. And his mind began to wonder whether, perhaps, this really *was* God's will, even in the service of a divinely appointed King.

In the service of the King! Yes. That was his authority. For himself he sought nothing, but for the King he would use his intelligence, his wisdom, even his honour. For him, *le Roi le veult* excused everything.

Only his conscience was not fooled.

CHAPTER 17

The crash of the axe on Catherine's little neck seemed to end an epoch. The King had suddenly aged. The athletic, immensely attractive young giant was now a mountainous old man, fifty-four inches round the waist, fifty-seven round the great barrel of a chest. He sighed continually. He ate and drank even more gluttonously. He spent hours reading and annotating devotional books. At a banquet he gave for sixty-one ladies, not one of them seemed to interest him. He was in a bad way indeed. Catherine had more than cuckolded him. She had destroyed his youth.

For Thomas Cranmer, also, life was for a time easier: less time at his manor houses in Kent, with their tormenting memories of Margarete; more time in London, attending meetings of the Council.

But the twelve prebendaries of the Chapter of Canterbury made the most of his absences. Conservatives and reformers were evenly divided – and were at it hammer and tongs: about sermons, about images and idols, about the celibacy of the clergy. Cranmer went down and bade them show more Christian love to each other, but apparently he united them only in their hatred for himself: because they eventually wrote to the King accusing Cranmer of heresy. Two of the prebendaries, Serles and Willoughby, galloped to London carrying a mass of evidence: far more than was necessary to burn a dozen Archbishops. It was, so far, the most dangerous crisis in Cranmer's life. And it was one of which he was entirely ignorant.

Scene: Lambeth Palace. Morice to Cranmer: 'Your Grace, the King's barge is about to pass under Lambeth Bridge. If your Grace – ?'

'Thank you, Ralph.' For once in his life Thomas acted on impulse. He jumped up from his chair, hurried outside.

It was an April evening, soft, brilliant, the clouds that had brought the day's showers now stacked like crumpled linen low on the horizon. From far away, yet heard clearly on that still evening, came the suggestion of music: lutes and viols, played by nymphs among the reeds of old Thames!

Thomas walked up on to Lambeth Bridge. He guessed the source of the music: the royal barge, all crimson and gold, white oars moving in unison like the wings of birds, was approaching majestically in mid-stream.

The splash of oars, the sweet music, came nearer. Now he could see, sitting alone on a mass of crimson cushions in the stern, the vast bulk of the King. Thomas stood in the middle of the bridge, held up his right hand, and prepared to bless his Majesty as he passed under.

The sight of his august Sovereign, bathed in evening sunlight and borne so magnificently on the tide of his own noble river, filled Thomas with an emotion too deep for tears. The friendship that linked these two most dissimilar men did not save Thomas from the lash of the royal tongue. It did not save Henry from the reproofs of his Father in God. Yet it was a very real thing for both of them. And Henry, seeing that sturdy figure ahead of him, shouted an order.

Thomas Cranmer saw the sweep of the oars check; and the barge turned towards the bank.

Thomas regretted his sudden impulse. Despite their friendship, he was never at ease with this ebullient monarch. No one was. An invisible headsman stood always behind his chair.

But he was caught. He hurried down to the landing stage.

The immense barge came alongside. There was great activity with boat hooks and folding steps. Then obsequious servants helped Thomas aboard, and led him to meet his Sovereign.

Thomas bowed low. The King, lolling on his cushions, waved him graciously to a seat. He gave him the captivating smile that was seldom seen nowadays. His mood was as mellow as the calm evening. 'Ah, my Chaplain. This is well met. It is too long since you and I talked.'

Thomas bowed lower, and sat down. The King's mood puzzled him. He seemed to be bubbling over with good nature, but also with secret amusement, as he had been in the good old days of planning disguisings or japes. Thomas said, 'Your Majesty honours your poor servant.'

'Not so, Thomas. We are growing old, you and I. Why should we not sit like gossips in the chimney corner?' He looked suddenly forlorn.

Wine was brought, and sweetmeats. The boat cast off. Soon they were sweeping along at an exhilarating pace in the very centre of the river.

Henry crammed in a handful of sweetmeats, swallowed, rinsed his fingers delicately in a finger bowl. Then he said, 'Now, what shall we discuss? Heresy?'

Thomas looked at him fearfully, expecting the small mouth to have set hard as a mantrap after uttering this ominous word. Instead, Henry was still smiling. His manner was arch, almost mischievous.

But the word had been spoken. 'Heresy, your Grace?'

'Heresy, Thomas. Tell me, Thomas, who is the greatest heretic in Kent?'

'I – do not know, your Majesty.'

Henry shook his head in mock reproof. But he was actually chuckling as he pulled a bundle of documents from the cushions and pushed them into Thomas' hands. 'I have news for you,' he said. '*You are*, my Lord of Canterbury.'

A breeze of evening scampered across the water, shook the barge like a playful terrier, and was gone rejoicing. The King's words, and the sudden rocking movement, robbed Thomas of both sense and speech.

And the King was still smiling. 'Read, my Lord,' he said, drinking deeply of the wine.

Thomas' poor eyes struggled with the accusations. They were dangerous, damnable, clever. They could destroy a man. But he had had time to collect himself. He said, 'May I humbly petition your Grace to appoint a Commissioner to examine the truth of these charges?'

'It is already done, my Lord. You are he.' The King was enjoying himself hugely.

'But – your Grace? *I* am the accused in this matter. I cannot be both judge and accused.'

'You can if I say so, man.'

'But – Sire? The world will suspect – ?'

Henry was becoming impatient. 'God's Blood! The world can suspect what it likes. I know you, Thomas.' Suddenly he looked sly. 'Perhaps I know you better than you think.'

'Sire?' Now what was coming?

'I know that you regard your bedchamber as exempt from the Six Articles.' He put a friendly hand on Thomas' arm. 'How have you kept her so dark, man?'

Thomas said, 'We – do not cohabit, your Grace. She lives in Germany.'

'A Lutheran, I think you said?'

Cranmer nodded.

Henry's voice was beginning to slur, his eyes to lose their focus. He said, 'I have never known. Does the Ordination drive out the devil that lords it in a man's loins?'

Thomas smiled wryly. 'No, your Grace.'

Henry's unfocused eyes struggled to fix themselves on Cranmer's face. In a grand, magniloquent manner, he said: 'Bring her back, Thomas my friend. I would not have your devil lonely o'nights.'

Thomas stared at his Sovereign in wonder and disbelief. Yet he said, 'But your Grace, marriage for the clergy is forbidden by the Six Articles. How could I – head under your Grace of the English Church, cohabit with a wife and retain my self-respect?'

Henry said contemptuously, 'You did it before, my Lord. So make your choice: wife, or self-respect? I know which would bring *me* more comfort,' he added in a sudden flood of self-pity.

His eyelids were beginning to droop like those of a tired baby. Thomas rose, bowed, and stood irresolute. Were these few half-drunk remarks sufficient authority to bring back Margarete?

The King roused. 'Master Bargeman! Bring your vessel round to Lambeth Pier.' He stared up at Thomas. 'Be discreet,' he said, firmly and soberly. Then he fell asleep as though he had been struck over the head.

He stood in the dusk of that April evening, staring out of his study window, rehearsing, analysing every word that had been spoken. When dealing with Henry, such caution might mean the difference between life and death.

Then: 'Candles,' he shouted.

Servants came running. Lights were suddenly everywhere. He sat down, seized a quill and began to write. It was an impassioned letter, dictated by loneliness, love, and a need for the strength and comfort that only she could give, and by what Henry called the devil in his loins. It begged her to return. Lovingly he signed the letter, sealed it carefully, and gave it to his faithful Morice to dispatch to Germany. Then he went to bed to pray, to consider fearfully the meaning of the heresy charge, to imagine, with fear and joy, the return of Margarete to his arms and to this bed.

And to listen to (and stifle if he could) the voice of conscience, asking him how he thought a man of honour could enjoy pleasures which he himself denied his underlings.

There was the clatter of hooves in the night. Thomas pulled on a robe, went downstairs to see what this ominous noise could mean.

Morice met him on the stairs. By the eerie candlelight Thomas saw the horseman beside him, and recognized with relief a courtier friendly to the reformers.

Ralph Morice said, 'Your Grace, Master Denny is come from the King, who commands your Grace's immediate presence at Whitehall.'

'Welcome, Master Denny,' said Thomas with his unfailing courtesy. But his mind was racing. A few hours ago he had left a somnolent and affectionate Henry at Lambeth Pier. What possible crisis could have happened since then?

The invaluable Morice said, 'By the time your Grace has dressed a horse will be ready for your Grace.'

It was amazing. A few hours ago Henry had been an old man, drowsy with wine, ready to be lifted from his barge and put to bed by his gentlemen. Now Thomas found him, at two in the morning, pacing the long gallery of Whitehall in a state of high nervous excitement.

At their entry the King swung round. With a furious gesture he dismissed Denny. Thomas, seeing the anger on that so-recently friendly face, fell on his knees.

'Oh, get up, man,' Henry said brusquely. 'Now then. I've had more complaints. And these from the Council. No gaggle of Prebendaries this time, my Lord.'

Thomas felt the blood drain from his face. The Council! Men not one of whom he trusted. And Henry clearly had listened to them. For now he said, 'You're for the Tower, friend. It is the Council's will.' Then he said, slowly and formally, 'And *I* have confirmed that will.'

Thomas was trembling. But he said, 'I humbly thank your Majesty for this warning. Nor do I fear the Tower, since I know your Majesty will ensure me a fair hearing.'

Henry looked at him in amazement. 'O Lord God,' he cried. 'Can't you see that once they get you there, stripped of your high office, they'll bind you up so that even I can't save you?' He stood gnawing his lip, staring at his Archbishop. Then: 'Oh, you are a fool, Thomas,' he burst out. 'Here.' He was tugging a ring off his fat finger. 'When they arrest you – as I promise you they will – show 'em this ring and appeal to the King personally.'

Thomas said, 'I thank your Grace for his regard for his humble servant.'

Henry said, 'I don't know why I waste my time saving someone too feeble to try to save himself. It's only because you may still be useful to me, remember that, Master Thomas.'

'I pray heaven that I may be, Sire,' said Thomas, and bowed himself out.

What was left of the night was sleepless. Thomas knew he was in dreadful danger, even with the King's ring next to his heart. The Council were ruthless and determined men who, once they had seen their chance, had fallen on Cromwell with relentless brutality. And if they could despatch the hard and cunning Cromwell so easily, surely they could despatch the simple Cranmer before he could get the royal ring out of his pocket.

And, at Whitehall, he found his fears had been justified. When, heart in mouth, he made to enter the Council Chamber, an officious servant said, 'Not so, your Grace. If your Grace would wait here,' and he indicated a bench occupied by servants and messenger boys.

For nearly an hour Thomas, Archbishop of Canterbury, sat on that lowly bench, fortified by his own natural humility. Then at last the door of the Council Chamber was opened, and the servant, with a contemptuous gesture, indicated that he should go through.

Thomas rose, and walked into the ornate room with dignity. There at the great table sat his colleagues of so many meetings, and not one met his eye, not one but looked hard and reproving, not one who rose in greeting.

Since there was no seat for him, Thomas stood at the end of the table, in calm and dignified humility, for had not his heavenly Master stood thus before His judges? But when he saw his old enemy Gardiner, Bishop of Winchester, rising to make the charge, his heart failed him. They were all eager to hound him to his death. But Stephen Gardiner would be the one most fervent, most implacable, in this work.

'Thomas Cranmer, you are charged with the most damnable sin of heresy.'

Thomas said, 'Then let my accusers state their case, my Lord of Winchester.'

'What? Here? In the Council Chamber? Oh, no, your Grace. The Tower's the place for that, as you well know. You will not be a Councillor there.'

It was a chilling remark. In the Tower, surrounded by the fearful engines of interrogation, the highest in the land stood naked and helpless as on the day he was born. Thomas said, with a touch of desperation, 'The Tower? Is this the wish of all you my friends at this table?'

Still they did not meet his eye. But each one, by a movement of the head, or of a hand, or by a grunt gave their assent.

Gardiner shouted, 'Summon the Guard.'

There was a clash of arms. The doors were flung open. Thomas knew the humiliation of a mailed hand on each shoulder.

Something snapped. 'Take your hands off me,' he shouted.

The heavy hands did not move. Gardiner said, 'Guard Captain. See your prisoner safely to the Tower.'

Thomas, furiously angry, said, 'One moment, Winchester. If I am to be judged, it will not be by underlings. It will be by the King.'

Stephen Gardiner smiled unpleasantly. 'I think not, Master Archbishop.'

Thomas opened his hand. In the palm lay a ring. Thomas held out his hand towards the table.

Dukes, Earls, high officers of State gazed at that ring, terrified as rabbits gazing at a stoat. Oh, they had been too bold! They should have known that Henry would always protect his lickspittle Archbishop.

Some of them, so skilled were they in survival, recovered quickly. 'Your Grace,' said old Norfolk, 'we wished only to give you this chance to quash the malicious lies of the common sort.'

But now, suddenly the King's huge bulk was among them. Completely ignoring the others he went and took Thomas' arm. 'What, my good old friend? Why, you look like a hind facing the cruel huntsman.' And now he turned and faced the Council. 'Surely, my Lords, none of you has aught against this simple priest?'

Gardiner said, 'Your Grace, it would be very treason to have aught against one whom your Grace holds in such high favour.'

'Treason indeed, my Lord of Winchester,' Henry said drily, 'And remember, a Bishop can be quartered as easily as any man.' He glared round the table. 'And so can Dukes, and Lord Chancellors and Chamberlains. Remember that, my Lords.'

Gardiner bowed very low. Henry, in an entirely different tone, said, 'Come, Stephen. Shake hands with Canterbury. All of you, take this good and gracious Prelate's hand, lest I suspect my Council of mischief.' He turned to Thomas. 'Thomas, invite these your friends to dine tonight at your house. It will be a merry party.' And he limped gaily from the room, smiling happily.

Stephen Gardiner was the first to shake him by the hand.

Gardiner's fingers gripped hard, as hard as the instruments of persuasion in the Tower. There was no more friendship in that grip than in the hissed words that accompanied it: 'The King will not live for ever, Master Cranmer.'

To suggest that the King might not live for ever was treasonable, punishable by death. But Gardiner knew his man: Cranmer would not betray him.

Norfolk and Suffolk knew of course exactly what the King's game had been. By allowing the heresy charge to go forward he had frightened the life out of his reforming Archbishop. And by the gift of the ring he had warned the Council that they touched Cranmer at their peril. And so he kept the balance of power firmly in his own hands.

But Thomas was still a less experienced Henry-watcher. He had, it seemed to him, missed the Tower by the skin of his teeth. He knew now that his fellow Councillors were out to destroy him. And, as Gardiner had pointed out, the only thing that stood between him and his accusers was an old, sick King.

And just when his enemies had shown their hand, he had given another hostage to fortune: Margarete! Miraculously he had kept her secret before. Could he possibly do it again?

As instructed, Thomas gave them dinner at Lambeth. But it was not a merry party. Over that great dining-room brooded the figure of the absent King. The room was heavy with fear and mistrust. Lips smiled ingratiatingly on my Lord of Canterbury; but eyes remained hard, and calculating, and watchful. And Thomas, who would like not to have an enemy in the world, knew that every man in this room desired his death; and would have it once the sick and ageing King was out of the way.

He was fearful of many things. His enemies had declared themselves, and as a result of a few maudlin words of Henry's he had written off impetuously to call Margarete back to him. And the days passed, and the ecstatic, excited reply he had expected from Germany never came.

Suppose the letter had fallen into the wrong hands? There was enough on that single sheet to bring him to the scaffold. Suppose Margarete was ill, unable to travel? Suppose she had set out, and her escort had been unable to save her from wild animals, robbers, marauding soldiers? And behind all these fears he heard the endless nagging of his conscience. These pressures not only sapped his will. They sapped his inner strength, making him weak and flaccid.

In this dark night of the soul it seemed to him that he had but one friend, one person whom he could trust and with whom he could relax: Ralph Morice, his secretary now for over ten years who loved and admired this man who held himself in such bitter contempt.

Morice was fascinated by this very human master. While he sometimes deplored his master's weaknesses, he knew that for him the Archbishop could do no wrong. And Thomas knew that Ralph would always make him feel that perhaps he was not quite the contemptible creature he thought himself.

Thomas was taking a glass of wine alone in his garden. The evening was still, perfect, golden. The peace of God, which passed all understanding, filled this garden. Yet Thomas was not part of it. He was at odds with himself and the world: irritated, restless, uncomfortable, afraid. Now here came Morice. Thomas knew that if anyone could bring him peace, it was this man. Besides, he had a favour to ask: one he could ask of no other man. Only Ralph could find out what had happened to that letter. Only he could be trusted to bring back Margarete safely through all the dangers of Europe.

Yet this favour was not the reason for the warmth of his welcome: 'Ah, Ralph, my dear fellow, sit down. Pour yourself a glass of wine.' He sounded cordial, relaxed.

'Thank you, your Grace.' But Ralph remained standing. And now Thomas saw that his secretary was strangely ill-at-ease. He must find the reason before he asked any favours. Other people's troubles always took precedence over his own. He said, gently, 'What is it, Ralph?'

Morice said stiffly, 'I wish to plead for a friend, your Grace.'

'What is it, Ralph? A benefice, a preferment?'

Ralph said, 'My friend already has a benefice, your Grace. In my gift, thanks to your Grace's kindness. He is Richard Turner, Curate of Chartham. And a man I hold in the greatest friendship and love.'

It was as though a breeze of evening swept down on the garden's still leaves. It was conjured up by the name of Richard Turner of Chartham.

Now Richard Turner was not a name to conjure with. Yet it brought a killing cold to that summer garden because he was the friend of the Archbishop's secretary, and because his was one of the names that Thomas' conscience was wont to repeat at three in the morning. Thomas felt the blood drain from his face. He said, 'What is it you wish?'

Morice was very pale. He spoke in short, gasping phrases: 'Is it true, that your Grace, instructed by the King, has ordered Richard, a gentleman and a scholar, to be whipped out of the County?'

Thomas said, 'He was accused of heresy, Ralph.'

'From which *you* discharged him. You discharge him, then you order him whipped.' By now Morice was almost incoherent with indignation. 'I seem to think Pontius Pilate in *his* weakness made a similar judgment.'

So it had come! The one person through whose eyes he had been able to see some nobility in himself, had at last seen him as he was: a latter day Pilate, cynically abandoning principle to expediency.

He said, helplessly, 'Le Roi le veult, Ralph.'

'And is that an excuse for every act of weakness, every betrayal?'

Many men would have blustered, refused to be so addressed by a secretary; would have defended themselves angrily. Thomas said sadly, almost pleadingly, 'There is another saying: *Indignatio principis mors est.*'

Ralph lowered himself on to a chair. He stared at his master in a kid of wonder. 'And you put that before injustice, before the hurt and humiliation of a fine man?'

Thomas was silent.

Ralph in his eagerness pulled his chair forward, until his knees were almost touching Thomas'. 'Your Grace, do two things for me,' he pleaded.

'Two things?' Thomas said bleakly.

'Save my friend. And help me not to despise a loved master.'

Despise! The word had been used. Now everyone despised him: the King, the Council, and above all, he himself. Yet he cried, with a touch of spirit, 'I have not always been servile. I angered the King many times, pleading for More, for Fisher, for Cromwell, even for Queen Anne.'

'And in every case to no avail,' Morice said sadly. 'Perhaps your Grace did not plead hard enough.'

Thomas sighed heavily. 'Ralph, I have many enemies. They have accused me to the King of harbouring every heretic in the realm.' Then he said firmly, 'I can do nothing for Master Turner.'

'So a priest whom you have discharged of heresy is to be whipped – for heresy?'

Thomas appeared to have shrunk into his chair. 'I *dare* do nothing.'

'Then *I* will do something,' said Morice, jumping to his feet. He looked down at the pitiful figure in the chair. And his anger left him. He had always loved and admired this man. Now suddenly he loved and pitied him. He said, 'I have friends at Court. With your Grace's permission – ?'

Thomas nodded: 'Do your best for your friend. And – ' he rose slowly from his chair, 'do not utterly condemn your other friend. He is a man of many weaknesses, Ralph.'

The two men looked at each other long and hard. And then together they went into the house. But Thomas knew that, if he was to retain any honour, he could never now ask another favour of Ralph Morice.

Still there was no Margarete, no letter. His self-loathing intensified. So why should a fine woman like Margarete return to such a creature as he? And then he thought: by now Doctor Luther will have given her a dispensation to marry another. And he was surprised and disturbed to feel the knife of sexual jealousy twisting in his heart: surprised, because in spite of all his self-contempt he had thought himself above such human feelings. But – another man entering *his* sweet domain – he discovered in himself dark caverns of hatred that appalled him.

And then, at last, a letter. She was lying at the Fleur de Lys in Dover, awaiting him. She referred to other letters, clearly lost (and in whose hands, he wondered. His enemies would pay well for anything that would bring down Cranmer the Heretic).

Chapter 18

The sea was still at its endless game with the shingle. They walked on the beach as the sun went down behind the grim castle, and the shadows of the hill reached out across the town.

She was older, less of a loved daughter, more of a wife and helpmeet. She thought more, spoke less. Or could it be, he wondered, that there was something wrong. He said, 'Are you weary after your journey?'

'No, thank you. It is most pleasant to walk so.'

Pleasant! A lukewarm word! There *was* something wrong.

In his present mood of self-denigration he was convinced that even she had gone over to the enemy. He said, harshly. 'What is troubling you, wife?'

She was too honest a person to dissemble. She said, 'I quarrelled with my uncle, Osiander. He did not want me to come.'

His heart sank. He had been both selfish and foolhardy to bring her to England. And his dear friend Osiander knew it, and had said so. He said, 'There are dangers, as I said in my letter. And I was selfish to expose you to them. But – I have needed you so much, beloved.'

She said quickly, 'Oh, it is not danger. But Osiander said – forgive me, dearest – he said you were behaving dishonourably. That you were prepared to hang a married priest and his wife, while living again secretly with me.'

He was silent. She said quietly, 'Tell me it is not true, beloved.'

He said, 'It is not true. The King himself told me to call you back.'

'Thank God for that. I knew my uncle must be wrong. You would never behave dishonourably.'

He said, 'Do not expect too much of me, dearest. I have seen myself very clearly.' He added, scarce daring to ask: 'Does my old friend Osiander despise me?'

'No. Of course not. Not despise. But – ' she sounded doubtful – 'he thinks you have betrayed the Reformation.'

Betrayed the Reformation! And for the first time he asked himself whether he had ever really stood for the Reformation. Had he ever *really* cared about Indulgences, the Real Presence, Images, Transubstantiation? Or had he simply used all these to act as pander to a tyrant King. To bring Henry to bed with this woman or that? Had he robbed the common people of their loved images and superstitions, not in the service of Christ but of an absolute monarch? Had he, in fact, imposed on the people of England a hotch-potch of a Reformed Church without ever realizing what he was doing?

He said unhappily, 'It is true that the King told me to call you back. Yet – it would still be possible for a married priest and his wife to be hanged. In honesty I must tell you that.'

She gave a little cry of horror. He peered down at her face, lit by the evening sun. It was hard and set. 'Now even you despise me,' he said sadly.

She looked up, then. 'No, Thomas, I do not despise you. You are a good man, a kind and gentle man. But you should never be an Archbishop. You lack the steel.'

She was being tender with him. But he understood her thoughts. He was a weakling, fearful and timorous. If she did still love him it was with pity, with a love that must always have an alloy of contempt.

Yet, being a good wife, and knowing she had brought him low, she now gave herself to raising him up. She cared for him, cosseted him, flattered him, until this humble man was in danger of becoming as proud as Lucifer. And then, one evening, when the last of the sunlight painted the windows' traceries on the tapestried walls, she led him to out-Lucifer Lucifer by holding out her arms to him and, when she held him safe, saying, 'Beloved, I am carrying your child.'

He stared at her in amazement, his throat, his eyes, suffused with tears. Then: 'Margarete!' he cried. 'Margarete,' and buried his face in her shoulder.

After a time she took his head in both her hands, and stared at him long and hard. 'I – thought you would be pleased,' she said.

'I am,' he cried. 'Oh, I am. I thank God. Your child and mine. Your flesh and mine, made truly one.'

'But – ?' she said, unsmiling. She knew him too well.

He was silent. Despite Henry's gracious magnanimity on the barge – a wife was still a hostage to the world. A child would be another: a hostage more difficult to hide, more helpless than a wife.

He smiled. 'There is no "but",' he said. 'Tonight we will sing our heartfelt Te Deum, wife.'

But in his heart, fearful as always, he was making plans to protect his wife in the coming months, and his child in the coming years.

And protect her he did through the slow months until, one day, she suddenly grabbed his hand; and, with a frightened smile, said, 'Beloved! Now – '

He was immediately back in Cambridge, reading St Jerome to the good monks. For him, birth would always have its mirror image of death. He rushed into his study. 'Ralph, the doctor, quickly. And, oh, whatever we need, tell the servants to prepare – ' He was distraught.

Ralph Morice hurried off. Thomas went back to his wife, and most improperly helped her undress. By the time the servants arrived they were scandalized to find her in bed, attended only by the Archbishop. They bundled him roughly out of the room. His feet led him down to the private chapel. He prayed, achingly, fervently for her. He had no idea how long it was before there was a tapping at the door. Abandoning God, he rushed and opened it. The doctor stood there: a man who though he had attended Margarete for years, did not know whether he had delivered a wife or a concubine. He said, stiffly, 'The woman is delivered of a girl child.'

Thomas ran upstairs. And there she lay, exhausted, drained, but smiling as only she could smile. And, in her arms, a tiny, perfect replica of her sweet self. Truly, truly thought Thomas, my cup runneth over.

A month later he was able to christen his small daughter Margaret at a secret ceremony in the private chapel. Another Margaret!

And, the following year, he christened a son: Thomas. Another Thomas! Another Margaret! Two innocent hostages to a cruel world.

And not only a cruel world now: a disintegrating one. Henry, with all his outrageous faults, had held his world together for thirty-eight years. But now the reins were falling from his hands. Thomas knew that death was close to a King who had shown him friendship. And without that protection Thomas would be naked and helpless.

Yes. The King was an old, sick man, unable to go upstairs in his palaces. In fact he would have been confined to his privy chamber but for the 'trams' which moved his great bulk painfully from room to room.

Despite plasters made from marshmallows, oxide of lead, rose water and dragon's blood, his leg ulcers refused steadfastly to heal. They gave him continuous and hideous pain. It was clear that the interesting meeting between him and his Maker could not be long delayed.

Thomas watched this breaking-up of a once noble vessel with dismay and sadness.

Nor was the breaking-up taking place only in Henry's rotting flesh. The Court, the Council, became as diseased as the King. Ruthless men watched Henry's decline with cold, detached interest. They made their plans. They whispered into the King's ear. And suddenly, it appeared, the Duke of Norfolk and his son the loutish Earl of Surrey were about to murder the entire Council and set Prince Edward on the Throne. Father and son were arrested, and many others. At Court, treason was like a stench in the air. Some were for Mary Tudor; some for that frail little boy Edward. You placed your bets, well knowing that the stake was your life.

Cranmer, who had most to lose from the death of the King, walked from room to room of the great Palace of Whitehall, sombre in his black gown and velvet cap, and plotted with no one. Yet he knew that the accession of Mary would quickly be the end of him; and that a sickly King Edward VI might only delay his martyrdom by a few years.

Yet he did nothing to save himself. It was not in his nature. He simply waited, as he had always waited, to serve his master. But this time not to the bed of some nubile young Queen; but to the Courts of Heaven, where God the

Father, surely, would be waiting to show His trusty and well-beloved Henry respectfully round the place.

Yet, in the event, Thomas was not there.

It cannot be said that Henry's doctors eased their patient over the last threshold. In the death chamber, by the light of many candles, they crept about the vast bed, pouring noxious liquids down his throat, cauterizing his raw ulcers with burning irons, fussily measuring his urine; while, in the shadows, watchful, silent, tense, the Council waited.

The King was dying; everyone in that fetid chamber knew it.

Yet no one dared say so. The very suggestion that the King might die was treasonable. The doctors were in a quandary. Everyone knew that the one man Henry would want in his last moments was Cranmer. And Cranmer was fifteen miles away at Croydon and no one dared send for him.

The situation was fraught with danger for them all. Every so often a physician would pad across the room and consult anxiously with the Council. Each time he would be sent back, rebuffed, to his duties. It was the doctors' job to decide when Henry needed his Chaplain, and then to send for him. Members of the Council were not messenger boys.

But in the end Sir Anthony Denny went boldly over to the great bed and whispered, 'Your Majesty, would it not comfort you to talk with Thomas Cranmer?'

Henry lay as one dead. The huge body already stank of corruption. Only the snoring breath showed that there was still life there.

Then the small eyes opened, and focused with difficulty on Denny's face. 'Why should I need a priest, Anthony?'

Denny took a deep breath. 'Because you are dying, Sire.'

The fat red fingers clutched suddenly at the bedclothes. A look of astonishment flitted across the bloated face, and for a moment the eyes stared in fear. Then he said calmly, 'Yes. I would talk with Thomas.' And, in a sudden, loud cry, 'Let him come quickly.'

It was a foul night, the roads icy, a river fog crawling about the space between frozen earth and freezing sky.

But Cranmer, riding north as fast as was possible, was unaware of his surroundings. A deep and terrible sadness wrapped him as tight as his cloak. The rages, the cruelty, the wanton injustices, the ruthlessness, all these were forgotten. His fears about the succession, about the plotting for position among the nobles: these were put aside. All he knew now was that his friend was dying. All he remembered was the warmth, the brilliance, the life-enhancing gaiety of that best of companions, Harry Tudor.

He came into the bedchamber. A few looked up. No one greeted him. He crossed to the bed. He knelt.

He thought he had come too late. 'Thomas Cranmer, your Majesty,' he whispered.

A hand rustled across the bedclothes, caught his, and held on to it desperately. Thomas said, 'Can you speak to me, my son?'

Henry heaved as though his great chest were bursting.

But only a dry rattle came from his throat. Then he fell back on the bed, exhausted. But Thomas' hand was still held in that desperate, chillingly cold grip.

Thomas said, 'My son. Give me some sign that you trust in the Lord.'

He waited, weeping, for a sign – a nod, a smile, an opening of the eyes.

None came. He said again, 'My son, give me a sign that you trust in the Lord.'

A tear trickled down Henry's cheek. The cold hand released Thomas'. Then, suddenly, found it again, and gave it a faint squeeze.

It was no more, really, than the fluttering of a wounded bird. But it told Thomas Cranmer that Henry Tudor would be seen at the Gates of Heaven, not as a tyrant and lecher, but as the Golden Prince he had once been, before the world and the flesh and absolute power had had their dreadful way with him.

Chapter 19

It was a time for the weeping of children, and for the tears of old men.

The young Elizabeth wept, not for her father, but because dashing, gallant Thomas Seymour, who romped with her was now married to her stepmother, the widowed Catherine Parr.

Edward VI, the young King, wept because his constant boyhood companions were pain and sickness.

And, among the dripping oaks of Charnwood Forest, a little girl wept because her harsh and unloving parents were sending her to stay with that same gallant Thomas Seymour, on his promise 'by God's precious soul', to marry her to the boy King. And she did not want to be a Queen. She just wanted to go on being Lady Jane Grey, studying her beloved Demosthenes and Plato at Bradgate House.

Even the thick-skinned old men of the Council wept because Edward Seymour, Protector of the King, treated them with such scorn and rage that they despaired of ever pleasing him.

Alone of all that Court, Thomas Cranmer wept for the passing of a friend. In his grief, he allowed his beard to grow. And this beard, long and white and untrimmed, made him look for the first time the man approaching sixty that he really was.

Yet, grief and fears apart, this was one of the few placid and happy times of his life. The savage, inhuman penalties for theological error had been reduced to indefinite imprisonment without trial. The marriage of priests was no longer forbidden, and he was able to live openly with his dear Margarete.

For the first time in his life he had a home. Margarete sat as hostess at his dinner table, and sparkled. They entertained friends, and there was laughter, and wit. And Thomas, at the head of the table, could not take his eyes off this wife who charmed everyone; or off those two loved wantons, little Margaret and Thomas, laughing, playing, merry as the day is long.

Friends were many, almost all on the reformed side, men who now could breathe freely, laugh freely, and talk without glancing nervously over their shoulders: men, not of rank, but of honesty of purpose; tradesmen, parish priests, schoolmasters; men like Edward Whitchurch, an old friend who had helped with the printing of the English Bible, a man nearer to Margarete than to Thomas in age, a cheerful bachelor always ready to be a merry uncle to the children.

Yes. Happy, peaceful evenings: the candles creating their soft pools of light; the wine, rough and sweet; and, above all, friendship and peace in every heart; and, to look forward to, a day of absorbing work tomorrow.

For during these peaceful days, Cranmer, respected and resplendent head of a great Church, was working on a complete and compact Book of Common Prayer.

He was doing the work for which his nature most fitted him: creating, out of the jumbled devotions of ancient

Christendom, a book worthy of his bright vision, so long ago, of the great Cathedral Church of Canterbury.

And he was writing it in English; and by so doing, his genius was helping to mould that young and vigorous language into something strong and sinewy and of a strange music.

At last, after so many years, he had burst from the bonds of his own frailty. At last he was a man, full of wisdom and learning and authority. The September of his days was as mellow as the cornfields and the orchards in the Kentish autumn.

Gardiner was in prison. Edward Seymour, who controlled not only the mind of the young King but also the whole country, was an ardent reformer not so much from religious conviction as from the fact that there were still riches to be had from the monasteries.

And, to Thomas' great relief, the Lady Mary came seldom to Court. Her brother's Protestantism offended her. She maintained her Catholic household at Kenninghall, hearing the Mass daily, and bided her time, strengthened by the common belief that her frail stepbrother was unlikely to reach manhood. And then? With God's help she would give England back to the Pope. And make sure that men like Cranmer should never again be able to mutilate the body of Christ's religion.

Yes. Quiet days. But even in a time like this a man like Thomas is always listening, watching. Is this quiet ominous? Is it like the silence before a storm?

Yes. The fear *was* justified. In the silence, the clouds crept up, like an invading army, and seized upon the sun. The earth grew dark, the sky was a burden laid upon the earth, a few drops of rain fell, heavy as toads.

The storm, that had been gathering for years, broke. Thomas was in the eye of the storm.

Edward Seymour, once all powerful, had gone to the block years ago. So had his brother, Thomas.

The man who had sent them there, and himself swallowed all their powers, was John Dudley, Earl of Warwick.

Dark, saturnine, brooding, he was one of those rare men whose lust for power is so unbelievable that other men fail to take them seriously until they themselves are trussed like flies in the spider's web.

Such men will seize an opportunity to gain a small advantage. Then they will build on that advantage quickly, remorselessly, climbing on the backs of others whom they then destroy, until they have gained the supreme power for which they lust.

Warwick's opportunity had come with the disorders of 1549, themselves sparked off by poverty, enclosures, and the introduction of Cranmer's Prayer Book, the people's greatest objection to which was that it was in English.

The rebels' petition to the King had infuriated Cranmer, since it began, 'We will have all the holy decrees of our forefathers observed, kept and performed; and whosoever shall again say them, we hold them as heretics'.

Thomas had always accepted personal insult with humility. But one thing his gentle nature could not and would not stand was defiance of his King. 'We will have…'? The idea of peasants thus daring to address their King had shocked Thomas into a reply of rare indignation. 'Was this manner of speech at any time used of the subjects to their Prince since the beginning of the world?' he wrote. But he had done more than write. For once he became a powerful, forceful Prince of the Church. He not only went to St Paul's and addressed the Lord Mayor and Aldermen and the people, telling them that the rebellion was God's punishment for their evil living; he also procured German mercenaries to put down the revolt, and urged the commanders to use the utmost severity.

The Protector Somerset however, had appeared less enthusiastic in crushing the disorders, and this had been Warwick's opportunity. With his army of mercenaries he had defeated the ringleader Kett and his rebels, and then used this success to undermine the Protector's position. Without pause he filled the Council with his creatures, and began to work on the mind of the young King, whom he quickly persuaded to create him Duke of Northumberland.

Northumberland was an even more ardent reformer in church matters than Somerset had been; and for exactly the same reason: greed. But Cranmer moved too slowly for him, and soon found himself buffeted by Northumberland's rough anger; an experience that badly prepared the ageing priest for his eventual confrontation, not only with the terrible Duke but with his boy King.

June, 1553. And the lawns and gardens of Lambeth Palace had never been lovelier; or so thought Thomas and Margarete. Edward Whitchurch, that beloved 'uncle', had made a seesaw out of a fallen trunk and a board, and was supervising the children's game, and his laughter rang as loud and as unforced as theirs. Margarete said, 'I think that of all our friends, Edward is the best.'

Thomas was surprised, and angered, to feel a stab of jealousy. He said, 'Indeed, I think so too,' and he spoke with sincerity. Yet now the sunshine was suddenly less bright.

He was bitterly ashamed. That he, a man of God, should know such an unworthy emotion! He looked at Edward Whitchurch, who was now romping with the children as he himself had never romped. Suddenly he felt an old man. He looked at his still-young wife and remembered Osiander's warning: there are not so many honest wives at the English Court.

Still the gardens basked in the warm sunlight and the peace of God. But a tiny arrow had lodged in the heart of Thomas Cranmer. It would not easily be removed.

And, in the Kingdom outside these garden walls, the peace of God was less evident.

Again, a King of England lay dying, shut away from the sweet sunshine in his heavily curtained bed, corpse-like, fevered, his only companion the man who had directed his thoughts throughout his short reign: John Dudley, Duke of Northumberland.

Another for whom the summer sunshine was only a sadness and a torment was Lady Jane Grey. She looked out of the windows of Northumberland's town house, and remembered with a longing intense as a physical pain the little hills of Bradgate, and the drowsing oaks.

But Lady Jane was not only sad and homesick. She was terrified. She had known that under Henry VIII's Will she was named as third in succession to the Throne; and that was a comfortable place to be, with a young King on the Throne and his two sisters named as his successors.

But now it was being said that Edward was like to die. And a month ago she had been married, despite all her pitiful protestations, to Northumberland's son Guilford Dudley.

Now Jane was no fool. She took it for granted that her new father-in-law, whom she loathed, was using her as a pawn in some dark game. And there was no one to whom she could turn for help. Certainly not her husband. Certainly not her parents, who ever since the marriage had looked like cats who have been at the cream.

And Jane was right. Northumberland *was* playing a dark game. He had persuaded Edward to make a Will barring Mary and Elizabeth from the Succession, and name Jane Grey as his successor. He had then married Jane to his son Guilford. Now all he had to do was bully the Council into giving their approval of Edward's Will. Then, with a sixteen-year-old girl both Queen of England and his daughter-in-law, he would have all the power that even he could wish.

Cranmer knew nothing of this. He had heard of the wedding, and even someone as charitable as he had assumed the worst about Northumberland's motives. But when he was peremptorily summoned to Greenwich Palace, his fear was that his Prince was *in articulo mortis*.

But the room in which he found himself was occupied by one person: the Duke of Northumberland.

Closeted with Henry VIII, Thomas always felt that he was in the tiger's cage. Closeted with Northumberland, he felt he was in the snake-pit.

Cranmer bowed courteously. 'How is his Majesty?'

'Well enough to have made his Will, my Lord.'

'I am glad to hear it. The last – '

Northumberland wasn't listening. He cut in, 'He has barred Mary and Elizabeth. And named Jane Dudley as his successor.'

'Jane – Dudley?' Cranmer was lost.

'Jane Grey. She married my son. You must have heard.'

'Of course. But – he has no right. King Henry specifically named the Princess Mary.'

'God's Blood, man. Do *you* of all people want a Papist back on the Throne? She'll burn you.'

Thomas paled. But he said bravely, 'That is not the point. His Majesty cannot legally – '

'Henry did.'

'But he was authorized by Act of Parliament.'

'Exactly. Well, we've no time for that sort of nonsense. All we need is the Lords and the Judges to sign this Engagement. Most of 'em have done. That's why I've sent for you. Just put your name there.'

Thomas' mouth was very dry. 'I – cannot sign that,' he said. 'It is high treason.'

'You haven't even read it,' Northumberland said contemptuously.

Thomas read it. The signatories undertook to support Edward's devise and to uphold it with their lives.

Thomas said, 'I demand to see the King. Alone.'

'You may see the King. But not alone.' He opened the door. 'Northampton, Darcy,' he yelled, like one calling servants.

The Marquis of Northampton and Lord Darcy, now Lord Chamberlain, came running. Northumberland said, 'His Grace demands to see the King. Escort him.'

'I wish to see him alone,' said Thomas. To his surprise he found he was very angry.

'Impossible.' Northumberland took back the Engagement, sat fanning himself with it. Thomas, with his escort, went into the royal bedchamber.

At the sight of the King, all his anger and agitation disappeared in great waves of compassion and revulsion.

Since his last visit terrible things had happened to the dying King. His head had begun to swell horribly, his hair had been shaved off, his skull covered with plasters and angry scabs. His skin was blotched like rotting apples.

Thomas knelt at the bedside, choking back his tears. He said, 'Your Majesty must abandon this devise.'

The body lay still, corpse-like. Then slowly that putrescent head turned, and a pair of tortured eyes looked at Thomas coldly. '*Must*, your Grace?'

'It is treason. Against your august father.'

'We,' said Edward, with a tiny burst of strength, 'are above treason.'

It is impossible to argue with a dying man. But Thomas pleaded and begged. Until in the end Edward gathered up all the strength left in his wasted body, and sat up in bed gasping and quivering.

For one hideous moment he heeled over, and that scabrous melon-like head hung over the kneeling Thomas. Then, with another tremendous effort, he righted himself and cried, 'My Lord of Canterbury, I as your true Prince command you to obey my will.' He fell back on to the pillows, exhausted. 'You cannot know, Thomas, how much it grieves me that *you* of all people, *you* should be the only one of my Council to doubt me in this matter.'

Such reproach from his Sovereign nearly broke Thomas' heart. After all, if all the learned Judges had thought it safe to sign, surely he was being cautious? Besides, his King had commanded him.

On the other hand – to sign one's name to such a document was to ally oneself irrevocably to Northumberland's fortunes. And, if *they* failed, and Mary came to the throne – then that signature would serve for his own death warrant.

Northumberland was waiting, patient and sardonic. 'Well, has he made up your mind for you, Master Archbishop?'

He took up the pen. He said to Northumberland, 'I could say that I am signing to save the Reformed Church of this country, and the Reformation. I am not. I am signing because my King commanded me – and because I am the most contemptible of men, and cannot stand alone.' And he staggered weeping from the chamber.

Northumberland sanded the fresh signature, and went back to fanning himself with the document.

So, the unending struggle for power reached yet another crisis, with each man staking his head (and the heads of many innocent bystanders) on the outcome.

How much longer could the King be expected to live? demanded Northumberland.

A fortnight at the outside, hazarded the physicians. Right! So the sooner he got Mary into his hands the better. The Council wrote a pathetic letter to Mary, begging her to visit her dying brother, who was calling on her name night and day.

Mary was no fool. A letter signed by, among others, the man who had declared herself bastard: Thomas Cranmer, whom she had almost come to think of as Antichrist: such a letter needed the most careful thought.

Quickly she assembled a retinue, and set off. But instead of heading due south, where her unhappy brother lay longing for her, she headed due north, and went to her house at Kenninghall in Norfolk. She arrived there on the day her brother died. It was July 6th. Shrewd, angry, bitter, she set about recruiting her loyal followers.

CHAPTER 20

Pretty Lady Jane was terrified. And she did not know why.

But something sinister was happening. Her attendants had wakened her at dawn. She had been bathed and powdered and scented, and dressed in a robe of oyster silk and a coronet of pearls.

Why? Why? She kept asking. No one replied. Then at ten o'clock they silently and suddenly left her. She was alone in the great reception room.

The house was silent, though from the courtyard came the clatter of hooves, the scrunch of carriage wheels. But she was left until eleven o'clock for her imagination to present her with fears that grew more and more bizarre as the morning passed.

Yet when finally she discovered what was afoot it was far worse than anything she had imagined...

The great double doors opened. A host of people entered the room, as stately and slow as a Spanish pavan: His Grace of Canterbury, Suffolk (her father), Northumberland, their Duchesses, Judges and Lords of the Council. And every one of them knelt before Jane!

All except her father, who stepped forward and took her hand and said, 'My daughter, your cousin Edward is dead. You, my daughter, are Queen of England.'

Queen of England! It was too much, too dangerous and frightening a thing to be. Mary would deal terribly with anyone who tried to oust her from the Throne. So, even, would Elizabeth. Besides, she did not want to be a Queen. She looked fearfully round: at the gloating faces of her parents, at scowling Northumberland, at the one compassionate face in that room – Canterbury's.

She went down in a dead faint. The Dukes of Northumberland and Suffolk were appalled. Their claimant to the Throne needed to be of stronger stuff than this.

Even Cranmer, the one person who understood her fears, felt his compassion tainted with selfish doubts. Was this frail studious child really the person to take and hold the Crown? And against a hard-bitten Tudor like Mary?

And where was Mary?

Jane's pathetic pleas to be allowed to live in peace were either ignored or rebutted angrily. Sick and weak with despair and fear she was taken by barge from Sion House to take up her royal residence in the Tower. She was proclaimed Queen of her capital City.

Mary, hearing of her brother's death, wrote to the Council commanding them to recognize herself as Queen.

Since the Council had already recognized (and indeed proclaimed) Jane as Queen, there was only really one answer to this letter. The Council wrote to Mary, pointing out very reasonably (though not perhaps very tactfully) that she couldn't be Queen because she was a bastard, and therefore must show herself a loyal subject to Queen Jane.

Northumberland gave this dangerous letter first to Cranmer for signature. Thomas did not pick up his pen. He looked pale and sick. 'Come, your Grace,' Northumberland said brusquely. 'You are in too deep to draw back now.'

It was true. Thomas was in deep. Oh, if only he had not so weakly signed that damning Engagement. If only he had refused, given up his high office, fled the country if necessary, ended his days with his dear Margarete and his friends in Nuremberg.

But he hadn't. He had signed away his life. And now he must do it again. He picked up the pen and signed.

But it is not possible to be despondent for ever. Jane *was* Queen, and if Mary instead had been proclaimed she might already be making a list of heretics. And that list would be headed by the name of Thomas Cranmer. He realized something else: it was his King who had commanded the Council to set Henry's Will at nought and proclaim Jane Queen of England. Mary was wrong. She had failed utterly in her duty of Christian obedience to the King her brother.

Yet rumours, dreadful rumours, began to reach the Council. The gentry of Norfolk and Suffolk were flocking to Mary's house in Kenninghall, offering to fight for her. In Buckingham and Oxford she was proclaimed Queen. It was even said that she had moved to Framlingham Castle, near the Suffolk coast, where her cousin the Emperor Charles V could easily send her aid.

The rumours grew worse. More and more nobles were flocking to Mary. Northumberland rode off at the head of his troops to crush the revolt. Cranmer stayed behind in the Tower attending on Queen Jane, helping to protect London, and writing endless letters to the noblemen and officers of every shire urging them to be loyal to Jane.

But it was a dreadful time. His heart ached for the young Queen, pale and listless while her father tried to bully her into some semblance of a Queen. His mind was hungry for news of what was really happening in the country. And all he got was more rumour: the fleet, sent to Yarmouth to prevent Mary fleeing the country, had threatened to throw their officers into the sea if they didn't join Mary. The officers, very sensibly, proclaimed Mary Queen and placed the fleet at her disposal.

Broadsheets supporting Mary had appeared on the London streets, and had only been discouraged by cutting off a few ears. Forty thousand men were crammed into Framlingham Castle, all fervently supporting Mary.

Then real news began to come in. Northumberland had marched his men from Cambridge to Bury St Edmunds, and then back again, a manoeuvre that seemed to suggest a certain lack of resolution. Bishop Ridley tried to explain to the people at Paul's Cross why Jane must be Queen, and the people had angrily refused to listen. In the sumptuous royal apartments at the Tower, Cranmer and the little Queen waited for one good bit of news to lift their hearts.

And none came.

Tensions were at breaking point. Army faced army; sickles and pruning hooks faced swords and halberds. It needed only a spark now to set the tinder aflame.

But the hot, dry summer days passed; and still the flames did not crackle into life. Without much argument, without much conscious thought the people of England had made up their collective mind. They liked Mary, they wanted Mary, they wanted Great Harry's daughter for their Queen.

This collective decision swept like a silent wind across the country. Northumberland's army melted away. Fear lurked in the eyes of the Lords of the Council. Mere survival was suddenly sweet. Power could wait for another day.

Only Cranmer was untainted by these fears. In his mind there was now no question of Mary becoming Queen. King

Edward had named Jane on his deathbed. And Mary, in trying to usurp the Crown, was guilty of disobedience to her Sovereign, the greatest sin of all to Thomas' mind. He wrote to Lord Rich, ordering him to support Queen Jane, and he had the letter signed by sixteen Lords of the Council.

But, that same day, four of the signatories of that letter held secret discussions with the Lord Mayor of London, and persuaded him to proclaim Mary Queen.

The Proclamation was made in Cheapside. The news spread through the capital like a forest fire. Everyone rushed on to the streets, the bells of every church were rung, bonfires were lit, the fountains were soon running with wine, a great Te Deum was sung in a crowded St Paul's. Never had the stolid English rejoiced so spontaneously or so whole-heartedly.

But for the dark and silent Tower the clangour of the bells, the distant singing, had a sombre message. Queen Jane, left alone but for her ladies, feeling disaster in her bones, was not reassured when the door was flung open and her father rushed into the room, wild and disordered, and cried, 'You can stop sitting under that canopy, my girl. *You're* not Queen of England any more, Mary is.'

Jane rose and walked away from the royal canopy. With great dignity she said, 'I have never done anything with greater happiness, Father. I became Queen only in duty to yourself and my mother.'

The Duke, beside himself with fear and rage, said, 'Now don't imagine *that* will save you, you crafty little vixen. If you try blaming your mother and me you'll soon be in even worse trouble.' And he rushed out and straightaway went and proclaimed Mary on Tower Hill.

That night, while all London rejoiced, the people in the royal apartments of the Tower were as wretched and hopeless as the poor devils in the dungeons below them: knowing, with awful certainty, that they would very soon be in the dungeons themselves. High treason was a phrase that murdered hope.

And Thomas Cranmer? His world was collapsing about him. He had seen his duty with awful clarity: to oppose with all the strength of his being the disobedient Mary. And he had been betrayed.

England had two proclaimed Queens, both guilty of high treason. One must inevitably lose her head, and now it looked as though it must be Jane. Yet surely a just God would not let a usurper, and a disobedient one at that, come to the Throne?

But if He did? Mary was a Papist. It would be the end of the Reformed Church in England, the end of his Prayer Book and his Bible, the end of Thomas Cranmer. Now his opposition to her, though as strong as ever, had ceased to give him courage. He was again the fearful, anxious scholar he had always been. The only possible course open to him was to beg for mercy. And that was something he could not, would not, do. Not from pride; rather from some refusal to treat with one who had flouted Christian obedience to a King.

But if Queen Jane was behaving with dignity; and Thomas Cranmer was coming to terms with almost certain death, the Lords of the Council assembled at Baynard's Castle were in a state of panic.

Frantically, they were writing letters: to Mary, describing themselves as 'your most humble, faithful and obedient subjects having always (God we take to witness) remained so since the death of Edward', and saying that although they had had to dissemble they had now proclaimed her Queen.

They also wrote to Northumberland ordering him to submit to Mary, and threatening to declare him traitor if he did not do so (though by the time this letter arrived he had already proclaimed Mary at Cambridge).

Yet once again Cranmer's signature was required. Even though they had betrayed him, they still had the conspirators' desire to implicate as many of their number as possible. But where *was* the Archbishop?

He was with Queen Jane. In her bewildered state of mind she had sent for the one person who had shown her kindness.

At his entrance she had flung open her arms in a gesture of happiness and cried, 'Your Grace! I am no longer Queen. Is not that wonderful?' Then she became immediately serious. 'But – I am still fearful. What has happened?'

'Mary has been proclaimed Queen, your Majesty.'

'Oh, do not call me by that horrible title,' she cried.

'I am sorry. But to me you still are, and should be, Queen.'

She sank down on to a stool, gestured to him to be seated. 'What will they do to me, your Grace?'

He was silent. He looked grey. At last he said, 'You and I are both in great danger, my child. We are both guilty of treason. But – you are young, and you had no wish to be Queen, I know. I think the Lady Mary – Queen Mary, will be merciful.'

'You mean – if I go back to living quietly at Bradgate? Oh, your Grace, that would be so wonderful that I weep to think of it.'

'I think – ' he said with his shy smile – 'I think that is very possible.'

'You don't think – she would – cut off my head?'

'No, no,' he murmured, shaking his head. (Oh, if only that was the worst they could do to one!)

'You are so kind. Will you pray for me, your Grace?'

'With all my heart.' But now there was a messenger, booted and spurred, stamping through the doorway. 'Your Grace. The Council require your presence at Baynard's Castle.'

The Lords of the Council started at his entrance. They bowed low. They weren't quite sure of themselves with Canterbury. An easy, amenable fellow they would have said at one time. But now, with the chief bully away in Cambridge (and ready for the block if they weren't mistaken) they were not so sure. You never quite knew which way his mind would work.

They gave him the letters. He carried them over to a blaze of candles and read them both with care. The Lords of the Council watched him anxiously.

Then, to their surprise, he sat down at the table and without a word signed both letters. Then he walked from the room, wearily dragging his feet, still without a word or even a glance for his fellow Councillors. It was finished. The Reformation in England, the reformed Church, he himself – all were finished. To sign, or not to sign, mattered nothing. Things would take their own bloody and terrible course now, whatever was said or written. The Lords of the Council had only one thought left in their collective heads: to save their necks. And the common sort, witless, mindless, were even now shouting for the usurper. The Voice of England was speaking.

As he rode back to the Tower the streets were still noisy with bells, and singing, and the scraping of fiddles. Drink was pressed on this lonely, black-robed traveller; filthy hands tried to pull him off his horse to join the dancing.

Sometimes, he was recognized by his long beard and greeted with mock reverence or even insults.

None of this touched him. He was cocooned in despair. Everything was lost. Was it true, what Osiander had once said, that he, Cranmer, had betrayed the Reformation by the weakness of his nature, and his lack of zeal? That he had only moved when Henry told him to?

No. Though he was one always ready to cry *mea culpa*, he did not think this was wholly true. In Edward's reign he had worked tremendously to give the new Church a form and a liturgy in keeping with the new thought. And he had risked his life to put the Protestant Jane on the Throne (though even that, he admitted bleakly, had in the first place been due to fear rather than to reforming conviction).

Despair. Through his pliant nature he had failed his God, his fellow reformers, his country. And now he must die.

And, to add to all these troubles, there still lodged in his heart that tiny arrow, tipped with the poison of jealousy.

Chapter 21

Survival was all that mattered now. All roads, it seemed, led to Framlingham. The Great North Road, the winding Suffolk lanes, were crammed with gentry, nobles, priests, commoners, clerks, all hurrying to assure Queen Mary of their allegiance and, if there was any possibility of being linked with the Jane Grey party, to beg for pardon for a fleeting aberration.

To everyone's surprise, Mary pardoned all who sought pardon (except for the Northumberland family and their advisers and Bishop Ridley).

Thomas Cranmer did not go to Framlingham. Nor did he seek pardon. He stayed at Lambeth carefully putting his affairs in order as he awaited arrest. He urged foreign Protestants to flee the country, illegally without passports if necessary, rather than stay and be trapped.

But his most terrible problem was Margarete and the children. As the widow of a traitor her position would be an impossible one. Her only hope, even of survival, was to be smuggled out of the country and back to Nuremberg.

And here, he told himself, he had three problems: first, to persuade her to leave him to his fate; second, to make the highly dangerous plans for her secret voyage; third, for both of them to find the strength for this amputation.

For amputation it must be. When she had gone before there had been some chance of a joyful reunion. This time, the only possible reunion would be in Heaven.

There was an alternative, of course: to flee the country himself, and seek refuge with the German Protestants.

This thought was so wonderful that it brought tears to his eyes. It was so tempting that he immediately recognized it as being of the Devil. 'Get thee behind me, Satan,' he whispered. *His* place was here, in England. He would die a Protestant martyr, and strengthen the waverers. If he fled, countless English Protestants would follow his example, leaving England open to the Papists. It was a fearful decision to make. But he was a brave and determined man in September, 1553.

Riding back to Lambeth he told himself that he must break the news to her as soon as he arrived home. There was not an hour to lose. At any moment the knock might come at his door. No time for explanations, plans. No time for tears, no time even for farewells.

He left his horse with a groom, and walked through the garden to the house. He walked slowly, a man who carried one of the heaviest of human burdens, the knowledge that he is about to break a loved one's heart.

The sound of laughter led him to the orchard.

Young Thomas was perched in a tree of apples, passing down fruit to his mother and sister. It was an occupation that was causing tremendous laughter and giggling. The young Thomas cried 'Father!' and slid down from the tree, and Margaret ran and flung her arms about his legs; and Margarete came and kissed him fondly. 'Thomas, my dear, you look tired.'

He couldn't do it! Yet he knew he must. Even now, the Officers of the Crown might be riding over Lambeth Bridge.

He said, almost curtly, 'Come to my study.'

She looked startled, followed him.

He opened the study door for her, held a chair. She sat down, troubled. He sat down at his desk. Suddenly he smiled. 'Do not look so fearful, Liebchen.'

She tried to look more cheerful. 'What is wrong, Thomas?'

He said, 'Catholic Mary has usurped the throne. England will be no place for Protestants.'

The colour drained from her face. She stared at him. 'You mean – we must leave England? Dearest, we should be safe in Nuremberg,' she said wistfully.

'*You* must leave England,' he said. 'You – and the children.'

'And you?' she asked sharply.

'I must stay. My duty.'

She said, 'We go together. Or not at all.'

He said, quietly, 'Would you come between me and my duty to my God?'

'You have also a duty to me and our children,' she said stubbornly.

He said, '"Thou shalt love the Lord thy God with all thy heart. And thy neighbour as thyself." God comes first, Margarete.'

She jumped to her feet. 'I am not your neighbour, Thomas. I am your *wife*, flesh of your flesh. Dear God, has human love no place in your heart?'

She had hurt him deeply. 'Love?' he said in amazement. 'Why else do I want you all to be safe in Germany? While I – ?' he could not help adding.

She was silent. Then, 'What will they do to you?'

'That depends. On whether they try me for treason – or for heresy.'

She gave a choked cry. Then she said angrily, 'Do you really think I would run away and leave you to face – that?'

He said, 'Do you *really* think I could face that, knowing you were – in their reach?'

She said, 'Thomas, you are my husband. I am your wife. Whatever happens, I must be by your side.' She came and sat at his feet, clasping his knees.

He kissed the top of her loved head. It was no good. He could argue no more tonight, torment himself no more.

But – '*heaviness may endure for a night, but joy cometh in the morning*'. One of his favourite psalms. And it was true. The morning brought the most wonderful piece of news he had yet heard: he was ordered to supply an inventory of his goods, so that the Council could arrange a pension for him, provided only that he ceased to be Archbishop and to make any public pronouncements on religion. He fell on his knees, and thanked God mightily for thus softening the hearts of the wicked. He and Margarete knew a deep thankfulness that the question of her leaving the country had been so quickly resolved.

Yet this statesmanlike forbearance on Mary's part was Cranmer's undoing. Both the Court and the people began to gossip. Bonner wrote disparagingly that 'Master Canterbury is become very humble and ready to submit himself in all things, but that will not serve.'

The rumour spread throughout the country that Cranmer had offered to celebrate Mass before Mary at St Paul's, and had ordered one Thornden to say Mass in Canterbury Cathedral.

Morice said hesitantly, 'Your Grace, things are being said which I think you should know.'

Thomas looked up greyly. 'What is being said, Ralph?'

'Your Grace, forgive me. But – the people are saying you have bought your freedom by submissiveness and humility.'

'Submissiveness and humility are Christian virtues, Ralph.'

'I thought you should know, your Grace.'

'So that I may stiffen my backbone? What else do they say?'

Morice said, 'Far, far worse. They say – ' He repeated the rumours about the Mass.

Thomas stared at his secretary in amazement. 'About *me*?'

Morice nodded.

'And that – that is why I have escaped arrest?'

'Rather, your Grace, that *that* is how you bought your freedom from arrest.'

'Monstrous! How *dare* they? Oh, Ralph, I am a poor creature in many ways. But – to buy my life with a Mass!'

As soon as his secretary had gone this cautious man had one of his rare outbursts of impetuosity. He seized his pen and wrote out a declaration against the Mass. The allegations that he had offered to say Mass before the Queen were, he said, lies spread by Satan who had himself invented the Mass. And Thornden was a 'false, flattering and lying monk'. He decided to append his archiepiscopal seal to the declaration and to affix it to the door of Paul's and of every church in London.

With a new Catholic Queen on the throne (and one who had every reason to hate him) this was a brave, defiant, but self-destroying action.

And he knew it. Once more he set his house in order. Once more he tried to persuade Margarete to take the children to Germany. To no avail. All he could persuade her to do was to move to the house at Ford.

Just in time. On September 13th he was summoned before the Council, who accused him of sedition in his declaration against the Mass.

The following day he was summoned to the Star Chamber. Gardiner was presiding. Several of the Council Members were men who had served on Jane's short-lived Council. Clearly, Queen Mary was determined to be merciful.

But not to Thomas Cranmer. As he stood before the Council he watched the hard, gloating face of Gardiner; and knew that for him there was to be no mercy.

Eventually he was taken out, to spend an anxious hour while his judges debated. Then he was brought back.

His knees were weak, his head was swimming. Gardiner, pulling his robes about him, fixed a steely eye upon him and said, 'Thomas Cranmer, you were the most fortunate of men. Despite your damnable treason in supporting the usurper Jane, despite your vicious usage in the past not only of our Queen but also of her saintly mother, Queen Mary was prepared to allot you a pension and let you end your days in peace. But, alas, your seditious action in declaring against the Mass has revived the guilt of your treason which can no longer be overlooked. You will be imprisoned in the Tower while your case is considered.'

The doors crashed open behind him. A mailed hand fell on each shoulder. And he had known it all before. But then, he had had Great Harry's ring in his pocket. Now he had nothing. Suddenly he was very afraid.

Despite his humility, he was dismayed to find himself handed over to a common gaoler who had difficulty in signing the receipt for his body. It boded ill.

The gaoler led him along the dark, echoing passages he remembered so well. And at last said, 'Here you are, Number Six in the Garden Tower. Nice name, isn't it? And next to the Watergate. You'll hear plenty of coming and going, even if you can't see a thing. Go on. Get in,' the man said impatiently. 'The Duke of Northumberland was in there till they topped him. So it should be all right for you.'

'In – there?' said Thomas. He peered into a small cell of rough stone, with a table and a stool. Already a malevolent, damp cold was reaching out to touch his face. 'Thank you, gaoler,' he said courteously. And stepped into the cell.

The clash of metal on metal, the grating of a huge key, departing footsteps. And a darkness and a blackness such as he had never known.

He began to shake so violently that he could scarcely stand. He groped his way in the darkness and found the stool. He sat down, and struggled for control.

But his body was quite beyond his authority. His teeth chattered, his every limb jerked spasmodically. It wasn't fear. It was the shock of hearing that key turn, of knowing that that door stood irrevocably between him and the sunlight.

After what might well have been several hours, his body was calmer. But his teeth still chattered from the pervading cold.

So it was time to get his mind into some sort of order.

Bitterly he reproached himself for not having ensured the safety of his wife and children. Yet what could he have done, in the face of Margarete's determined loyalty?

In the nature of things, he also needed to consider his own condition. A more worldly man than he would have already seen what bribery could do in the way of food and wine and comfort. But all Thomas' thoughts were on light. Light! The one thing without which he might indeed lose his reason.

After what might have been a few hours or half a day (there was no means of knowing) the door squealed open and he was blinded by the light from a lantern. The gaoler banged a jug of water down on the table and a crust of bread.

Thomas' mouth was parched. He could only croak. 'Candles? I have money.'

'Candles is a penny.' He took Thomas' coin, pulled a candle out of his pocket, lit it at the lantern, and stuck it to the table with its own wax.

And he stayed thus for two months, knowing nothing, hearing nothing, knowing only that his cell grew ever colder and damper. Winter was coming. And if he did not die by other means, he would die of the murderous cold.

Yet it was as well that, buried alive, he did hear no news. The Queen, incensed by Cranmer's declaration against the Mass, abandoned all thoughts of being merciful. Cranmer, she decided, must be the scapegoat for everything. Others were pardoned. But for Cranmer there would be no mercy.

Parliament enthusiastically supported her. They agreed that Cranmer had divorced Henry and Katherine against their will, in ways unlawful and corrupt. His name was vilified. And it was not difficult to stir up the people's hatred. Was not this the man who had taken away their loved images and superstitions, had foisted on them an English liturgy that they needed to try to understand, instead of the incomprehensible Latin. The sooner Mary executed him and brought a little colour back into things, the better they would like it.

Thomas knew nothing of this. All his intellect had to feed on was his imagination. But that was a plentiful storehouse indeed. Had he not seen men racked, quartered, burnt?

So he prayed, and thought, and feared. Until one morning his cell door screeched open and two soldiers seized him roughly and, weak from confinement as he was, half carried, half shoved him up into the world of the living.

Blinded by the thin November sunlight, it took him some time to realize what was happening. He was given a bucket of cold water in which to wash, and a clean habit, and a comb for his hair and beard. Then they led him to an open space and indicated that he should stand beside a solitary figure: a man, all in black, leaning on a heavy axe.

This sinister vision filled him with thankfulness. So death had come sooner than expected. 'Today shalt thou be with Me in paradise,' he murmured.

Other figures were now being marshalled on to the open space: three young men, and a slim girl dressed from head to foot in black. And now he recognized them all: Ambrose and Henry Dudley, Guilford Dudley, and his wife Jane, the nine-day Queen.

Poor child! He forgot his own fears in pity for her. She had been leaning heavily on her husband. But now she was dragged away, and the soldiers roughly formed the prisoners into single line behind the man with the axe.

Quickly a line of halberdiers formed on each side of the prisoners. A muffled drumbeat began. The melancholy procession set out for its unknown destination, the bright axe now carried aloft before them.

After two months in a living tomb, he found walking almost impossible. Once he stumbled and fell. Two halberdiers dragged him to his feet and shoved him forward again. But now, after staggering and floundering for a mile (to the great amusement of the crowds) he saw where he was being taken: the Guildhall. And he knew, with searing disappointment, that it was not death but trial that faced him.

Clearly, Mary Tudor had not done with Thomas Cranmer yet.

Norfolk, back in power once more, headed the Commission of peers and common law Judges. In a few hours it was all over; Cranmer and the other men were sentenced to be hanged, drawn and quartered at Tyburn; Jane to be burnt or beheaded at the pleasure of Queen Mary.

Then they were marched back to the Tower, each contemplating his or her own terrible fate. Yet, fearful as each one's burden was, Thomas Cranmer had an additional load to bear. He had stayed in England determined to face martyrdom for the sake of the Reformation. And now, instead of dying as a heretic, he was condemned to die for high treason, a crime he abhorred.

He was incensed. He, Thomas Cranmer, who had steeled himself for martyrdom, was condemned to die a shameful and agonizing death as a traitor! It was monstrous.

Worse followed. One December morning, when a damp rime hung the walls of his cell, his door was flung open and the Constable of the Tower entered.

Thomas, courteous as always, rose to his feet, though he had to support himself by clinging to the table. Was this the end? If so, God give him strength in his frailty.

The Constable, without a word, handed him a document. Thomas held it to the light of the candle. But poor eyesight, and the trembling of his hand made it impossible for him to read. He said, 'Master Constable, read it I beg you.'

'It is an Act of Attainder, passed by Parliament, declaring you to be guilty of high treason,' he said flatly.

Thomas sank on to his chair. 'Master Constable, since my return from Guildhall I have been denied pens and paper.'

'On instructions from above,' said the Constable.

'But you would not deny them to me when I say I wish to write to her Majesty?'

The Constable pursed his lips. 'No.'

Thomas wrote an abject letter to the Queen begging for pardon. Rather than be hanged for treason he would demean himself in any way required.

The Queen did not reply. She never risked contaminating her immortal soul by reading letters from heretics.

Nevertheless, a week before Christmas the Council, in a seasonable concern for the health of their prisoners, decreed that the Dudleys and Cranmer should be allowed to walk in the Tower gardens.

Once again he stepped outside his icy cell. Once again he came up blinking into the winter sunlight.

His heart stirred as it had not done since he had lost Margarete. The world was sweet, even on this December day. To walk leaning on his staff was sweet, to stand still and gaze at distant London was sweet, to bow to the Lady Jane and receive her curtsey was sweet, even though he was strictly forbidden to speak to the other prisoners.

So they walked, with their burdens of death on their shoulders, and in their step a slight spring, since it was well known that for a prisoner to be granted this liberty was often a sign that he would be shown mercy.

He had written to the Queen, begging for pardon. Soon afterwards he had been allowed to walk in the gardens. Surely it must mean that he had touched the royal heart?

And, sure enough, the good news came. Mary decided she would not punish for treason against herself a man who had been guilty of treason against God. She would not execute Cranmer for treason. She would execute him for heresy. But first she would allow him to take part in a Disputation which would soon show that he and his followers were ignorant and unlearned heretics.

When Thomas heard this news he fell on his knees and thanked God from a full heart. He would be a martyr after all.

The imprisoned Dudleys, walking in the gardens, also regarded this as a sign of leniency. And they were right. Mary

Tudor had little stomach for executing her personal enemies. It was only to those she judged the enemies of her God that she was merciless.

Yes. Thomas Cranmer was uplifted. Death was inevitable. But now his death would be a witness to the new faith. He would not have died in vain.

Yet – was death inevitable? Once again he heard rumours: another rebellion, this time by Protestants from Kent led by Wyatt, and by Suffolk in the Midlands.

A Protestant insurrection! He was deeply saddened and appalled. Rebellion was something he both hated and feared. And then he had another, alarming thought. If the rebels won, they would rescue him from prison and reinstate him. And, since he believed that anyone who rebelled against his lawful Prince went straight to Hell, he would be swept down with them. Instead of a martyr's crown, the brand mark of the Devil.

So he prayed earnestly for the defeat of the only people whose victory could have saved him from the flames.

And his prayers were answererd. The revolt was put down. One February night he was awakened by a tumult at the Watergate, just outside his cell: shouts, yells, the sound of blows, of staves striking flesh, cries, screams, whimpers. Prisoners were being delivered at the Watergate, and the officers of the Tower were having a little brutal enjoyment at their expense.

Violence! Brutality! Thomas called himself weak and squeamish. But it sickened him. He prayed to Another who had known what it was like to be helpless in the hands of cruel men. He prayed, knowing that soon the day must come when he himself must be the mistreated prisoner.

And even as he thought and prayed thus, he heard the key turning in the lock. Two gaolers seized him and bundled him out into the passage. They steered him through narrow passages crowded with men – soldiers, prisoners, wounded and dying men. It was pandemonium. The gaolers forced a way through for him, trampling and kicking those who strewed the floor of the narrow corridors.

At last his escort stopped. A cell door was unlocked and opened. He was pushed inside. The door was locked behind him.

It was a larger cell. But his poor eyes could make little of it in the candlelight. There was a bigger table, there were human figures, black and grey, vague as ghosts, grouped round the table. He peered at them anxiously.

A voice, a warm, friendly, welcoming voice cried, 'Thomas!'

It was the first friendly voice he had heard for months. It unmanned him completely. 'Ridley!' he cried, and wept uncontrollably.

Nicholas Ridley took his hands 'Thomas! Your Grace. We are indeed honoured. Are you to lodge with us?'

'I know nothing,' Thomas said brokenly.

'We shall make a brave four,' said Ridley. 'Here are Hugh Latimer and John Bradford. And now we have our Archbishop for good company.' He led Thomas to a chair talking away all the time. 'Doubtless they needed your cell for the rebels. So they brought you here, thanks be to God. Why, it will be like the old days at Lambeth when you and Morice and I talked the sun down the sky.'

He sounded cheerful, even carefree. But he had been shocked at the appearance of his old master. The Archbishop looked lost and feeble. He trembled, he almost tottered.

Hugh Latimer, whose sturdy mind was set in a frail body, understood Thomas' needs. He produced a cup of water. Thomas drank shakily, the water dribbling down his ragged beard.

The water revived him a little. And he began to realize that, for the first time for many months, he was among friends: friends moreover who shared his beliefs and his dangers.

He also learned, at last, some details about the Disputation. It was to be held at Oxford. And Latimer and Ridley were to be present with him.

This was joyful news indeed. For a long time now he had known the loneliness of the deserted Christ. Every voice had been contemptuous, every face hostile. Now he was among friends again, even though they were as despitefully used as he.

The prison cell became a study. The four men argued, discussed, read such books as they were allowed, prepared their arguments for the Disputation even though as yet they could only guess at the subjects. Outside, the counter-Reformation was getting into its stride. Queen and Council were clearing away the legal tangle that prevented them from burning heretics, Protestant theologians were facing danger and death to escape from the country; married priests sadly put away their wives; Jane Grey was beheaded; Mary put her own sister Elizabeth in the Tower but refrained from cutting off her head; Cranmer's Book of Common Prayer was banned; the dead Katherine of Aragon was remarried to the dead Henry VIII, thus legitimizing Mary, who was preparing to marry Philip of Spain; and the colonies of Protestant refugees from abroad were despatched back to their own countries and the savagery of the Catholic Emperor, Mary obligingly telling him which ships they were on. The cruel fires were burning across the face of Europe. It would not be long now before they were lit again in England.

Chapter 22

Margarete, sick with worry, lay hidden at Ford. She saw no one, heard no news. All her attempts, all her pleadings, to visit her husband, proved futile.

Then, one day, there was the clatter of hooves in the stable yard. She looked out fearfully from a window.

It was Edward Whitchurch! She ran to the door. 'Edward! What news? What news of Thomas?' In her relief she seized his hands. 'Oh, I do not even know whether he is alive or dead.'

But he remained grave. 'He is alive. But the news *is* bad, Margarete. He has been found guilty of heresy.'

He had to put an arm about her to save her from falling. Slowly, they walked into the parlour. 'There is worse,' he said. '*You* are in urgent danger of arrest and imprisonment.'

She said scornfully, 'That is not worse. *I* do not matter. But – poor Thomas.'

He said, 'And your dear children? What of them, when both you and Thomas are imprisoned?'

She was silent. Then she said brokenly, 'Could not you, Edward, do something, make some arrangements, something – ?'

'I am in as great danger as you. I too must leave England.' His voice became commanding. 'Now Margarete, there is a ship lying near Dover. Everything is arranged.'

'No,' she said. 'Do you really think I would leave England when my husband – ?'

He cut in harshly. 'If you do *not* leave England you sign your own death warrant. And you condemn your children to beggary and starvation.'

She gazed at him piteously. He said, more gently, 'Thomas is beyond any help *we* can give him, Margarete.'

'Give me a week,' she said. 'I cannot – '

'Not even a day,' he said. 'Even now could be too late. Any delay endangers my life as well as your own.'

She pondered. Then she said, 'I am a married woman, Master Whitchurch. I can go only with my husband's permission.'

He was exasperated. 'The ship sails in a few days. How *can* I get Thomas' permission? Besides, he himself has begged you to go. You know it.'

'I cannot travel with you without his permission,' she said woodenly. 'It would be most unseemly.'

He said bitterly, 'You are endangering all our lives. Fleeing without passports is dangerous enough. But – '

'Dear Edward,' she said softly. 'I would not add to *your* risks. But – it is necessary, my friend.'

A key turned in the lock. The heavy door swung open. A gaoler stood in the doorway. The four prisoners stared at him fearfully. He beckoned to Cranmer.

'Hurry up. You've got a visitor.' He led him down the long corridors to a waiting room.

A visitor! Margarete? 'Dear Jesus, let it be Margarete,' he prayed.

But it was a man. 'Five minutes,' said the gaoler.

'Edward, my old friend!' They embraced fondly. Yet he still felt the sting of jealousy in his heart.

Edward said, 'Now listen, Thomas. I have a passage on a ship to France. I also have a passage for Mistress Cranmer and your children.'

'Oh thank God,' cried Thomas. 'And thank *you*, Edward. Those three dear mopsies have been my care day and night.'

Whitchurch said, bleakly, 'Mistress Cranmer will not travel with me without your permission.'

'Foolish girl,' he said fondly. 'Tell her I not only give permission, I *command* her to go with you.' He looked at his friend searchingly. 'Edward, will you answer a man in the shadow of death truthfully and honestly?'

'Of course, Thomas.'

Thomas said, 'Are you in love with Margarete?'

Whitchurch looked startled, embarrassed, afraid. Then he said, 'Yes. Thomas. But there has never – '

'I know that, man. But I ask because – Edward, it would ease my burden if I thought that – when I am gone – you might take Margarete to wife. And be a father to my children.'

Both men were silent. Then Edward said, 'You are a good man, Thomas. It will not be my fault if – ' But there were no words left, only tears. The gaoler reappeared. Their parting was brief and hurried. Thomas was led back to his cell. He was, for that short walk, a happy man. Margarete and the children were almost on their way to freedom. And he had boldly plucked the poisoned arrow from his heart.

Chapter 23

On March 12th, 1554, Cranmer, Ridley and Latimer left the Tower on their journey to Oxford and the Disputation.

After the tomb-like atmosphere of a cell in winter, the brisk and boisterous March day was like a great draught of wine. Instead of shadowed arches, they looked up at clouds, dancing free across a limpid sky.

Thomas Cranmer in particular was uplifted. A month ago he had been on the verge of collapse and breakdown. Now, thanks to his friends, he was strong, self-assured. He was a scholar of international renown. What had he to fear from men like the Prolocutor Weston, a man he had once kept in his house to receive religious instruction? And the four friends in the Tower prison had chosen and rehearsed their arguments until every one was word perfect.

Yet, on arrival in Oxford, they were taken straight through the city, not stopping until they reached the North Gate, where they were unceremoniously bundled into the Bocardo, the common gaol, and lodged in separate cells.

After a month, Ridley and Latimer were taken to stay in private houses in the town. Thomas was left in gaol.

He was plunged into a disabling loneliness and homesickness. Sadly he remembered, oh so much: summer evenings at Knoll, with his Margarete, dinner with friends at Lambeth; even that strange interlude with the King on the Royal Barge.

But the next day, almost to his relief, he was brought before the Commissioners. Now, once more, he had regained his composure. He politely refused to sit down, and stood leaning on his staff, answering questions humbly and respectfully. He was at last given the three questions to be discussed – The Real Presence, Transubstantiation, and the Mass as a sacrifice. Two days later, the Disputation began.

It was held in the Divinity Schools of Oxford University. Cranmer, Ridley and Latimer each had to argue against thirty-three opponents, chosen from the most learned doctors of Oxford, Cambridge and Convocation.

Cranmer stood for six hours arguing in Latin above the jeers and chatter of the crowd. The next two days it was the turns of Ridley and Latimer, who were both abused and vilified.

Then, on the Friday, Cranmer was taken from prison to St Mary's Church, where Weston and the Commissioners informed him that he had been proved wrong in the Disputation, and invited him to recant.

Angrily Thomas said, 'I will not recant. And I protest that I was given no chance to state my case, arguing with five persons at once and unable to make myself heard.'

Before he could even finish his protest he was taken out and Ridley was brought in. Then Latimer. Then the three together were brought in. 'Do you recant?' demanded Weston.

They shook their heads. 'Then,' said Weston, 'you are condemned as heretics, and are no members of the Church.'

They had been tried, found guilty and condemned. The Disputation was concluded with a procession through Oxford. And Thomas knew that this glorious display of the Church militant and triumphant symbolized the end of all he had worked for, the end of the Reformation, the end of his life on earth.

CHAPTER 24

Bloody Mary (as she came to be known) was a kindly, devout and merciful woman. When Northumberland tried to usurp the Throne for his daughter-in-law, she pardoned almost all the conspirators, and flatly refused to execute Lady Jane Grey. Even to Cranmer she was prepared to show mercy.

She decided that, rather than risk a charge of vindictiveness from her tender conscience, she would pardon this old enemy. Surely to forgive him would commend her to Him who had said, 'Love them that hate you'.

Then, before she could even arrange his pension, he wrote a virulent declaration against the Mass. This, followed so soon by the Wyatt Rebellion, was her road to Damascus. Now she saw her Christian duty clear before her: with the help of men like Stephen Gardiner and Bishop Bonner, to bring back England into the arms of a sorrowing and merciful Pope. She consulted her Chancellor, asked his advice.

Stephen Gardiner smiled thinly. But those who knew him would have realized it was a smile of rare satisfaction. 'It will not be difficult, your Grace. The common sort will be delighted to be given back their images and their ritual.'

'And their true Faith,' Mary said sharply.

'Of course, your Majesty.' His smile faded. 'There is, however, one area where things may be difficult, where opposition may indeed be violent.'

Mary's thin lips looked suddenly as tight as a trap. Gardiner realized, with a surge of joy, that he was looking at the face of a fanatic. She said, 'Then *we* shall be more violent, my Lord.' She took a deep breath. 'Who *are* these traitors?'

He said calmly, 'The nobility and the gentry, your Grace.' He saw her look of surprise. 'Oh, they will attend Mass, and believe what they are told to believe.'

He saw from her face that he was on dangerous ground. 'Naturally. Because their Queen is bringing them back to the true Faith.'

'But – ?'

'They might not find it quite so easy to return the lands and money your Majesty's revered father gave them from the dissolution of the monasteries.'

They were both silent. At last Mary said, 'We must not be unfair to gentlemen whom my dear father honoured. That would indeed lie heavy on my conscience, Master Gardiner.'

Gardiner nodded. Then briskly, 'We must burn the reforming Bishops; but with full legality, lest any accuse us of vindictiveness.'

She said, 'If I burn his Grace of Canterbury, my own heart will call me vindictive'

Gardiner said firmly, 'If you do *not* burn Master Canterbury, your whole country, all Europe even, will call you infirm of purpose.' He dropped his voice. 'God Himself may feel that you are neglecting to do His will.'

Mary was silent. To have been given the powers of a Prince, and then neglect to use them in His service. It would be a terrible indictment if it were ever true. She said, and it was almost a whisper: 'Cranmer will die.'

Gardiner hid his sigh of relief. He said, 'Of course, what would help more than anything to restore the Papacy in England would be if Cranmer recanted before he burned.'

'If he recanted, he could not be burned.'

'Not as the law stands at present, your Grace. But – laws can be changed, as we well know.'

And for nearly a year and a half, after witnessing that triumphant return of the Church he had tried to banish from his country, Cranmer lay in the Bocardo gaol. Frail, sick, filthy, he was shut up in a hostile world. And when, on September 7th 1555 he was served with notice to appear on a charge of heresy in front of the Pope's Commissioners, the summons came almost as a relief.

In theory, Cranmer had to be tried by the Pope himself. In these circumstances, Pope Paul IV appointed James Brooks, Bishop of Gloucester, to be his judge.

When Thomas, stooped and ragged, entered the Court, he refused to uncover to Brooks, the Pope's representative. But he uncovered and knelt to Mary's representatives. Christian obedience to a Sovereign was still his guiding light.

But if seventeen months' solitude had left their marks on his haggard body, they had also left them on his mind. It had grown sluggish. And faced by a brilliant prosecutor he floundered in his efforts to defend himself.

A transcript of the proceedings was sent to the Vatican. And while the verdict was awaited, Mary increased her pressure on Cranmer. Stephen Gardiner was now dying. But another of Cranmer's enemies had taken his place by her side. Cardinal Pole had arrived in England, charged by Paul IV with restoring the Papacy. And he, like Mary and Gardiner, realized that this weak old man must die, and die shamefully. And, if a recantation could be got out of him, and a reason be found for still executing him, then the Reformation in England could be laid to rest and forgotten.

So, after his trial for heresy, he was sent back to his lonely cell in Bocardo, where he was visited by the Emperor's Spanish confessor, de Soto.

De Soto had already been sent to persuade Latimer and Ridley to recant. But Latimer had refused to see him and Ridley had been as forceful as de Soto in argument. As a result Cranmer's courteous and gentle reception misled him into telling Mary that a little more pressure might break the Archbishop's resistance.

The pressure took a grisly and horrible form. On the morning of October 16th, the key turned in his cell door. Four men with halberds led him forth.

He began to tremble, as he had trembled when he was first lodged in the Tower. The soldiers looked at him scornfully. And led him to a narrow stone spiral staircase.

'Where are you taking me, friends?' he asked the soldiers.

'To witness a little diversion, in case you was finding prison tedious,' said one of them cheerfully.

They came out on the prison roof. He was led across the wide area of the roof to a parapet. Then two of the soldiers seized his arms and held him firmly. 'Now! Look down there,' he was ordered.

He found he was looking down on to the town ditch. And on to a vast concourse of people, who formed a circle round two men chained to a stake, two men round whom faggots were being piled.

'Ridley!' he cried. 'Latimer!' Violently he struggled to shake off his guard. As well try to shake off two bears.

But now he had been seen. A murmur passed through the crowd, like a breeze through a cornfield. 'Master Cranmer. Master Cranmer.' Some shook their fists. Many pitied him.

Human justice took its slow and terrible course. There were prayers, exhortations, sermons, before lighted torches were flung on to the faggots heaped about two living men and a great sigh rose from the throats of the crowd and was lost in the crackling of the flames.

During the burning, two of the soldiers held Cranmer firm, twist and turn as he might; and a third forced his eyes open with unkind fingers so that he missed nothing. When at last they returned him to his cell he was in a state of shock. For hours he lay collapsed on the floor. He had seen what no human being is strong enough to see: the sight of two friends treading a fearful road that he himself must surely follow.

Yet, as soon as he had a little strength, he dragged himself to his feet. His shaking fingers groped for, found, a pen. He found paper.

Sometimes his shaking hand sent the pen jerking wildly across the paper. Yet, in the end, he had recorded Latimer's last triumphant cry: 'Be of good comfort, Master Ridley, and play the man; we shall this day light such a candle by God's grace in England as I trust shall never be put out.'

A candle! His two mistreated friends had lit a candle that should never be put out.

He, Thomas Cranmer, could put it out! By weakness, by cowardice, he could destroy all that their courage and steadfastness had achieved. Yet if only *he* could find courage and steadfastness somewhere in his miserable soul, he could turn that candle into a veritable star.

De Soto, arriving smug, and confident of victory, got short shrift. Thomas was so uncharacteristically rude to him that he refused to go again. Thomas was left to himself.

Yet after a time he began to long even for de Soto.

Thomas was not a particularly gregarious man. But he had been in solitary confinement for most of two years. Where the fear of death could not break his will, he began to fear that the denial of human companionship might do so.

Then, a miracle! He was transferred to the house of the Dean of Christ Church College. Clean clothes, good food and wine, the company and conversation of scholars. He began to see what he had almost come to think of as a foolish dream: life as it could be, should be: free, civilized, pleasant.

It was a haunting, tempting sight.

Then, suddenly, this subtle and dangerous period of temptation ended. The Pope had sat in judgement, excommunicated him, ordered that he be handed over to the secular power for punishment. He was burned in effigy in the streets of Rome; and found himself back in Bocardo.

From his solitary cell he looked back with bitter tears to life as it could be, should be. In his loneliness he cried out for one friendly voice.

And there was none. Only his enemies were all around him, silent, unseen: a whole world of enemies.

And more than a world. Where was God, that he had let Ridley die so terribly? Why did not God, to whom he prayed without ceasing, give some sign that he, Cranmer, was right and the Pope was wrong?

Could it be that the Church, founded by Christ Himself on the rock of Peter, was still God's Church, and that Ridley and Latimer had suffered, and he was about to suffer, for fighting against God's will? Could *that* be the terrible truth?

In that case, he faced not only the flames of death, but the everlasting fire of Hell: fire of which our earthly fire is no more than an image in a mirror!

Thou art Peter, and upon this Rock will I build my Church. And he, Thomas Cranmer, puffed up with pride like Lucifer, had led a misguided army against that Rock, and had failed, and his army was beaten, and scattered, and only he was left, a solitary prisoner rejected by God, to face death and the fires of Hell. There was only one possible salvation: repentance. With the last of his feeble strength he wrote out his first recantation.

More recantations followed. He even attended the Mass he had so bitterly condemned. None of this interfered one jot with the course of power politics. He was degraded, first dressed in the vestments of an Archbishop, and then mockingly stripped of them. He was made to put on priests' vestments and was stripped of them. His head was shaved to destroy his tonsure, and his fingers were symbolically scraped to remove the unction of his priesting.

This harsh ceremony was carried out in the Church of Christ Church College; by an old friend of Thomas'. Thomas Thirlby, a man with whom he would at one time have shared his last crust; and the coarse, cruel Edmund Bonner, Bishop of London, an implacable enemy.

Thomas woke on that morning feeling sick and ill. He was about to be driven out of God's Church. Already he had forfeited God's love. Now this was to be made manifest in human terms.

Bishop Bonner began the ceremony with a vitriolic attack on Cranmer, gloating over his degradation. He tore off his vestments with relish, shaved his head so carelessly that the blood flowed, scraped his fingers so that he tore the flesh. Then, when all was done, they delivered him formally to the secular arm for execution. Bishop Bonner ended the ceremony by saying venomously, and with an evil stare: 'Now you are Lord no more.'

Yet as he dragged himself back to Bocardo, faint with hunger and weariness after the long ceremony, an unknown man gave his own warm cloak back to him against the February dusk, and provided fish for his supper, and spoke kindly to him.

He was perhaps the last to speak kindly to Thomas Cranmer on this earth.

CHAPTER 25

The awful preparations were set in train. Officials cleared the town ditch of rubbish, and set up a stout stake in a good open space with a nearby bench for the gentry, and a portable pulpit for the prayers. They also indented for a hundred and fifty faggots and some kindling wood. And, in case it rained, and made it necessary to hold the first part of the ceremony indoors, they built a high platform in St Mary's Church. At the same time Dr Henry Cole, Provost of Eton, whom the Queen wished to preach the sermon, arrived in Oxford. And he visited Cranmer on March 18th.

Henry Cole did not beat about the bush. He said, 'You are to be burned on Saturday, March the twenty-first, Cranmer.'

The announcement, so long expected, came like a blow on the head. But Thomas gave no sign. He said, in a firm voice, 'I am not afraid to die, Doctor Cole. Yet I am troubled by a mountain of sin.'

Henry Cole gave a short laugh. 'You would indeed be a hardened sinner if you were not, Cranmer.'

Thomas' mouth was dry. 'Repentance – ?' he began.

'Repentance may save even you from the fires of Hell. It will not save you from the earthly fire.'

Thomas said, 'Yet – repentant heretics are not burnt. Surely what you say is unjust?'

Cole said, angrily, 'Would you accuse your Prince of injustice?'

'I would accuse the State of injustice. My son has been robbed of his inheritance. Since I was convicted of treason (and God knows no man was ever more loyal to his Prince) all my goods were forfeit. Is not this unjust, Doctor Cole, since I am not to die for treason?'

Cole was astonished. 'You can think of such worldly things when your immortal soul is about to be cast into Hell? Mend your mind, Cranmer. And touching the other matter, your heresies have been so vile that, even though you repent, it is needful that you be punished for them in the fire. And – there is a third matter I shall touch on in my sermon.'

So weak was Cranmer's state nowadays that consciousness ebbed and flowed like a sluggish tide. A few moments ago he had been alive with anger, now an ebb had set in. He made a great effort. '*What* matter, Doctor Cole?'

'Touching the martyrdom of Sir Thomas More and Cardinal Fisher. Northumberland's death atoned for More. Another death is needed to atone for the saintly Fisher. Yours, Cranmer.'

Thomas stared at him in amazement. 'You mean – I am to die – in revenge for my old friend Fisher?'

'Those are the Queen's orders.'

'But – this is monstrous. To die for Fisher, whose life I tried so hard to save. That is – a hard thing to accept, Doctor Cole.'

Henry Cole said, 'Well you will need to accept it, Cranmer. And the Lord have mercy on your soul.' He knocked on the cell door. It was opened from outside. He was gone, cold and mean as the Lent wind.

On the following day, Thursday, the Spanish friars came to help him prepare his speech from the stake.

It was a lucid, well-thought-out speech, in which Cranmer did not spare himself. He began by saying he was a wretched caitiff who had committed sins without number. He exhorted the people not to love worldly pleasure, to obey their King and Queen, to love their neighbours and to give to the poor. He then recited the Creed, adding that he believed every article of the Catholic faith, every article set forth in the General Councils, and every clause word and sentence taught by Our Saviour and His Apostles.

Then he came to 'the great thing that so much troubleth my conscience, more than any other thing that ever I did; and that is, setting abroad untrue books and writings, contrary to the truths of God's word; which now I renounce and condemn, and refuse them utterly as erroneous, and for none of mine.'

'But whatsoever I wrote then, now is time and place to say truth; wherefore, renouncing all those books, and whatsoever in them is contained, I say and believe that our Saviour Christ Jesu is really and substantially contained in the blessed Sacrament of the Altar, under the forms of bread and wine.'

It was a full and abject renunciation of his life's work. It stabbed the Reformation in the back. The Spanish friars were pleased with their work. On only one point they could not make the old man budge. He would not include in his text the *Ave Maria*.

The friars went away. He was alone once more.

He had embraced the Catholic faith. God, by so terribly withdrawing the light of His countenance, had shown him the errors of his life. Now, however, there would come a sign from God of anger abating, of some promise of mercy.

None came. He prayed aloud, bruising his knees against the stone floor. He lifted his eyes, shouting to God for a sign, weeping in an agony of despair.

No sign came. The stars wheeled against the velvet night. But the Presence of God was not in his prison, nor in his heart. Nor, he desperately feared, in his Eternity.

All night he prayed: until the stars paled, and his square of window was suffused with the pinks and blues of a new day, of his last whole day on earth.

And, as with the night, the daylight brought no sign.

But it brought the detestable Doctor Cole and the friars: still eager for their *Ave Maria*.

He had given them everything: recantations, confessions, an abject renunciation of everything he had once believed in. And still they were not satisfied.

But they found they were dealing with another Cranmer. Fear of imminent death and Hell fire had enfeebled his body to such an extent that his emotions were as wild as unbroken horses. And now anger was in command. He said, 'I have given you everything. I will give you no *Ave Maria*.'

Dr Cole sneered. 'Will you risk Hell fire for an *Ave*?'

The words were like a douche of cold water on Thomas' devouring anger. He checked, looked at Cole with senescent cunning. 'What do you mean?'

Cole said, 'You are still being recalcitrant. It could be that your recalcitrance over an *Ave* cancels all your other repentance in God's eyes.'

Could that be why there was no sign in the night? His anger had ceased now. He was again an old man, bewildered. He turned to one of the friars. 'Is this possible? If so, I – might recite an *Ave*.'

'God is not mocked, Cranmer'.

It was an unfortunate phrase. It took Thomas back to when he had stood alone in his sorrow. And the Master of Jesus, gloating over the death of this married priest's wife, had said, 'God is not mocked, Cranmer.'

The inhumanity of those words had left a scar on his mind like a whiplash. A scorn and hatred for the speaker's cruelty had never left him. And now these tormentors had all suddenly taken on the pale, ascetic features of that Master of Jesus. And once again a consuming anger filled his mind. He hammered with both fists on the cell door, shouted for his gaoler. The man came running. Thomas was panting heavily. 'Take these gentlemen away,' he said breathlessly.

'But – the *Ave Maria*?'

Thomas did not reply. He was caught in an anger such as he had never known: the trembling, inarticulate anger of old age, directed against so wide a range of targets: those who harassed him; his ageing enfeebled limbs, his muddling senses; God, even, uncaring on His Throne.

Above all, his own frailty. He had betrayed the new religion. He had betrayed his friends, men who had gone unflinching to the block, the stake, the hangman's knife. Perhaps, before he was flung into Hell, he would be shown those beings seated in glory on the right hand of the Father.

Yes. They were in glory. Men on both sides, he suddenly realized: More, Fisher, Latimer, Ridley, Frith. In glory: not because they had believed aright (once again he did not know what *was* right). But because they had been true men, men of high courage.

His anger against himself deepened. And not only anger: contempt, hatred, loathing.

One question demanded to be answered: could I find in myself such courage?

He refused to look at the question. It was like a beam of white light, searching for his eyes. And he refused to let it find them. He dragged himself round his cell, crouched, eyes down, as though to escape this searching beam.

Then, at last, the question pinned him down. And he could not answer 'No'. Nor dare he answer 'Yes'. But he sat down at his table and began to write, copying out his speech, agreed with the friars, for tomorrow.

But he did not copy out the last paragraph, in which he had renounced all his books, and stated his belief that Christ was really and substantially contained in the blessed Sacrament of the Altar.

He did not copy this. Instead, he began to write:

'And now I come to the great thing which so much troubleth my conscience, more than anything that ever I did or said in my whole life. And that is setting abroad of a writing contrary to the truth; which now here I renounce and refuse as things written with my hand contrary to the truth which I thought in my heart, and written for fear of death, and to save my life if it might be. And that is all such bills and papers which I have written or signed with my hand *since my degradation*, wherein I have written many things, untrue. And forasmuch as my hand offended, writing contrary to my heart, my hand shall be first punished therefore: for, may I come to the fire, it shall be first burned. And as for the Pope, I refuse him as Christ's enemy and Antichrist, with all his false doctrine. And as for the Sacrament, I believe as I have taught in my book against the Bishop of Winchester, that which my book teacheth so true a doctrine of the Sacrament that it shall stand at the last day before the judgement of God where the Papistical doctrine contrary thereto shall be ashamed to show her face.'

He was fearful. He himself (or some force outside himself, he did not know which) had forged a weapon that could slay the abject creature he so hated, and bring him to the imminent pains of martyrdom; that could make him worthy to be received not only by the noble army of martyrs, but by Him who sat on the right hand of the Father.

He made a copy of what he had just written. He hid both copies in the bosom of his habit. His earlier speech, the one written for him by the friars, he laid carefully on the table, ready for morning. Cautious as ever, he still had an escape route in case his desire for martyrdom failed him when he saw the stake and the faggot. Indecisive as ever, he still did not know which paper would bring him to Heaven, which to Hell.

It was a wet morning, the sky and the grey town dismal. The faggots were damp.

So the first part of the ceremony was held in St Mary's Church: a grey light filtering through the high windows, a few candles sharp and bright in the distant shadows.

Everyone was there, in his Sunday best for the occasion. Divines, clerics, Bishops, their jewelled vestments colourful as peacocks in the gloom; Doctor Henry Cole, in the high pulpit castigating the heresies of the condemned man and producing the State's neat little excuse for burning a repentant heretic – that it was to atone for the execution of Cardinal Fisher.

There were the common people, fidgeting, nervous and restless as they always were during the long-drawn-out preliminaries to a burning.

And Thomas Cranmer was there, raised up on a rough wooden scaffold where all the congregation could see him, still in an agony of indecision as to which speech would bring him to Heaven, which to Hell.

Cole thundered on. Thomas, who wasn't listening, suddenly caught a phrase: Cole was explaining about Cranmer needing to die for the death of Fisher.

And finally his mind was made up. A religion that could avenge one man's death by burning the one man who had tried to save him: *that* religion could not be the way to salvation. He felt in his bosom and brought out the speech he had written yesterday, the one in which he had called the Pope Antichrist.

And he saw, even more clearly now, that salvation did not rest on what you believed. It rested on your willingness to suffer and die for what you believed. It was a terrible, terrifying discovery. It was something far too strong for a weak creature like himself to accept. He shivered as with an ague.

Yet when he began to speak his voice was strong. He held himself upright. When he described himself as a wretched caitiff and miserable sinner he almost smiled. And when he finished the Lord's Prayer he went straight on to exhort the people.

The Spanish friars looked alarmed. Where was the *Ave Maria* he had appeared willing to include? Surely – ?

But after that he kept to his text, and they began to relax. Until – 'And now I come to the great thing which so troubleth my conscience… '

Something was wrong! He was reading quickly, in a clear, powerful voice: 'I renounce all such bills and papers which I have written or signed with my hand *since my degradation*… '

Pandemonium spread through the church like a fire in tinder. The Spanish friars were shouting and gesticulating. They clattered up the steps and grabbed him. But not before he had shouted above the uproar: 'And as for the Pope, I refuse him as Christ's enemy and Antichrist, with all his false doctrine. And as for the Sacrament, I believe as I have taught in my book against the Bishop of Winchester.'

Roughly, with blows and curses, they bundled him down from the platform. But the people had heard enough. They were not fools. And now he dropped the second copy of the speech he had just read, where it was sure to be picked up.

He hurried eagerly from the Church, cheerfully mocking the Spanish friars who ran beside him. He cried out, 'I see Heaven open, and Jesus on the right hand of God.'

Deeply shocked, they reproved him for his blasphemy. But he was not listening. He had done with them, and with all the affairs of this troubled world. He ran to embrace the stake, as the bridegroom runneth to enfold the bride.

Later, when all was done, they found at the foot of the stake a black, leathery object, untouched by the flames. It was, they decided, his heart, which had proved too evil to burn. They threw it, with the rest of his ashes, into the town ditch...

And Jesus said: A new commandment I give unto you, That ye love one another.

Eric Malpass

Beefy Jones

Beefy Jones is a lovable rogue. Not very bright, but strong and kind-hearted, he lives with a gang of petty criminals and Jack-the-Lads in the disused loft of the church hall in Dandy. The Vicar, meanwhile, is blissfully unaware of this motley gang of uninvited occupants. Returning home early one evening, Beefy overhears a meeting of the Church Council where under discussion is the demolition of the church hall – their home. The gang then embarks on a series of adventures with one aim in mind – to sabotage the vicar's plans by any means they can in order to save their home. In this hugely funny and intriguing story, they find themselves plunged into a series of wild, madcap escapades with the willing, naïve Beefy always at the centre of the action.

The Lamplight and the Stars

Nathan Cranswick's third child comes into the world on the day of Queen Victoria's Diamond Jubilee. Whilst the Empire celebrates, Nathan's concerns are about his family's future. A gentle and wise preacher, he gratefully accepts the chance to move from the dingy, cramped house in Ingerby to the village of Moreland when he is offered a job on the splendid Heron estate. Anticipating peace and tranquillity for his wife and young family, his hopes are cruelly dashed when their new life is beset by problems from the beginning. A family scandal and the Boer War menace their whole future, but finally it is the agonising choice facing his gentle daughter which threatens to tear the family apart...

ERIC MALPASS

MORNING'S AT SEVEN

Three generations of the Pentecost family live in a state of permanent disarray in a huge, sprawling farmhouse. Seven-year-old Gaylord Pentecost is the innocent hero who observes the lives of the adults – Grandpa, Momma and Poppa and two aunties – with amusement and incredulity.

Through Gaylord's eyes, we witness the heartache suffered by Auntie Rose as the exquisite Auntie Becky makes a play for her gentleman friend, while Gaylord unwittingly makes the situation far worse.

Mayhem and madness reign in this zestful account of the lives and loves of the outrageous Pentecosts.

THE RAISING OF LAZARUS PIKE

Lazarus Pike (1820–1899), author of *Lady Emily's Decision*, lies buried in the churchyard of Ill Boding. And there he would have remained, in obscurity and undisturbed, had it not been for a series of remarkable coincidences. A discovery sets in motion a campaign to republish his works and to reinstate Lazarus Pike as a giant of Victorian literature. This is a cause of bitter wrangling between the two factions that emerge. For some, Lazarus is a simple schoolmaster, devoted to his beautiful wife, Corinda. For others, who think his reputation needs a sexy, contemporary twist, he is a wife murderer with a deeply flawed character. What follows is a knowing and wry look at the world of literary make-overs and the heritage industry in a hilarious story that brings fame and tragedy to an unsuspecting moorland village.

ERIC MALPASS

SWEET WILL

William Shakespeare is just eighteen when he marries Anne Hathaway, eight years his senior. Anne, who bears a son soon after the marriage, is plain and not particularly bright – but her love for Will is undeniable. Talented and fiercely ambitious, Will's scintillating genius soon makes him the toast of Elizabethan London. While he basks in the flattery his great reputation affords him, Anne lives a lonely life in Stratford, far away from the glittering world of her husband.

This highly evocative account of the life of the young William Shakespeare begins the trilogy which continues with *The Cleopatra Boy* and concludes with *A House of Women*.

THE WIND BRINGS UP THE RAIN

It is a perfect summer's day in August 1914. Yet even as Nell and her friends enjoy a blissful picnic by the river, the storm clouds of war are gathering over Europe. Very soon this idyll is to be swept away by the conflict that will take millions of men to their deaths.

After the war, the widowed Nell leads a wretched existence, caring for her husband's elderly, ungrateful parents, with only her son, Benbow, for companionship and support. But Nell is a passionate woman and wants to share her life with a man who will return her love. Meanwhile, Benbow falls in love with a German girl, Ulrike – until she is enticed home by the resurgent Germany.

This moving story of a Midlands family in the inter-war years is a compelling tale of personal triumph and disappointment, set against the background of the hideous destruction of war.

TITLES BY ERIC MALPASS AVAILABLE DIRECT FROM HOUSE OF STRATUS

Quantity		£	$(US)	$(CAN)	€
☐	At the Height of the Moon	6.99	11.50	15.99	11.50
☐	Beefy Jones	6.99	11.50	15.99	11.50
☐	The Cleopatra Boy	6.99	11.50	15.99	11.50
☐	Fortinbras has Escaped	6.99	11.50	15.99	11.50
☐	A House of Women	6.99	11.50	15.99	11.50
☐	The Lamplight and the Stars	6.99	11.50	15.99	11.50
☐	The Long Long Dances	6.99	11.50	15.99	11.50
☐	Morning's at Seven	6.99	11.50	15.99	11.50
☐	Oh, My Darling Daughter	6.99	11.50	15.99	11.50
☐	Pig-in-the-Middle	6.99	11.50	15.99	11.50
☐	The Raising of Lazarus Pike	6.99	11.50	15.99	11.50
☐	Summer Awakening	6.99	11.50	15.99	11.50
☐	Sweet Will	6.99	11.50	15.99	11.50
☐	The Wind Brings Up the Rain	6.99	11.50	15.99	11.50

ALL HOUSE OF STRATUS BOOKS ARE AVAILABLE FROM GOOD BOOKSHOPS OR DIRECT FROM THE PUBLISHER:

Internet: **www.houseofstratus.com** including author interviews, reviews, features.

Email: **sales@houseofstratus.com** please quote author, title and credit card details.

Hotline: UK ONLY: 0800 169 1780, please quote author, title and credit card details.
INTERNATIONAL: +44 (0) 20 7494 6400, please quote author, title, and credit card details.

Send to: **House of Stratus Sales Department**
24c Old Burlington Street
London
W1X 1RL
UK

Please allow for postage costs charged per order plus an amount per book as set out in the tables below:

	£(Sterling)	$(US)	$(CAN)	€(Euros)
Cost per order				
UK	2.00	3.00	4.50	3.30
Europe	3.00	4.50	6.75	5.00
North America	3.00	4.50	6.75	5.00
Rest of World	3.00	4.50	6.75	5.00
Additional cost per book				
UK	0.50	0.75	1.15	0.85
Europe	1.00	1.50	2.30	1.70
North America	2.00	3.00	4.60	3.40
Rest of World	2.50	3.75	5.75	4.25

PLEASE SEND CHEQUE, POSTAL ORDER (STERLING ONLY), EUROCHEQUE, OR INTERNATIONAL MONEY ORDER (PLEASE CIRCLE METHOD OF PAYMENT YOU WISH TO USE)
MAKE PAYABLE TO: STRATUS HOLDINGS plc

Cost of book(s):__________ Example: 3 x books at £6.99 each: £20.97

Cost of order:__________ Example: £2.00 (Delivery to UK address)

Additional cost per book:__________ Example: 3 x £0.50: £1.50

Order total including postage:__________ Example: £24.47

Please tick currency you wish to use and add total amount of order:

☐ £ (Sterling) ☐ $ (US) ☐ $ (CAN) ☐ € (EUROS)

VISA, MASTERCARD, SWITCH, AMEX, SOLO, JCB:

☐☐☐☐☐☐☐☐☐☐☐☐☐☐☐☐☐☐☐☐

Issue number (Switch only):

☐☐☐

Start Date: ☐☐/☐☐

Expiry Date: ☐☐/☐☐

Signature: __________

NAME: __________

ADDRESS: __________

____

POSTCODE: __________

Please allow 28 days for delivery.

Prices subject to change without notice.
Please tick box if you do not wish to receive any additional information. ☐

House of Stratus publishes many other titles in this genre; please check our website (**www.houseofstratus.com**) for more details.